THE FACE OF DEATH

She came at the intruder, the bar above her head, and her first swing barely missed the terrible mask, gouging a hole in the bulkhead. She didn't get a second chance. The intruder's left hand shot out and struck her throat with incredible force, breaking her trachea with one blow.

She began to strangle at once on her own blood, but her rage was so great that even in her death agony, she found strength to rip off the intruder's mask. Her eyes widened in horror as she slipped to the floor, hugging the mask to her chest. Her lips formed the word *You!*—and the intruder smiled . . .

Ace Books by Simon Lang

THE TRUMPETS OF TAGAN

TIMESLIDE

HOPESHIP

HOPESHIP

SIMON LANG

ACE BOOKS, NEW YORK

This book is an Ace original edition,
and has never been previously published.

HOPESHIP

An Ace Book/published by arrangement with
the author

PRINTING HISTORY
Ace edition/January 1994

ISBN 0-441-34306-6

ACE®
Ace Books are published by The Berkley Publishing Group,
200 Madison Avenue, New York, NY 10016.
ACE and the "A" design
are trademarks belonging to Charter Communications, Inc.

PRINTED IN THE UNITED STATES OF AMERICA

10 9 8 7 6 5 4 3 2 1

For Theresa the beloved,
who danced with me at the eleventh hour
on the bridge at Avignon,
and thereby saved my life . . .
and for Edward,
the Black Knight.

Special Thanks to:

Dr. Charles L. Remington, Yale Peabody Museum, New Haven, CT;

David S. Fischer, M.D., New Haven, CT;

Alan Ouimet, Federal Bureau of Investigation, (ret.), Guilford, CT;

Dale Carson, Madison, CT;

Dr. Alan Ouilette, DVM, Madison, CT, (203) 421-3300;

and especially to:

Harmon John Ward III, architect, of Anahcim, California, for his intelligent questions, his considerable knowledge and most particularly for his friendship.

PROLOGUE

SHE WAS NAMED for an ancient dream, a faded memory, a half-remembered quest.

Long ago, so the legend went, on an unimportant planet halfway to the Rim, there had been a seagoing vessel populated with medical people sincerely concerned for their fellow beings. It was said that this ship and its people had sailed from country to backwater country, ministering to the lame and the halt, to the ill, the poverty-stricken, and the hopeless. The good done for the many by the few was astounding, and under their hands, and by the grace of God, medical miracles were commonplace. The blind saw. The lame walked. And most amazingly, even for those patients who subsequently died, someone at least had tried.

Someone had cared.

For the caregivers themselves, the experience became one of the spiritual and emotional highlights of their lives. For the recipients, the big white hospital ship was the only recourse they would ever have from their daily diet of despair.

The ship's name, like her mission, was *Hope*.

One day, the story continued, for reasons economic or political (no one remembered, or bothered much about it), the good ship *Hope* was decommissioned. Her people, forever changed, returned to their daily lives, and the poor and the ill of all the small and unimportant countries had to get on the best they could without her, or die in the attempt.

But then, such was the stuff of legends.

Centuries later, with the inception of the Galactic Federation, the *Hope* legend was somehow revived, and a movement was begun to reinstate the spirit of USS *Hope* on an interstellar basis.

Under pressure from religious and civic groups, the Federation, reluctant until now to address the issue, found that it could, after all, spare for this worthy humanitarian cause a century-old hulk that had been sitting for several decades in dry dock over NYCity, Earth, collecting past-due rental invoices.

Declared unfit for military use, but still marginally spaceworthy, she was quickly outfitted and staffed by volunteers, and—her accommodations rigorously Spartan but her standards flying high—USS *Hope* wheezed out across the solar system at her top speed of sublight 4, determined to fulfill her calling. It was to take her three months even to reach her first planetfall. She wallowed determinedly through local star systems that way for several decades, keeping the legend alive and doing what good she could.

Meanwhile, she existed on charity. Various groups raised funds for her with everything from Ksatriya dances on Krau to shrimp-boils on Eisernon and neighborhood bake-offs on Earth, and doors on a dozen planets opened routinely to earnest uniformed youngsters collecting offerings in containers marked 'Support USS *Hope*.'

Things might have gone on that way indefinitely, but ten years ago, by some happy circumstance, the Federation had appointed Priyam Mykar Sharobi as Fleet Surgeon (and incidentally, *Hope*'s Chief of Staff), and all hell broke loose.

In short order, Sharobi—a tough, feisty, quarter-breed Sauvagi who knew everyone worth knowing, and was not much impressed—had arranged to have his hospital moved into the largest, fastest and most modern multiwarp starcruiser in the Fleet; had decimated *Hope*'s medical ranks of the well-meaning and the sloppily sentimental in favor of the competent, the incisive and the daring; and had demanded the crippled Donelang Kris, the most hated Xhole in the Federation, as *Hope*'s Captain.

By the time she was rechristened, in formal ceremonies at Federation Central, the USS *Hope* was formidable indeed.

Situated as she was in the latest state-of-the-art vessel, she was prepared for virtually any conceivable situation except outright warfare. Environments for the nine separate galactic species, and all the many hybrids thereof, were wrapped inside her mammoth duralloy hull, and three empty, easily programmed sectors remained constantly on standby, in the event of the discovery of a new intelligent people whose aspect and metabolism might differ from that of the other nine. Her medical school and research facilities were the best in the galaxy, as were her staff and crew, and her residential accommodations, peculiar to each species and including parks, luxury apartments, athletic facilities and shopping malls, were flawless.

Thus fortified, Sharobi made his warp-speed rounds from ship to hospital ship, Fleet and civilian vessels alike, subjecting each to a rigorous scrutiny and tersely inviting careless personnel to shape up or ship out.

Then, careful that he betray no trace of silly sentimentality in what was, after all, simply good medical practice, Priyam Mykar Sharobi ordered the good ship *Hope* on the first leg of her long-overdue mission of mercy to the galaxy.

And he, and his people, and the good ship *Hope*, had been at it wholeheartedly ever since.

The early morning air was warm and soft, and the rain had been falling steadily from the low gray clouds for days. It washed clean the myriad greens of the jungle, slicked the palm-thatched roofs and sluiced down the compound's muddy streets, making its way toward the River.

In Nalinle's mind, as in the minds of the whole clan, there was only one river in the world, and it needed no other name. It was simply the River, just as the village they lived in was the Village, and they were the People. There were other villages somewhere, they supposed, for others like themselves lived far off in the Jungle; but no one gave them much thought. It was sufficient simply to hunt and to fish, to raise children and to sing songs together around the evening campfire, before going home to a quiet hut and a gentle wife. For most of them, it was life enough.

But Nalinle was a man who wondered. Standing there by the half-wall of his stilted hut, watching the rain fall warm and easy, he wondered where it came from, and where it went. How the River knew where it should flow. And what coaxed the moons into the sky, night after night.

When the village children scampered shouting through the puddles, he wondered why it was that his only surviving child—a son, Mikai—lay twisted and helpless while other children could run with their fish lines down to the River.

"Nalinle." Mali's voice was tired. "You will not leave me alone?" He turned to look at her. Standing there by the firebowl in the center of the hut, she seemed a stranger, old and worn from bearing children who had died too soon. Her fragile bones made her imminent pregnancy seem all the larger, and her scalp lock, once black and lush and glossy, now was thin and dry, the color of dead leaves. The hoop in her right ear seemed huge and out of place.

He made no answer, and she sighed and knelt heavily at the firebowl, threaded a fine shave of root on a sharpened stick, and held it over the coals. Nalinle came to squat beside her.

"The runner said, 'Thirty days, Hopeship will be at the mountains at G'ham.'"

She shook her head. "I do not understand 'thirty.' Is it more than 'many'?" In their culture, any amount more than six was termed simply 'many.' Only Nalinle wondered and counted, cutting marks on sticks. Only Nalinle cared how much was more than many. He tried to explain.

"Look, Mali." He held four fingers close to his face. "It took him four days to run here from his village with the news." He spread all six fingers of his left hand once, twice, thrice and again. The fifth time, he carefully bent four of them down with the fingers of his other hand. "Twenty six days and Hopeship will be gone."

"I do not understand," she said.

They stared at the fire together, saying nothing, while the root sizzled and the rain fell steadily outside, pit-pocking puddles. Nalinle made a waking dream of Mikai splashing through them with the other boys, running down to the River. He imagined the size of the fish his son would bring home, and the taste of it, broiled with *tyym* leaves. It was so real a dream, he was sure some god had sent it as encouragement, and it heartened him.

"If I take the boy and run," he continued, excitement making his voice less steady, "if I make good time and run swiftfoot through the jungle, I can reach the Hopeship before it is gone. They can make him well, Mali. The runner said they are like gods! They will make him whole!" Mikai made a gurgling sound of excitement, too, thrashing a bit on his mat, but Mali lowered her head.

"Six times I have cheated you, Nalinle," she whispered. "Five that should not have died, and one that should not have lived." He caught her shoulders, turning her to him, while the forgotten food sputtered on the coals.

"*Mikai will live!*" he said. "I will *make* him live!"

Her face flashed up in a rare moment of passionate grief. "For what—Nalinle! So he can go on babbling in a corner all his life?"

"Mali!"

She held her belly with both arms, rocking herself, tears streaking her cheeks. "The new child will be strong, I swear it! This time I will do it right! I have made many sacrifices to the River. Our child will be strong this time!"

"And Mikai? The son I have?"

She shrugged as if wincing away from pain. "Five have died before him," she said. Nalinle got up wordlessly, crossed to Mikai and gathered him up in his arms. The thin, gangly boy clung to him clumsily. Fearfully.

"I die . . . ?" he mouthed hoarsely, drooling against his father's shoulder.

"No, Mikai!" He buried his face against his son for a moment. "You will be *well*!"

"Nalinle, the headman says you will die the death if you go beyond the Boundary. No one has ever gone so far. It is tabu."

Mali's tears made tracks down her smooth green cheeks. "For your new son—and for me—I ask! Nalinle, *stay!*"

Nalinle made no answer. He looked around the hut, from the woven grass half-walls to the hand-hewn poles that held up the thatch, to the pegs for their few belongings and the sleeping mats (all but Mikai's) rolled neatly against the wall. He smelled the succulent morsel roasting over the fire, and the lush, wet, fecund odors of the encroaching jungle.

"We will eat," he told her, "and then we will go."

Slowly Mali took the hoop from her ear and handed it to him. "Take it. They will want something for helping him. . . ."

Nalinle blinked. "Your wedding hoop. It is dear to you."

She wiped her eyes with the heels of her hands. "Take it! It is all I have of myself to send with you!" He replaced the hoop in her ear, cupped her face in his hands, and inhaled deeply her dear, familiar breath.

"Not so, Mali," he said gently. "You are sending Mikai."

He had been trotting for hours. Underfoot, the swampy ground had firmed and risen and dried, and sparse grasses blew in the hot wind under tall hard trees that were nothing like the juicy greenery of the lowlands. What rain there was fell harmlessly, scarcely more than a mist, as they came at last to the painted poles that marked the Boundary.

Nalinle hesitated only a moment. The act of stepping beyond the poles reminded him of his manhood ceremony, a crossing, a going past of a place he could never return to. His belly contracted involuntarily as he licked his lips and held Mikai a little tighter. Shifted his pack. Looked back over his shoulder toward the Village.

It called to him, silently but strongly. The clan fire. The other men's voices, laughing and talking. Mali's breath. Everything on the inside of the invisible line between the Village and the Boundary was familiar and comfortable and safe; everything outside it was strange and somehow threatening.

But outside the Boundary, the runner had said, was a range

of hills, thinning slowly to savannah, and from those hills he would see the mountains at G'ham.

It was almost evening, both moons slowly rising behind broken clouds, when Nalinle took the step into the unknown, put his bare foot over the Boundary and carried Mikai to the crest of the hill that rose before him. He stared unbelievingly for a long moment, then squatted slowly, resting Mikai against the grass.

Up high like this, with the jungle cover of leaves and lianas gone, he had for the first time in his life a panoramic view of the near world, and it was more than he could take in at once.

There was so much space, with birds flying free in it, and the sun dipping behind the hills. On their ridges, clusters of tall trees thrust boldly upward toward the sky, like Boundary poles, and in the dale below, long evening shadows gathered in a dense forest. Water traced a far, thin silver line through a valley, and each hill sat on the knees of its neighbor, growing taller and taller until they faded into the blue grandeur of nearby mountains.

"See, Mikai," Nalinle said in wonder, indicating them with a lift of the chin. "There they are. They are really there! The mountains at G'ham." Mikai laughed hoarsely, mouth wide open, and waved his arm and hand like a water-bird's wing. His eyes were shining.

"It will *be* there," Nalinle continued, as if pronouncing a magic spell. "It will be there, the Hopeship . . ." He picked up the boy and began to walk again, over the crest of the hill and down the other side, moving faster and faster as he talked. "*They* will know what to do . . . They will *know* . . ." He was dog-trotting now, his words exploding out of him as he ran down the hill and toward the forest in the gathering dusk.

". . . they will do something . . . and you will be *straight* . . ." He hugged the boy to himself ferociously, his voice ferocious, too, and rough and desperate. His eyes were wet. "They know *how* . . . they *know* how to make people better. . . ." He struggled with the agony of dangling between grief and hope, and finally cried:

"They *will* do *something*—for you! They *must!* . . . They *must!*"

He broke into a clumsy, plunging run down the remainder of the hill, and, as if his voice would carry all the way to G'ham and the ship, he burst out in a long desperate cry that echoed against the hills:

"*H-o-p-e!* Wait for us . . . !"

CHAPTER

I

THE ALARM BEGAN a regular, steady chiming in the medical Ready Room, and the shipwide com cut in.

"Incoming. Incoming," the pleasant metallic voice announced dispassionately. "Attention triage and trauma personnel: wounded incoming. P-2. P-7. P-10. Zero-Zero. Monitor Gates Six and Seven, please. Incoming. In "

"That's us." Tommy Paige flung down his only royal flush of the shift and jumped to his feet along with Artie Michaels and PprumBurr, heading for Admitting at a dead run, for a P-2 injury was nothing to play with. On a sliding scale from one through ten, anything under a P-4 was a dangerous business indeed.

The access corridor between the Ready Room and Gates Five through Ten was sealed off for sterilization, and even now, techs garbed in pyrosene coveralls and helmets were hosing down the bulkheads and deck with live steam. Artie slammed the heel of his hand against the plastex seals in frustration.

"Damn, I forgot! They brought those Scup patients through here from planetside this morning. It'll be sealed all day! Come on, maybe we can squeeze through the loading bay!" He pulled at the bar.

"Are you crazy?" Paige demanded, jerking him back. "Somebody drops a crate on your head, we've got a mess on deck! Come on, we'll cut through Maintenance!"

"Incoming, incoming," the pleasant metallic voice repeated monotonously. "Attention, triage and trauma personnel. Incoming at Gates Six and Seven—"

They burst through the Maintenance portal and raced between scores of racked skimmercraft, Artie hurdling oil slicks the scrubbervacs had missed and Paige dodging several twitchy orange servos in a beautiful piece of broken field running. PprumBurr soared lightly above it all, humming in close harmony with a tech who slid into the grease pit under a skimmer, caroling:

"Yo, Lenny! Grab the oil pressure on B-a-a-a-a-y Five!"

The bulkhead LCD began the pressure readout as they ran, and all around them there were the busy goings-on of men at work, the glare of welders' torches, and the satisfying smells of fuel, hot metal and space.

Artie flung open a manually operated portal on the far side of the bay, and the three emerged into the quiet, decorous corridor just outside of Admitting. They stepped into an adjacent scrub room, stood briefly under the flash, threw on fresh tunics (while PprumBurr shoved its proboscis into a sterile mask) and took their stations at either side of the skids.

Their patients had already arrived, for they could hear the emergency pumps flooding the airlock, and Gate Six irised open abruptly, propelling a Navy ambulance toward them at breakneck speed. Paige and Michaels jumped for the grab bars on the skimmer's sides and physically dragged it to a stop, its flashers still rotating, while the Droso, PprumBurr, flew up and quickly released the locks. The two Navy medics pulled the lone MAX and readied the bulkhead hatch as an Earthling female passenger deplaned, hesitant amid the flurry of activity. She was wearing a plastex splint on her right wrist, and she seemed tired and confused. PprumBurr flitted down and approached cautiously to speak to her.

"I mmm PprumBurr," it offered politely, simulating human speech by vibrating its wings at various speeds and pitches. The sound was similar to that of paper held before an oscillating fan, or of a green twig dragged along the pickets of a fence: a fluttery dry hum originating, not in the Droso's thorax, but in the blurred flutter of the wings themselves. "Mmay I helpp you?" She showed no repugnance toward it, only mild surprise, it noted, which was flattering. It pulled its manipulators deliberately across its eyes in a debonair fashion, calculated to enhance its attractiveness, but unfortunately, the female seemed oblivious to its charm.

"Please," she said. "I'm Audrey Lassiter. My husband has been injured. I was told I should see someone from Social Services upon my arrival."

"Come wizz mme, ppplease," the Droso invited, bobbing its head politely. "Rightt thzz way." With a last, reluctant glance at her husband's MAX, still racked in the skimmer, she followed it out.

"This one's Dr. Charles Lassiter," the medic told Paige confidentially, handing him the pak from the MAX's flat stern. "Your P-7. He's stabilized but Dr. Anderson said to make sure you saw the flag on him."

Paige saw. Dr. Charles Snow Lassiter, high-level Interpol operative, was flagged for a psychiatric rule-out. The report was a standard rundown of his considerable physical injuries; the fact that he had repcatcdly threatened the life of his rescuer; and the usual notes and routine vitals. The flag was the problem.

For a man in Lassiter's position, Paige knew, it would be professional death to have word get around about a psych flag, even if he turned out later to be as sanc as Solomon. Interpol was notoriously touchy about the mental health of its agents. A premature, and probably false, assumption like this could ruin a man's career.

Paige's own brief history of Krail slavery had jumped up and chewed his own rear, and painfully, too, several times. He was, he admitted, getting rather thin-skinned about it. Pity to have it happen to Lassiter, he thought.

As admitting physician, he could retard idle speculation by red-coding the flag, which would keep the information under strictest confidence. Only he and the charge nurse would have access to it. If necessary later (if, say, the rule-out was positive, and Lassiter really had a significant mental problem), he could always pull the code and make the information common knowledge. Until then, under a red code, it would stay confidential.

It wasn't exactly a kosher maneuver, but it wasn't strictly forbidden, either. Paige had been known to walk the crumbling edge of risk before. And enjoy it, too.

He decided to take the chance.

He helped horse the MAX into the bulkhead hatch, sent it hissing down to Sickbay on a cushion of compressed air, and pushed the com stud.

"Sickbay, you've got an incoming P-7 on Tube Five. Name: Charles Lassiter. Charge nurse, please note the flag, and red-code. Repeat, charge nurse, please red-code the flag."

"Ulrika Drac, Sickbay, Doctor," the com responded coolly. "Flag noted and coded."

PprumBurr returned just as a second ambulance catapulted in at Gate Seven, the neighboring slot, braking sharply to keep from ramming the barrier. The retro blast blew the Droso hard against the ceiling, where it clung quivering, buzzing furiously and pulling its antennae through its oral manipulators in a rare show of insectile annoyance. A glistening drop of poison trembled on the tip of its stinger.

"Incoming arriving at Gate Seven," said the com unit's voice tardily. PprumBurr somersaulted in midair, settled back on deck, shook itself and retracted its stinger with some dignity.

"Zznnnmmabittjj!" it buzzed, much perturbed.

Navy medics piled out to help deploy the first of the two MAXs, and swung it quickly into the adjacent hatch, where PprumBurr quickly double-checked both the MAXpak and the patient's ID, and coded him down to Sickbay in a rush of compressed air.

"P-10 away, Ttube Four, Zzickbay," it reported. "Zztand by for nncoming P-10, on Ttube Four. Nname Donnovann." It signed and returned the Navy men's paperwork as Paige and Michaels pulled the second MAX.

"Here's your P-2, Tommy," Artie said, as he tossed him the pak. "You're not going to believe this! It's Dao Marik! Remember him?"

"Marik?" Paige blurted, unbelievingly. "It can't be!" He consulted the MAXpak. It checked. Patient: Dao Marik, GFN. Second Officer, USS *Skipjack*.

He pressed FULL REPORT and the pak printed out quickly:

'Einai, male; Age: thirty-four,' followed by various statistics regarding height, weight, routine blood work and vitals. A comprehensive medications list. Previous surgical notes. Description of trauma: A P-2 injury in which a projectile weapons blast had blown away much of his left shoulder and chest, breaking the left clavicle, damaging the left brachial artery and left heart and causing massive blood loss, complicated by a right temporal subdural hematoma from an earlier trauma.

The MAX reported that it was sustaining a minimum blood pressure and automatically assisting respiration, but that Marik's condition was still precarious. Paige coded for an increase in vasoconstrictors and stimulants, and found himself running through probable protocols even as they prepared to transport the alien to Sickbay. His mind was racing. Marik was here, and he was injured. Marik, whom he had always considered his friend, and yet . . .

And yet.

"Isn't he the guy who killed you that time on Xholemeachc, Tom?" Artie wanted to know, as he released the inhibitor bands and rotated the cylinder.

"Matter of fact, he is," Paige grunted, helping the medics swing the MAX into the hatch in the near bulkhead. "Hefty shot of curare, right in the belly. Took me out like a light."

"So I guess you owe him one now, huh?" Michaels persisted, as Paige programmed Marik's destination into the code pad on the bulkhead and hit the com.

"Sickbay, you have a P-2 incoming, Tube Three. Name: Dao Marik. Stand by for incoming P-2." He turned back to Artie. "I'm sorry, what—?"

"I was just saying, you owe him, now. You know, even-Steven. Tit for tat. He killed you, now you owe *him* a killing."

Paige slammed the hatch shut and thumbed the stud, and a gasp of compressed air whooshed Marik away.

"I guess you could say that." Paige gazed thoughtfully at the dark rectangle of plastex over the hatch, under which a moment ago there had been the face of a man who had once, coolly and deliberately, made certain that Tommy Paige was very, very dead. *You owe him a killing, Tom. Like you wouldn't begin to understand, Artie,* he said to himself. After a long moment, he glanced up with a strange smile, shook himself free from dark reflections of Dao Marik, and slapped the wiry youngster on the shoulder.

"Come on, Big Artie, let's go collect PprumBurr and finish our game."

Dr. Neal Anderson, Chief Surgeon of USS *Skipjack*, sat in the sumptuous leather chair across the desk from Mykar Sharobi, sucking an empty pipe and studying through half-closed eyes *Hope*'s irascible Chief of Staff as he flipped through the printout on the new arrivals. The eminent Sauvagi, though a full head shorter than Anderson, was equally broad and twice as belligerent, a blocky and brilliant crossbreed with a mind like a steel trap and a disposition to match.

After a long while Sharobi grunted and straightened, tossing the copy onto the desk and locking his hands behind his head. "Says your Controller, Donovan, checks out fine and you're taking him back with you."

"That's right. They're calling him The Iron Man, over on *Skipjack*. Constitution like an army mule."

"So what we're dealing with, here, is two badly injured men: Marik, who's got a combination of gunshot wounds and a subdural clot—and Charles Lassiter, who was crucified, for pity's sake! *Crucified!* In this day and age! Great *Quel*, man!" the alien expostulated. "How'd he manage that?"

Anderson clamped the pipe stem in his teeth. "Timeslide injury. He rescued a bunch of Jewish children from the Nazis, back in twentieth-century Earth, and unfortunately they caught him and nailed him up on the door of the synagogue with their bayonets." He removed his pipe, peered into the stem, then put the pipe back into his mouth. "I don't mind telling you, I was really worried about his mind for a while. I even flagged him for the psych people, but . . . I might have been a bit hasty on that."

"Could be. These Interpol people are pretty tough, physically and emotionally as well. I'd guess we're dealing with simple post-traumatic stress. Clear that up in no time around here."

Anderson shrugged noncommittally. "Maybe. He did a lot of screaming about revenge, at first, doing Marik in, that sort of thing. Marik took him down, you see, kept him from a martyr's death. Lassiter seems to have come to his senses since then, though. Abject apologies and all that." He began rummaging through his pockets for his tobacco pouch.

"Marik saved Mrs. Lassiter's life as well, just recently, so Charles is doubly in his debt." Sharobi grunted noncommittally as Anderson continued to pat absently at the thigh pockets of his uniform, with no luck.

"But you know, Mike"—he paused to point his pipe stem at Sharobi—"being under a moral obligation like that could really rankle in a man like Lassiter: old Southern values and so on. Rich or poor, those people're proud as Lucifer."

Sharobi shook his shaggy head like an angry bison. "That can rankle in anybody! *Damn* Marik!" he growled, getting to his feet and beginning to pace irritably. "That boy is always running around spitting in Destiny's face! Saving fair maidens! Climbing the Pole at Ets-la! Chasing the Grail!" Anderson, who had heard it all before, leaned back comfortably in his chair, still rifling his tunic pockets as Sharobi warmed to his subject, pacing the room and punctuating his concern with angry gestures.

"He gets himself battered—and broken—and all torn up, at every turn of the compass—for these high ideals of his, this—this *chivalry* thing! And for what? Where does it get him?" He wheeled on Anderson. "Right here on *Hope*, that's where! That's how I first met him, Neal—"

"I heard," Anderson interjected, finally locating his tobacco in an inner pocket. Sharobi barreled on.

"—during the last war. They brought him in here practically on a shovel! Building fell in on him while he was trying to pull a rescue. In the middle of a rocket strike, no less!" Anderson slowly packed his pipe, tamping it firm with his thumb and waiting for Sharobi's indignation to blow over. The mellow fragrance of good tobacco wafted richly on the still air. He cleared his throat.

"I'm the first one to agree Dao isn't shy about risking his neck," he admitted, "but why would he—"

"Because Priyam Oman Shari-Mnenoplan was trapped inside."

Anderson leaned forward in consternation. "The old Master? Are you *serious?*"

Sharobi nodded slowly. "I'm afraid so. You see, Marik had gotten out safe, but he went back for the old man. They didn't make it out, of course." His voice dropped to a pensive mutter. "I understand it took over an hour to dig Marik out of the rubble. . . ." His head came up sharply.

"But I'll tell you something, Neal: if I'd been there, I would've beaten him to it. There's the rub, as you people say. Shari-Mnenoplan was my master, too, and there are only nine of us Priyamli left in the galaxy: me, Marik, and seven others. I wasn't there to risk my neck for the Old Master, so in effect, Marik did it for all of us. I owe this boy, Neal."

"He's a good man, Mike," Anderson admitted, and Sharobi growled his agreement.

"*Quel*, yes, he's a good man! He's a superb surgeon, he's bright and decent—and, dammit, much as I hate to admit it, I like him!" He blinked rapidly a few times, cleared his throat, and his voice took on its caustic edge again as he began to pace and gesticulate.

"And of course, he knows it! And takes advantage of it! So while he goes on bravely grandstanding, yours truly keeps having to wade in and bail him out! Patch him up! Send him right back out to do it all over again! Mark my words, Doctor"—he impaled the air in Anderson's direction with a didactic forefinger, scowling pugnaciously. "One of these fine days he's going to get in too deep for any of us to help him. Maybe then he'll come to his senses and stop playing boy hero!"

"Mike," Anderson observed mildly, taking the pipe out of his mouth, "you know Dao Marik, and I know Dao Marik. Do you really believe that?"

"Well—*Quel*!—what do *you* think?" Sharobi demanded. "Can't we talk some sense into him?"

Not a chance in hell," Anderson observed mildly, drawing a reluctant grin from Sharobi, who dropped his hand and wagged his shaggy head again.

"Well, let's have a look at him before you go, anyway. Or what's left of him. See what we can piece together for the next go-round."

It was dusk when Nalinle reached the clearing by the stream. The watercourse must surely be the River's child, he thought, because it looked just like its father. He considered it a good omen. It was as if the River had sent it with them to bless their journey. This, then, would be a good place to stop. The River's child would provide them food and water, and take care of them, for that was the business of gods. He was glad of this, for his chest and arms ached from carrying Mikai, and his stomach writhed with hunger. The dryness in his throat was almost unbearable. He laid the boy down carefully by the stream and fed him handfuls of water until the child turned his head away with a grunt; then he slaked his own thirst and splashed water all over his face and hairless head. Moved off a little distance and slumped against a tree, his legs stretched out in front of him, catching his breath. Looked. Listened.

The treetops, high above, were still colored with orange light, and a few last birds were winging between them, calling sweetly to each other. The wind, which had been strong on the hilltop, was perfectly still, as if it had heard something new and different. *How strange*, Nalinle thought. *Up high it is still day, but here among the trees, the night is already beginning to gather.*

"See, Mikai," he said, pointing, "how the night creeps up from the ground, and climbs the trees." Mikai's arm's flailed wildly in response, and he made a huge effort to speak, knocking himself over in the process.

"Ne'!" he mouthed hoarsely. "Boy! Uh'! Ne'!" His father's puzzled frown dissolved, and he smiled, propping him up again.

"Yes. You are right. The dark climbs up like the village boys gathering eggs from birds' nests." Mikai, his eyes bright and alert, laughed, drooling onto his chest, happy his father had understood him yet again. While he watched Nalinle picking up sticks for the evening fire, and striking sparks from his flint, he wondered what the night might find in the nest of day; where it came from, and where it went; but he had no way to ask that, or any of the hundred other questions that occurred daily to him in his prison of twisted bone and flesh.

Nalinle, blowing on the beginnings of a fire, went suddenly still, and spoke so softly that Mikai could scarcely hear him.

"Listen!" They listened together. There was the faraway chirping of sleepy birds, and the purl of the water over the mossy green stones. A whining insect danced around Nalinle's ear until he pinched it in a swift fist. There was another sound.

There, near the water: a faint scratching, a rustle, and then nothing. Nalinle made a 'quiet' sign to Mikai, got to his feet noiselessly, and padded to the bushes by the water's edge. He slipped between the branches, green on green, and disappeared from Mikai's view. After a moment, there was a scuffle and a loud, last piercing squeak, and Nalinle stood up and held up for Mikai's admiration a limp, furry prize. He whipped out his stone knife and gutted it quickly, then took the skin and entrails down to the stream bank.

"Oh, River's child, who has come with us, I share with you the food you have provided Nalinle and his son. Oh, River, lead us to the Hopeship so Mikai can be straight!" He threw the gifts into the stream, where they disappeared at once, wiped his messy hands on his bare chest, and went back to his fire and his son, satisfied that his prayer would be granted.

He chose two strong, Y-shaped branches, broke them evenly, and shoved them hard into the ground on either side of his embryo fire. He thrust a green stick through the carcass and suspended it on the two crotches, and then blew his smoldering mound of twigs, dry fibers, and spiraling smoke into a small, eager blaze. He fed it carefully until it grew strong enough to consume large pieces of broken branch, and squatted on his heels beside it, feeling the delicious warmth soaking into his sore muscles, in the cool night air.

The fire made a bright circle of light in the darkened forest, and Nalinle found himself half-dreaming as the juices began to bubble and brown on the roasting carcass. A tendril of chill breeze curled around his ankles. A few night birds called and were still.

"Ea'?" Mikai croaked.

"Soon." Juice sizzled and spat on the blackened logs, giving off a mouth-watering smell. "Soon," Nalinle repeated, almost to himself.

"I have a new thought, Mikai," he began, after a long while, and Mikai became very still, listening raptly. "There is a place outside of the Village, by the River . . . I go there often in the Time of Growing . . . and I see a strange thing. . . ." He gestured flat and smooth, as if he were looking at the River itself. "The water comes high, and brings mud far up onto the bank . . . so much mud, Mikai, sometimes fish die of it. . . ." He gripped his own throat. "It gets in here, and they die." He was solemnly puzzled, and spoke more slowly " but—later— when the water leaves this place . . . grass grows there, Mikai! Grass, and many green things, more than in any other place . . ."

He paused to tear up the carcass, snapping his scorched fingers, and licking them carefully. He broke the meat into small pieces and thumbed them, one by one, into Mikai's mouth, until the boy motioned that he was satisfied. Then he began his own meal, speaking as he ate and leaning forward to punctuate his words with expressive fingers.

"And so, I turned this over in my thoughts and said, 'Why should the wife of Nalinle . . . go far into the swamp to find grain?' " Mikai was watching him intently. "Why should we not *take* the grain . . . from the swamp . . . and put it in this holy place that the river favors . . . and make it grow close by!" He sat back triumphantly, enjoying the unadulterated admiration shining in Mikai's eyes. He did not see another pair of eyes, luminous and watchful, shining in the darkness beyond the fire.

"When you are straight, we will *do* this!" Nalinle waxed

eager. He had kept his thoughts bottled up for so long, pondering them alone for fear of confusing Mali, that he virtually exploded, waving the last, gnawed bone for emphasis.

"And again I said, 'Nalinle will make a promise to the River. I will pray and say, "River, come up every year and bless the grain . . . and I will stand beside you with my son Mikai, and we will praise you and never leave your side.'" I would say this very loudly to the River."

"N," Mikai said, scowling, waving his arms. His legs, tightly drawn against his thin body, churned impotently. "N!" he insisted. *You can't*, he thought. *What would we do when the storms come, and at night? We would have to sleep and eat sometime. We would want to hunt and fish. Maybe I would want to find a woman of my own, and give her my breath.* He opened his mouth wide, but the saliva dripping from his chin was the only protest he could make. "N!" he said once again. Nalinle smiled slyly.

"Wait, Mikai, wait . . ." He glanced toward the stream and lowered his voice conspiratorially, leaning close to his son. "Mali will take skins, and dry grass and branches of wood. And she will make a skin-Nalinle and a skin-Mikai . . . And when it is dark, and the moons and the River are asleep, we will stand the skin-Nalinle and the skin-Mikai on the bank. And the River will see, and be fooled"—he elbowed Mikai in the ribs and sucked the marrow out of the clean bone—"and we will go hunting—Nalinle and his tall, straight son."

"Uh'! Ou'! Ri'uh!" Mikai mouthed gleefully, laughing. "Uh'! Ou'!" He wobbled and plopped over onto the springy forest floor, laughing.

"Yes!" Nalinle chortled. "Yes, Mikai, the River will come up—and go out! Up—and out! Because of the skin-Nalinle and the skin-Mikai! And it will never know!" He selected a slim, straight branch from among the pile he had gathered, and carved a notch in it. "This is a special day. It is the day we came past the Boundary, and lived; and it is the day we decided to fool the River itself! This," he told Mikai impressively, showing him the notch, "is Day One!" Their eyes met in mutual understanding, and Nalinle grabbed his son, gave his

smooth green scalp a fierce, unaccustomed kiss, and thrust the
stick into Mikai's waistband. "You will be the keeper of the
days."

A twig snapped. A paw brushed through downed leaves. In
the darkness across the fire, something growled low in its
throat. Mikai froze like a fawn, eyes wide, and Nalinle sprang
to his feet, all senses alert, the firelight stark on his face. He
searched the darkness with eyes dulled from the bright flames
at his feet. *Where are they*? What *are they*?

There were several pairs of flat, luminous eyes—five animals, he judged, or five demons—watching from the shelter of
the undergrowth just outside the firelight. He grabbed a
burning brand and flung it with all his might at the nearest pair
of eyes. There was a surprised yelp and a brief disturbance in
the brush, and something snarled. One of the predators started
up a yowling song, quickly taken up by one or two of the
others, making Nalinle's scalp crawl. He grabbed a second
burning stick from the fire and charged them, shouting inco-
herently, for he was terrified. He laid about wildly with the
burning club, hitting furry animal bodies with heavy thuds, and
in seconds, the animals fled yelping away through the underbrush. He trudged back to the dim fire, bleeding from bites on
his arm and leg and trembling with fear and fatigue. "They are
gone, for now," he said. Tossed aside the doused torch. Kicked
dirt over the embers.

"But they will come back." He swung his pack onto his stiff
shoulders and levered Mikai's ungainly dead weight into his
arms. He picked his way carefully through the dark to the
water's edge and, wading in, began to jog upstream through the
shallows.

A night-bird's song came sweetly through the quiet splashing
of his passage, and some distance away, the predators yowled
their hunting song to the moons. Nalinle jogged steadily on,
seeing only the black forest of the night, and the silver highroad
of the River's child, leading him to the Hopeship.

The headache was gone. The absence of his throbbing
headache was the first sensation of which Dao Marik became

aware, and for a long while he simply lay there with his eyes shut, enjoying the absence of pain. His shoulder and chest itched madly, and he was not surprised to open his eyes and see that, still ensconced in his MAX, he was under a Regenerator. That accounted for the itching, then, he thought dreamily. The low-grade electrical current of the ReGen unit, matched to the current found in the distal extremities of developing organisms, was literally rebuilding his missing tissue, itching unbelievably as it did so.

Perhaps the pleasant drowsiness was from the antihistamines they would have ordered to control the itching. He felt sleepy and comfortable. The soft hum of the metallic unit encasing his chest, shoulder and arm was gently soporific, and smelled faintly of ozone and thunderstorms. There was another odor nearby, too, sweetish and musky, that made him vaguely uneasy. He tried to place it, but somehow it eluded him.

He tested his hands and legs fractionally, experimentally, and found everything to be in good working order. Explored the smarting at his right temple with cautious fingers and found a small, healing scar. Scar? he wondered. He felt surprisingly well for a post-op patient, even with the residual weakness. He was ravenously hungry.

The sweet, unfamiliar musky odor intensified, and something touched his forehead lightly. He looked up to see the great red multifaceted eyes of a Droso riveted upon him at very close range. One of its hairy manipulators continued stroking his forehead, while another found his jugular vein and rested firmly upon it for an extended moment. In spite of himself, Marik felt a lurch at the pit of his stomach. He had never been so close to a live Droso before (though he had dissected several Droso cadavers), and they had a well-deserved reputation for being as deadly a race as one might find in the known galaxy.

Primarily insectile, the Droso lived mainly on nectar and plant juices, siphoned up through their long probosces; but during their spring mating season, both males and females required a sizable ration of mammalian blood for the production of viable young. Please T'ath, it was not springtime for Droso, Marik mused sleepily. He was a bit short in the available blood department, just now. Not being sure what to do next, he simply waited. It was the Droso who spoke first.

"Einai," it began, vibrating its wings to a silver blur. "My name izz PprumBurr. I mmm phyzzician." It took Marik a moment to get used to decoding PprumBurr's unorthodox communication, after which it became reasonably clear and even rather pleasant, like bees murmuring on a warm afternoon.

"Zzharobi wazz here?"

"Earlier. Neal Anderson, too, I think, but he's gone back to *Skipjack*." He was surprised at how well he felt. "How long have I been here?"

The Droso scratched between its eyes with one oral manipulator, considering. "Three rr four dayzz. Nno, mmore. One week. I cann check, 'fyou like. Howzz head feelnngg?" it wanted to know. "Hurrtt?"

"No," Marik told it. "The throbbing's gone. That's a plus. I expected some post-op pain, too, but—"

"Nno pozzttopp. Nno zzurgrry on head," the Droso replied. "Nnew technnique. Drrozzo technique. Zzip—inn! Zzip—clott outt!

"Deliciouzz," it said reminiscently, as an afterthought. Its thin black tongue quickly swept its proboscis and its hidden lancet and disappeared again. Many things came to Marik's mind, but at last he said the only thing he really meant.

"Thank you—very kindly—Dr. PprumBurr."

With all six legs it made a curious little *demi-plié*, then reached over and adjusted a series of dials on his MAXpak before it stroked Marik's forehead gently again.

"Zzleep," hummed its wings softly. "Zzleep nnow."

Comforted and ineffably weary, Marik slept.

The predators were after them again.

The stream, the River's child, became narrower as they ran, a mere thin trickle of cold water and wan light gleaming in the eerie pre-dawn blackness. The animals were hunting them in earnest now, baying down the wind, and Nalinle plunged into a ravine beside the watercourse. He raced blindly on, lungs on fire, heart thudding in his chest. The baying faded, and he slowed. Stopped, listening. There was nothing. Leaned against a tree, eyes shut, panting. Mikai made a fretful, frightened sound, and Nalinle sobbed, between breaths, "No, Mikai . . . hush . . . I think we've lost them. . . ."

The baying resumed, a sudden shock of sound almost beside them, and Nalinle was off again, leaves slapping his face, in a headlong, stumbling run. He was tiring quickly now, and on the edge of despair. There must be a way out, a refuge, a hope—! He searched the pathways and brush desperately, and in his hopelessness, almost missed his only chance. There—below! A dense thorn thicket, woven of tough canes, each armed with long, sharp spines, enclosing a hollow big enough to conceal them both.

Nalinle grabbed a low-hanging limb, swung himself and Mikai off the ground and over the drop, and plunged feet first down the embankment. He rose bruised and shaking, but with nothing broken. A quick check satisfied him that all was well with Mikai.

Recklessly, Nalinle tried to force an entry into the thorn cage, and cried out as he slashed his hands on the thorns. The baying came closer. He grabbed a broken piece of branch and tried to use it as a pry bar, but the soft, rotten wood crumbled in his hand. They could hear the eager whimpering of the predators now, sniffing on the ridge above them for their scent. Any moment, they would find him and Mikai and tear them to pieces. He dragged the boy as close as he dared to the thorn cage, and, gritting his teeth, got his back under the edge of it, lifting the heavy canes by main strength. He ignored the hot bite of thorns raking his back, and the renewed baying of the beasts above him, and strained against the stubborn thicket. After a reluctant moment, it began to lift, the opening only a few hands high. Not enough. Mikai could not pass beneath it yet. He shoved his head under the thorns as well, and pushing with all his strength, he raised the edge a full cubit.

He reached down, the cage settling painfully on his head and shoulders, and grabbing Mikai's arm, dragged him under the protection of the cage. With an abrupt, stunning barrage of howls, the predators burst into the ravine and bounded toward them, just as Nalinle threw himself down and backward, tripping over his son as he dropped the curtain of thorns abruptly between himself and the rapacious pack. Unable to halt their forward momentum, the beasts crashed into it with shrill yelps and yodels. Nalinle, bleeding from a dozen deep scratches, smiled and patted Mikai's face reassuringly, but could not yet speak. He was dripping sweat, and the scent of his fresh blood drove the beasts mad. They pawed and gnashed at the thorn enclosure for a long while, snarling and digging at it, and whining when there was no way to reach the two humans inside.

"Twenty-six days . . . to the Hopeship, Mikai . . ." Nalinle's breath was ragged and he laughed a bit to cover it. " . . . twenty-six days . . . and you will be straight. . . ." He curled up in exhaustion, protecting the boy in the curve of his body, and, resting his head on his bent arm, was asleep almost immediately.

Mikai, however, stayed awake for a long time, thinking and wondering, looking up with bright eyes past his prison at the far and myriad stars.

CHAPTER

II

DOYON KAHARL, R.N., stood panting at the door flap of the medical outpost tent on Ildefor, fanning himself with an empty file folder. His thick mahogany fur stood stiffly on end, and he pulled the antistatic pump spray out of his pak again and gave himself another thorough once-over, until his fur lay flat. Even with the spray, he avoided touching the other members of the Medical Team, for the slightest contact gave both parties a nasty shock.

He squinted against the light and sighed heavily. He had been staring out into the savage sunlight and endless, empty sand dunes of Ildefor for two weeks, and still not one patient had shown up. The Senn, always reliable in these matters, had reported scores of scattered villages; and their native contact, an impressive fellow by the name of Sheikh Jamal al-Musa, had brought them three Scup patients and promised to send the tribes along. But he and his men had ridden away on their splendid horses, and, excepting the occasional swooping *tsai* and the endlessly circling *kaits*, they had seen no other life.

No one had come.

Heaving another sigh, Doyon retraced his steps into the huge, empty hospital tent, where the rest of the Team waited.

The tent was filled with a muted golden haze, as if the sunlight had oozed through the canvas, slow and liquid, like warm honey, and pooled on the warm fiberplast floor. The heat was all-encompassing. Even the examining tables and instruments felt as if they had just come out of an oven. There was no cool surface anywhere.

Theresa Paladino and Yoghesh Svilaby, their doctors, were sitting in camp chairs. Yoghi, his head tipped back, was snoring softly, and Theresa, dulled into half-sleep by two weeks worth of heat and boredom, leafed woodenly through a month-old magazine she had brought down with her from the ship.

Pawa and Esme, the two Einai nurses, had put aside their needlework and were watching Janicke Rom and Buflo Kodi, one of the Senn, shooting T'iq on the floor. The Senn set the rods and cast the dice, and Rom winced.

"*Pift*, another *ferhoven* deuce," he muttered, and Kodi chuckled.

"Never gamble with us Senn, friend," he advised, picking up the thin sheaf of credits off the fiberplast and pocketing it. "Custer tried it with my ancestors, and look where it got him."

"One more time," Rom suggested, peeling off a few more credits from his diminishing wad and tossing them down. "This time, *I* set the rods, and *I* get to shoot."

"Go for it, friend," the Senn said, licking his long canines and smiling. "Like they say, there's another one born every minute."

Beyond one of the nearby dunes, a trio of nomads, in kaffiyehs and burnooses, had been keeping watch since sunup on the aliens' tent. Their leader, a reckless youth who had not yet seen his twenty-fifth summer, was on an errand for the Caliph himself, and he took his responsibility seriously.

"These offworlders are our last chance to save the dynasty of my lord the Caliph Ishaq ibn Muhammad al-Ghazi. If we fail, and Prince Salman is forced to marry the Grand Vizier's daughter—"

"—the spavined camel!" Sethi groaned.

"Rather, Hamid Vizier's route to the throne, via the marriage bed," Kedar rumbled, scowling.

"Mind your tongue, old friend," Voldi advised, "or one of Hamid Vizier's minions may deprive you of it." He returned his eagle's gaze to the hospital tent below. "Surely they will have at least one suitable female to interest the Prince. All we have to do is find her."

Kedar scratched his graying beard. "Finding her, Voldi, is one matter; getting the Prince to notice her could be quite another."

"Without a wife, Prince Salman cannot ascend to the Throne of Antar," Voldi answered, reiterating what they all knew. "Since he will look at none of our women—"

"Aye, all he wants is his accursed books!" Kedar hissed in disgust. "No wonder the Caliph always has a headache!"

"—perhaps he will accept an alien woman."

"*Ya Allah*," Kedar murmured. "I hope so!"

"I don't know why you're so worried, Voldi," Sethi muttered. "If the royal bookworm defaults on his obligations, your family is next in line for the throne." He gazed out over the sand. "I'd look for her with one eye shut, if I were you."

"I am the faithful servant of my lord the Caliph," Voldi said, "and I intend to serve him—and Prince Salman—to the best of my ability! Besides, Sethi," he added, whacking him playfully, "if I became a Prince, who'd go stealing horses from the Parsi with you?" He whirled on the suddenly enlightened Kedar. "Not a word about that to my father, Kedar!"

Kedar stroked his beard. "You know I would *never* tell, young master," he promised. "I might ask him if he knows, but—I would never *tell* him."

"I need to get inside and have a good look around. You two keep watch," Voldi instructed, slipping his dagger out of its sheath. "Once the tribes come and they are too busy to notice me, I will go down and have my injury tended."

"What injury?" Sethi frowned. Voldi bared his left forearm and drew the dagger across it in one swift motion. The wound gushed redly, dripping into the sand.

"This one," he grinned. "Get me a strip of rag, will you?"

The ever-present flies began to gather as Kedar bound up the arm. "Now that you can call yourself a patient, what do we do?"

"We wait," Voldi said.

The sun stood still in the brassy blue sky. There was not a cloud to be seen, nor would there be, until the torrential autumn rains graced the desert with their all-too-transient green.

Overhead, a *tsai* circled endlessly, hunting for some tasty
mammal imprudent enough to forage at midday. Heat waves
wavered on the scorching air, and the low buzz of flies,
clustered on the blackened blood clots in the sand, was an
urgent inducement to sleep. Sethi yawned. A horse stamped a
foot and blew. A dry, aimless wind swept sand off the tips of
the dunes, polishing them to endless shades of buff and cream,
sable and gold, while their melting shadows stretched and slid
slowly down their flanks.

It was very, very hot.

Esme Cuf, tired of watching Rom lose his money, stood up
and stretched like her ancestor cats. She patted a delicate yawn.

"Ho-hum. Two whole weeks, and still no takers," she
complained. "Nothing ever happens around here." Hoping for
a breath of air, she strolled lazily to the brilliant shard of
sunlight that marked the door—and caught that breath sharply
in astonishment.

"Oh, good T'ath!" she exclaimed. "Look what's coming!"

The others hurried to crowd behind her as, from every point
on the compass, they saw on the horizon a wriggling, shimmering black phantasm, like one gigantic circular creature,
gradually closing in on the medical installation.

"What the hell is it?" Rom demanded, and Pawa gripped his
arm with nervous fingers.

"Is it alive?" she asked.

"Could be," Kodi muttered. "This reminds me of the time on
Canopus Five, where that big ringmold ate fifteen medics
and—"

"Mold doesn't grow on deserts, for Siv's sake, Kodi," Rom
interrupted. "Too dry. It's got to be something else."

"You want to bet me?" The Senn leered. "Come on, what've
you got?" But Rom silenced him with a graphic gesture.

"It's probably just a mirage," Yoghi Svilaby suggested
uncomfortably. "Something is moving far off across the desert,
and we're just getting the reflected image here." But Theresa
shook her head, still watching the thing approach.

"I don't think so, Yoghi. I think whatever it is, it knows

we're here. And it's coming on purpose." She looked up at him with her candid brown stare. "Straight for us."

After a long while, Voldi lifted his head, listening; got to his feet and climbed the slight ridge above them, scanning the horizon. Kedar scowled at Sethi, who shook his head. They had heard nothing.

One of the horses, and then another, snuffed the air and whickered, and Kedar slipped away to the camouflaged shelter to quiet them.

"Here they come," Voldi muttered. He pointed across the dunes, where dark lines of massed humanity approached from various directions, converging inexorably upon the big khaki tent below.

To the great relief of the Medical Team, the frightful black apparition had slowly reconciled itself into an uncountable multitude of black-swathed Bedouins making their way slowly and steadily toward the outpost.

They were so close now that the Team could pick out the occasional individual, walking apart from the others, and some of the men seemed to be carrying heavy, closed litters between them.

"I wonder what *that's* all about," Theresa Paladino mused aloud, and Yoghi Svilaby, the Team leader, blew out a held breath.

"We'll find out soon enough. At least we aren't going to be the entree for some kind of exotic slime mold, that's the main thing. Pawa," he said to the middle-aged Einai nurse at his elbow, "you're the triage officer until further notice. Get ready to start sorting them out. Esme can help if you need her.

"Kodi, how about you play clerk and record these people for us?" The Senn shook his massive head as he quickly picked up the T'iq pieces and stuffed them into his pouch.

"Uh-*uh*. Count me out, Doc. Sick people make me queasy. I'll just stand back here and watch."

"You'd refuse to help us?" Yoghi yelped, waving an arm at the oncoming throng. "With a mob like that coming at us?"

Kodi tucked his chin into his mane and pulled an offended face.

"We Senn already helped," he retorted defensively. "Hey, we did our job! We *found* these people for you!"

"Well, that's fine, but it's not much help right now, is it?"

"What do you want, two for one? We've got to find 'em and document 'em, too? What're you, some kind of white guy? Next thing I know, you'll want me to sign a treaty!"

"Don't let's get abusive, Kodi!"

"Look, Yoghi, you do your job, I do mine. You're the doctor, you do doctor stuff. I'm the scout, I scout. Ours is an old and noble profession, for pity's sake! And it doesn't include doing your paperwork!" He retired, offended, to the far tent wall, to smoke alone. Yoghi sighed.

"Okay, okay. Rom, you take over clerking, will you?" Janicke Rom nodded, pulled a table and chair outside the tent flap, broke out the Case Book and switched it on.

Ready, it said, and Rom ordered, "Stand by one."

The tribesmen were close enough now for individual features to be made out, and their collective scent, the smell of some sharp resin, of musk, and of goats, drifted in on the hot wind. Their voices, a muted cacophony of sibilant babble, made a sound like distant surf.

"It's going to be a long, long afternoon," Theresa observed cheerfully. "And I'm going to love every minute of it."

Esme broke out the hypodermics, loaded them with charges of broad-spectrum antibiotics, and set them by, just as the first desperate, hopeful group of natives crowded around the front of the tent, darkening the sun.

The air in the tent soon became close and noisy with the shrill chatter of women, the groans of the ill, and the wailing of children. Esme helped Pawa sort through the hundreds of patients, dividing them into three categories: those who must be helped immediately, those who could wait for help, and those whom no one could help. She had just handed one of the last group, a pitiful little bundle of soiled rags and stiffening limbs, back to its grieving mother, when she turned to the next patient in line and met the full blaze of a pair of warm black eyes. She blinked.

He was about her own age, she noted absently, several inches taller than she, and wore tunic and trousers of the same sturdy sand-colored material as his flowing burnoose. A golden amulet of some sort hung on a flat chain around his neck. There was a sword at his side and a jeweled dagger thrust through his sash. His black beard was trimmed close, and he looked like a young man accustomed to having his orders followed at once. He was also very handsome. For an alien, she corrected herself quickly. Handsome for an alien.

"Oh," she said. Pawa moved forward, but Esme, without looking at her, said, "I'll take this one, Pawa." She blinked again, and her patient began to smile, his teeth startlingly white in his swarthy face. He made a quick, graceful gesture from heart to lips to forehead.

"Peace," he said. *Nice voice*, she thought. *For an alien.*

"What are you doing here?" she asked. "I mean, what's wrong with you? Not that anything looks wrong," she hastened to add. "But—" He pushed back his sleeve, revealing the gory makeshift bandage.

"I cut my arm," he said. He was several levels above the natives they had been doctoring all afternoon, she thought. Quiet. Well-spoken. Obviously one of the gentry. She wondered who he was, and where he came from. He certainly was awfully attractive, if you liked the type. For an alien, of course.

Pulling herself together with a decided effort (after all, Esme, you are a *Nursing Professional*, and Nursing Professionals do not, *not*, NOT, get emotionally involved with their patients), she hooked a foot under the rungs of a chair and pulled it forward.

"You can sit here. Arm on the table, please." He complied, and as she unwrapped the soggy rags, he leaned forward to peer closely at her face.

"Your skin is green," he said with a tinge of wonder.

"Ummm. We have a whole planet full of people with green skin, where I come from," she murmured, tugging with a forceps at a stuck bit of bandage. "Want to scoot a little closer to the table, please?"

"Look at me," he said and she faced him squarely for a long minute while he studied her face with apparent delight.

"Well?"

"You are exactly perfect."

"Not quite," she demurred, laughing uncomfortably, "as any of my co-workers can tell you—"

"And your eyes have slit pupils," he continued, pleased.

"I'm an Einai." She smiled in spite of herself. "We all have green skin, and we all have slit pupils. And we like it that way." She freed the last thread, dropped the bloody rags into a waste receptacle and examined the slash in his arm with cat's-paw delicacy. "I'm afraid this is going to take a few stitches. How did it happen?"

"I told you. I cut myself."

"On what?" He whipped out the dagger and held up both sides of the shiny blades for her inspection.

"An accident?" He shook his head in the negative, holding her with his eyes as he put away the knife.

"You cut yourself on purpose?" He nodded, the smile gathering in his trim black beard.

"*Why?*"

"So I could come here and find you." There was no reason for her hearts to make that sudden jump. She began to cleanse the wound with sterile sponges.

"I cannot believe that a person of your obvious intelligence would deliberately hurt himself." She glanced up reproachfully at him, but he was still watching her with that amused and admiring dark stare that made her feel as if she had appeared in public with nothing on.

"Believe it," he said softly. "It was a small price to pay for finding you." She felt her face grow warm. It was time, she felt, to stop this nonsense here and now.

"I want you to understand something, sir. I'm a nurse here," she explained firmly. "I'm not here to- to-" She faltered to a stop. "I am *an R.N.*" She picked up the suture gun and switched it on. There was the tiny *z-z-zziiiinnng* of power coming up. She took hold of his arm, bringing the edges of the smooth, tawny skin together between her fingers. Checked the suture

gun, frowning. The electric thrill in her fingertips was surely
due to a malfunction somewhere in the unit. She wondered if
he could feel it, too.

"Do you feel a kind of an, ah—electrical field?" she asked.
"Here, where I'm touching your arm? A sort of a tingling—"
Bother the man! He was looking at her as if—well, as if simply
touching him could produce that electricity. Some people had
their nerve, she thought, her fingers still tingling. Yoghi would
have to check out the whole suture unit. It was obviously a
technological problem, and had nothing at all to do with the
alien.

"This may sting a little," she warned, but his expression
never changed, from the first burst of light to the last, and
through the bandaging. When she was finished, he rose and
flexed the arm. Nodded.

"It is good, N.R.N.," he told her. "Many thanks. What do I
owe you?"

"Oh, nothing at all. It's all free. A public service to your
planet from the good ship *Hope*." But he was having none of it.

"You don't understand, N.R.N. These people"—he gestured
at the noisy natives—"can afford to take charity, for they have
nothing else. But the son of Sheikh Jamal al-Musa pays his
own way." He reached for his *tsai* amulet and slipped the gold
chain off his neck and over her head before she had time to
protest. The *tsai* looked very content resting against its soft
new nest, he thought.

"Why—this is valuable, I can't take this!" Esme protested,
as he started to walk away. "Take it back! Sir! You can't leave
it here! Take it with you. Sir!"

"I'll come back for it later," he promised over his shoulder,
and he was lost in the crowd. She stood staring after him until
Pawa touched her arm.

"Esme, wake up," she said. "What's wrong with you?" Esme
startled, came back to a semi-reality, still seeing the smoldering
gaze, the striking white smile.

"Who was that man?" she asked, bemused. Pawa followed
her gaze and, seeing only the milling, barefoot natives,
shrugged.

"Which one? There are hundreds. Come on," she added briskly, "the queue is getting longer by the minute, and this next poor woman needs attention right away."

Sighing, Esme got back to work, the amulet heavy around her neck.

"I have found the woman." Voldi topped the rise, slid down the slope and leaned back against the hollow of the dune. "*Ya Allah!*" he exclaimed. "She is so beautiful, the very stones should sing!"

"Did you explain the great honor we are offering her?" Kedar rumbled. "Will she come of her own accord?"

"She wouldn't even smile of her own accord, until I coaxed her! Ah, but when she did—" He broke off and shook his head. "The stones should have sung," he repeated.

"So how do we catch her?" Sethi asked. "And when?"

Voldi sat up, smoothed the sand with his palm and drew a square in the dry sand with his finger, indicating various positions as he spoke.

"This is the hospital. Right now, the offworlders are very busy, especially the woman. But she must take her rest some time. After sundown, I think. She will come outside, *here*. You two stand lookout, *here*, and *here*, with the horses saddled and ready, and I will catch her myself."

"Are you sure the Prince will like her?" Sethi asked.

"Am I sure? Sethi, you should see her! Jade skin, eyes as gold as this—" He reached for his amulet and broke off, flushing. "Anyway, she has golden eyes, her hair is as black as a *kait*'s wing, and she moves like the wind across the dunes. How could even *he* not like her?"

"What happened to your amulet?" Sethi wanted to know, and Kedar eyed him suspiciously.

"You gave it to her, didn't you?"

"As payment for the medical attention, yes!" Voldi defended.

"Are you sure you don't want her for yourself?" the older man suggested.

"Of course not!" Voldi answered. "I am catching her strictly for the Prince." Kedar made no reply but continued smiling and stroking his beard, like a man who knew a secret, until Voldi, much annoyed, stalked away and flung himself down in the shadow of the horses' shelter for a nap.

Theresa had been right, Esme thought that night as she stepped outside for a break. It had been a long afternoon, followed by a longer night. Theresa had enjoyed every minute of it; Esme had merely gotten bone-tired.

Ten minutes, she had told Yoghi. After the crowded tent and the variety of disease, deformity and deterioration that went with it, ten blessed minutes alone in the quiet night would feel like a month in the country.

She took a deep breath of fresh, crisp air, stretching her arms wide, and started walking slowly around the tent, working out the kinks in her sore muscles. She rotated her head on a stiff neck; tried a few round-dance steps, humming to herself, even did a few half-hearted calisthenics before giving it up. The breeze was cool and the sky thick with stars. Fine sand made a faint *shush*ing sound under her feet, and her eyes, equipped with the night-sight of her feline ancestors, made out a serpent slithering away; a four-footed predator slinking along the shadow of a dune; and the thousands of wind-carved sand ripples, mimicking shallow water.

She reached for the amulet on her breast and studied it carefully in the bright starlight. It was a bird, such as she had seen often circling over the desert, its four wings extended, its short, broad tail fanned wide. Its eye and open beak held a tiny pair of brilliant jewels she did not recognize.

She turned it slightly from side to side, watching the play of starlight on the jewels and thinking about the odd encounter with the handsome young stranger this afternoon. Wondered dreamily who he was, and why he had come, and where he might be right now.

Thus occupied, she was not prepared for the sudden rush from behind her, the quick hand over her mouth and the thick rug over her head that muffled her cries as she was picked up bodily, slung over a saddle, and carried away far into the starry, starry night.

● ● ●

They were well beyond earshot of the medical outpost before Voldi and Kedar finally reined in their horses and waited for Sethi, who had hung back in case of pursuit. The rug-wrapped bundle writhed and jerked furiously, emitting muffled screams and imprecations in three galactic languages. Kedar gestured.

"Maybe you should let her ride behind you," he said. Voldi lifted the still-kicking bundle from his horse's withers and, as he stood Esme on her feet and pulled away the rug, started back as she came up like a wild cat, scratching and biting. She landed a few smart slaps before Voldi held her firmly still at arm's-length.

"You!" she raged. "How dare you! How *could* you! I"—she jabbed her finger into her chest—"have a job to do!"—she pointed in the direction she believed the hospital to be—"back there!" Kedar lifted a hand.

"Your pardon, lady," he broke in gently, and pointed off to one side. "It's that way." She glared at him for a moment, then blinked.

"Are you sure?"

"Quite sure. That way."

"Thank you." She glowered up at Voldi again. "Back *there!*" She pointed in the new direction, then dropped the arm with a wordless sound of fury and stamped her foot. "I demand you take me back at once, do you hear me? *Do you hear?*"

"All Ildefor hears," Kedar said mildly, and Voldi was much amused.

"Sh-sh," he cautioned Esme, a finger at his lips. "Patience. Sweet patience, N.R.N. I will explain." She subsided with a poisonously sweet smile, standing motionless as a cobra ready to strike. She might've beamed back to the hospital anytime, she knew; but to do so in front of planetary locals, except in an emergency, would be a violation of the Galactic Compact. Better by far to demand they return her to the outpost by ordinary means. By this point, ordinary means, in Esme's estimation, included the removal of their faces without benefit of anesthesia.

"*Do* explain," she said.

"We are offering you our planet's highest honor," he told her. "We are taking you into the household of His Royal Highness, Prince Salman ibn Muhammad al-Ghazi, to become one of his wives. We offer you a life of ultimate luxury, jewels, slaves—"

"Oh, fine! Just fine!" Esme frothed. "*One* of his wives? I know what this is, it's an alien proposition! This is rich! This is wonderful!" She jammed both fists into her negligible hips. "You think I haven't been propositioned before? You think I don't recognize the old 'How-about-a-little-coffee-and-couch-my-wife's-out-of - town - and - I'll - buy - you - a - brand - new - full - length - *kundu* - coat' routine? Well, forget it! This girl's not interested! I happen to be that anachronism called a nice girl! And this nice girl's going back, and she's going back right now! Are you going to take me, or do I walk?"

Voldi spread his hands. "Unfortunately, N.R.N., my vowed obedience to the Caliph prevents my returning you to your tent."

"Fine! That's fine with me! I'll walk! Fine!" No one moved as she started marching angrily off across the deep sand, but after the first few yards, Kedar shifted in the saddle and cleared his throat.

"Pardon once more, lady." She wheeled, ready to do battle yet again, but the grave older man merely indicated, with a long arm, a direction slightly to the right of the one she had been taking.

She lifted inquiring brows, raised her hand, and pointed in the new direction.

He pursed his lips and nodded soberly. She screwed up her face in chagrin, but seeing Voldi's wide smile, lifted her chin.

"Fine!" she snapped, and started off determinedly on the correct course.

Esme had walked quite a long way in a half-hour, she thought, always conscious of the two mounted natives riding several yards behind her. Her muscles were beginning to cramp but she ignored them and marched on.

"I beg you to reconsider," Kedar pleaded again. "It is very important that you marry the Prince." Esme nodded vigorously to herself, said something under her breath, and kept walking.

"He is a very intelligent man," Kedar pursued. "And he is rich beyond your wildest dreams—and some even say handsome!" Voldi pulled a long face at him, but he made an overhand, placating gesture, and resumed, "Anyone would be happy to be chosen his bride." Esme turned around and kept walking, but backwards now.

"Wrong," she snapped, stumbling a bit on the sliding sand, which she kicked. "*Ouel! Bosna kirit!* Wrong! *I'm* not happy, and *I'm* someone!" She turned around and continued her odyssey, the men riding slowly along behind her.

"You place me in an embarrassing position, N.R.N.," Voldi pursued. "I have promised His Highness to bring the Prince the most beautiful woman on the planet, or die. If I go back without you, I am either lost or a liar!" She fought back the smile that crept, unbidden, to her lips.

"That's your problem," she retorted. "Deal with it."

"It isn't working," Kedar observed, and Voldi murmured, "Patience, my friend. Remember the saying, 'A soft tongue can take milk from a lioness.'"

"I *beg* your pardon!" Esme stopped, wheeled and glared at him. "I very well *beg* your *perpendicular* pardon! Milk from a lioness indeed! You keep well away from me, if you know what's— You just *try* to— I guess because we Einai are—! Sure, *well!* Let me tell *you* something! I— You—" She sputtered to a furious stop.

"*Fine!*" She exploded, her eyes brimming, and turning around, began to run blindly away. There was a roaring in her ears, and the sand was deep and difficult to run through. She heard Voldi shouting behind her, but ignored him. Let him shout! She was going back to the hospital, and nothing was going to stop her!

"Wait, N.R.N.! he yelled frantically behind her, his horse now coming at a gallop. There was the metallic song of his scimitar whipping out of his scabbard. "Wait!" but she ran all the faster, scrambling and clawing at the deep sand, up one side of a large dune. As she was about to gain the crest, she heard another hearts-stopping roar above her.

A huge male lion was silhouetted against the stars. Its head swung toward her and it snarled a warning, its intense eyes lambent in the starlight. It snarled again, tail lashing lazily from side to side, and she floundered to a stop, breathing hard. Her hearts were pounding in her chest and ears, and she found herself so weak and shaky that she couldn't move, even when the beast started making its way eagerly down the slope toward her.

Dr. Theresa Paladino had finally sat down, put up her swollen feet, and opened her water carafe. After almost ten hours of steady work, she savored the warmish water that slid down her throat only to spring through her skin seconds later as perspiration. A cool breeze blew through the tent, chilling the moisture, and she pushed her hair back from her face with both hands and shut her smarting eyes. *What a great day*, she thought, *I must have treated a hundred and fifty people.* She was sinking into a lovely half-drowse when Pawa Gria, the older Einai nurse, touched her shoulder.

"Doctor, excuse me, but Esme is missing."

"What do you mean, missing?"

"She's not here. She told Dr. Svilaby she'd be back within ten minutes, and that was hours ago." Her face was lined with concern, and Theresa patted her arm.

"We'll go have a look. I'm sure she's fine. Remember, 'When you hear hoofbeats around here, it's more likely horses than zebras.'"

"Why should I remember that?" Pawa asked. "I didn't hear any—"

"It's an old Earthling saying. And it's a good one. It means, 'Look for the ordinary—like, maybe Esme wandered off a little too far—before you imagine fantastic things like, maybe Hassan-of-the-Desert carried her off on a white horse to an oasis somewhere, okay?"

"Certainly, Doctor. Er, could you tell me, who is Hassan—"

"Don't ask," Theresa advised. "Just don't ask."

Half an hour later, everyone was concerned. Buflo Kodi, pressed into service, read the tracks and told them that Esme had, indeed, come outside by the side tent flap, and had walked alone for perhaps fifty yards before she'd evidently been abducted by a man (definitely a man) riding—he displayed two long strands of horsehair—a white horse. Pawa caught her breath and stared round-eyed at Theresa, but wisely said nothing. Yoghi frowned at the scuffle graphically depicted in sand.

"We'd better alert the ship," he decided, leading them back inside the tent. "Follow routine procedures."

"You do that," Theresa told him. "Meantime, Kodi and I are going after her. By the time they get a Security Team down here, anything could happen." Kodi showed his fanged smile.

"I'm with you, Doc. I'll lay you ten to one I find her before sunup." Theresa slung her bulging medikit over her shoulder and slapped a ten-credit note down on an examining table.

"You're on," she said, and before Yoghi could raise the ship, they had started across the desert in hot pursuit.

Esme could feel the sand that had worked its way into her shoes, the cool night breeze against her skin, and her muscles aching with their unaccustomed activity. But all she could see was the hypnotic gaze of the lion that was making its way toward her.

Suddenly there was an explosion around her of hoofbeats, flung sand, and wild yells as Voldi and Kedar, scimitars raised, thundered past her toward the lion. Confused by this sudden turn of events, the big cat settled back on its haunches, its ears flattened, half-heartedly snarling and swiping at the men a few times before it surrendered and ran away over the ridge.

Voldi rode up, sheathing his scimitar. "Are you all right, N.R.N.?" She nodded, unable to speak for fear of weeping, for her legs and chin were frankly trembling. He reached down and swept her up before him on his saddle.

"I have indulged you as much as I am able, lady," he admonished, "but now we must make haste. We are due in Fatima by noon tomorrow, and we still have many leagues to go."

It was midnight when Sethi, his horse lathered and blowing, met them on the wharf at Jedda, reporting that a female alien with a large, hairy pet had begun a pursuit, but that he had confused the trail.

"He's not a pet," Esme corrected, as Sethi took off his headcloth and carefully wiped down his shivering horse. "He's a person, a Senn scout, and they can track anything, anywhere, anytime. They're the best trackers in the universe." Sethi, who had taken off his cloak to cover his mount, made a truncated bow in her direction.

"My apologies, N.R.N."

"And stop calling me *an R.N.*!" she burst out. "My *name* is Esme Cuf! My *profession* is R.N., Registered Nurse!"

"You are a medical individual?" Kedar exclaimed in delight. "*Al-hamdu lillah!* The Prince will pour a thousand blessings upon our heads!"

"Why? Is he sick?"

"Worse," Sethi told her glumly. "He is a scholar."

A felucca slowly hove into position against the wharf, its sail blotting out a geometric section of stars.

"Restrain yourself, hothead," Kedar chided over his shoulder, as he went down to speak to her owner. "Remember, it is well said that 'The ink of scholars is more precious than the blood of martyrs.' "

"*Esme?* Your name is Esme?" Voldi turned away and patted his horse's neck to cover his embarrassment. "Then I have been calling you wrongly. I have made myself a fool." She laid a hand on his arm.

"Mistaken, maybe, Voldi," she said. "Never a fool."

"Esme," he repeated, looking deep into her golden eyes. "*Es*-me." They shared a warm smile.

"Now that you know it, make sure you don't forget."

"Never, Esme," he promised softly. "I will never forget."

CHAPTER

III

IN THE MIDDLE of being fed his lunch, Dr. Charles Snow Lassiter, high-level Non-Official Cover for Interpol, had a sudden horrible thought. Something, he realized, was terribly wrong. He felt as if he had stepped unwittingly into a trap.

He stopped chewing a particularly succulent morsel of Chicken Kiev and stared with still, drawn face and wide eyes at his nurse, Ulrika Drac.

She looked German! How could he have failed to notice something so obvious? She was so fair as to appear insubstantial, with her tow-colored braid and her translucent, colorless skin. He had seen eyes of the same cold and unresponsive ice-blue before, on a rocky little island named Kós, in the Mediterranean Sea. They had regarded him then, as now, as something less than human, beneath notice. It was as if an arctic wind had blown on the back of his neck. She lowered the fork.

"What can be the matter, Charles Lassiter? You are not hungry, is it?" *You are not hungry, is it?* she had said. How familiar, the cadence, the accent. How horrible. Someone else, somewhere, someWhen had said, *Radios, is it? What else are you carrying, Herr Spy?* Then there had been the boots and fists and bayonets. And the door. The awful door.

He swallowed hard and drew away almost imperceptibly, resting his twisted hands against his chest. "You're not, um—" He cleared his throat. "Forgive me for asking, but—you're not *German*, by any chance, are you, Miss Drac?" Ulrika Drac drew back haughtily.

43

"I? Of course not! That is an *Erthlik* race! I am pure Krail, for a hundred generations!" Her chin came up proudly and her thin nostrils flared. "Now that you bring it out, I will tell it you: I was to replace the third consort of Beq nom-Pau himself, before I cried amnesty." Lassiter, immensely relieved, lifted his brows in admiration.

"Well, now, that *is* impressive."

This put a different face on the situation. She was a Krail, and a free woman at that. Not a German, after all. Merely a Krail. He relaxed and considered her situation.

Among the Krail, whose harsh, repressive laws permitted infanticide, abortion and multiple consorts, crying amnesty was tantamount to committing suicide. Krail women were destined to be used as pawns by their fathers, and later, by their husbands, in a complex game of social intrigue that included the elimination of rivals by violence, arranged marriages and the auctioning of politically promising sons to the highest bidder. Any woman who dared cry amnesty sacrificed family ties, friends, citizenship, any hope of marriage, and the protection of others of her race; even her family name was permanently replaced by the hated title 'drac': dragon.

On the other hand, once granted amnesty, she was free. Free to leave the planet (at the Imperium's insistent invitation), to seek an education elsewhere, to pursue her heart's desire.

For Ulrika Drac, this meant a long-dreamed-of career in nursing, but she had graduated at the top of her class only to find that there were virtually no openings for Krail women, even those with impressive credentials. The fault lay, not directly at Ulrika's feet, but at those of her people.

The Krail were an unpopular race among the galactic community, for, as a society, they had elevated racist elitism to an exquisite, if deplorable, art form. Only perfect babies were allowed to survive (the imperfect and stunted being abandoned on a mountain designated for that purpose). They traded consorts the way other species traded poker chips or takkat figures, and unlike the Einai, whose word for 'slave' closely approximated the Erthlik term 'employee,' the Krail ran an active slave trade, and held other non-Krail human species in overt contempt.

It was generally felt, among the citizens of the Federation, that we might just barely tolerate this offensive attitude for the sake of galactic peace, but—in the case of Ulrika Drac, at least—we would be reluctant to pay for the privilege.

Only Mykar Sharobi (who had discounted her resumé as no better than that of a thousand other hopefuls, but who had seen beyond her crust to her considerable courage) had been bold enough to take her on.

He hired her on the spot.

Ulrika was inordinately grateful, and while she was unable to verbalize that emotion, she acted out her feelings in the only way she knew: she Knew. She worked harder, and for longer hours, than anyone else. In her spare time, what little there was of it, she learned everything about everything—and everyone; read incessantly; absorbed information like the proverbial sponge, and retained it.

She made it her business to be *Hope*'s resident expert, and paraded the fact at every opportunity, thus incurring the abiding rancor of people who otherwise might have wanted to be her friend.

Ulrika Drac had never had a friend, nor had she regretted the loss. She didn't need a friend. Didn't want one. What she wanted, and sorely needed, was a mate. Most Krail women, secure in their seclusion, would have veiled their blushing faces at the very thought of pursuing a male; but Ulrika was gloriously different. Ulrika had cried amnesty. Ulrika was free.

And she was on the hunt.

Now, feeding the helpless Erthlik Lassiter, to whom she had been assigned as a special duty nurse, she found herself pleasantly warmed by his slow smile and the way he had of watching her through those thick, fair lashes. The daily routine of making his bed and giving him his baths and medications gave her an intimate and proprietorial feeling about him. She made him her particular project. Gave him back rubs. Carefully shaved his beard. She had taken to preparing savory little delicacies for him in the nurses' kitchen, of late, and coaxing him to talk to her when he was depressed. They had laughed aloud together two separate times.

Perversely, she found the warning flag that red-coded a possible psychiatric problem provocative and romantic, for (excepting Dr. Paige, who was an Erthlik and therefore didn't count) she was the only one on the entire ship who knew about it. It was exciting, like sharing a tryst with Lassiter; like keeping a lovers' secret.

It really was too bad, she thought in vexation, cutting up the rest of his chicken, that he was already married. She stabbed at a piece with the fork. Blast these backward aliens and their stupid monogamy!

Lassiter jerked back with a grunt, licking his lip, and she blinked.

"I'm sorry. Did I stick you with that? Here, try once more another bite." She forced a thin smile, showing long, perfect, blue-white teeth. He took the bite cautiously.

She had seen the wife. How could he stand it? A small, dark inconsequential thing. Never could tell what sort of racial mix lay under the sallow skin. No wonder he refused to give her children. *They would probably be dark disgusting little runts*, she reflected smugly, *not clean and white, like us Krail*.

Like Lassiter, with his clear blue eyes and lion-colored hair and freckled pale skin. Charles Lassiter deserved better than this Audreh person, she decided. She touched her severe yellow-white braid self-consciously. He deserved the best. The purest.

He deserved Ulrika Drac.

The question now was, she thought, shoveling the last of the mashed potatoes into his mouth, how do we rid ourselves of Audreh Lassiter? It was something to consider, to fantasize about. Never to take seriously, of course. After all, she was a health professional. But it would be amusing to think about, in idle moments. On lonely, restless evenings.

And besides, she comforted herself as she gathered up his empty containers, the future could be brighter than it appeared. *Hope* was, after all, a big ship. Who knew what might accidently happen, and to whom, that would change things permanently for the better?

In the meantime, she must pamper her patient. She must do everything she could to make him grateful to her. Dependent. Indebted.

Her pale blue eyes regarded him with the intensity of a mantis, and because she was willing to go to any lengths to ensnare this man, she steeled herself to make a revolting suggestion, one not even to be mentioned in polite company.

"Would you like me to—" She cleared her throat, moistened her lips, and forced herself to ask the question.

"Would you like me to give you some—" she repressed a shudder, "some *ice cream?*" Charles brightened.

"That sounds good. Thank you. A double scoop of butterscotch pecan ripple, please. With whipped cream, if you have any."

And because she was, first and foremost, a professional, Ulrika Drac managed not to gag until she had reached the empty anonymity of the corridor outside Lassiter's room.

She had just returned with the noxious concoction as Tom Paige sauntered into the room. She set her lips in a thin line, put down the dish and stood back, her arms folded across her flat chest. Paige pointedly ignored her, focusing instead on his patient.

"Dr. Lassiter? I'm Dr. Paige. I'm going to be taking care of you for the next few weeks."

"Thank you kindly, Doctor," Lassiter said, in his soft colonial drawl, and Paige smiled.

"I'd guess you are definitely a Southern Earthling."

"Close. A colonist. New Georgia." He hesitated. "May I ask you a question, Doctor?" The sandy-haired young man waited and Lassiter gnawed a bit at his lip. "You're not German—are you?" he asked abruptly, and Paige shook his head.

"No. Actually, I'm from New England, Earth. English, Irish and French descent. How's that?"

Lassiter wagged his head and gave a self-deprecating chuckle. "I don't know what's the matter with me . . . I find myself asking people that question a lot lately." Paige acknowledged the information with a nod and a small, noncommittal smile. He jotted something in his notes and consulted the chart.

"Let's see now . . . *Doctor* Charles Lassiter." He glanced up. "Are you a medical doctor, Doctor, or are you just terribly well-educated?"

"Medicine," Lassiter said. "John Hopkins, Class of '63."

"Good! Then I'll have less to explain. Let's have a look at you." He unwrapped the bandages on Lassiter's hands and examined Anderson's creditable repairs. Both the original trauma and the surgical wounds were healing nicely, but there had been considerable nerve damage, resulting in deformity of both hands, leaving Lassiter without their normal use.

Paige noted that the ring and little fingers of the right hand were clawed in a classic low-lesion ulnar palsy. He examined the hand carefully. The knuckles were overextended and the finger joints tightly flexed, and there was the predictable inability to abduct and adduct the fingers. Paige tested the thumb adductor and found no function there, either. It would take a while for Lassiter to regain fine-motor control in that hand, he reflected, not to mention regaining sensation.

"Can you make a fist for me?" he asked, and Lassiter obliged. The hand rolled up from the fingertips, the knuckles bending only after the fingers were fully flexed. "Try to flex the MP joints, and keep the fingers straight." Lassiter tried, with no result, and shook his head.

"Sorry." He studied the hand as if it belonged to someone else. "Froment's sign, isn't it? Ulnar nerve damage."

"That's right." Paige turned his attention to the other hand. The left thumb was carried hard against the palm, and Lassiter lacked the ability to pull it away on his own. The thumb, index and long fingers, as well as portions of the ring finger, were numb to the touch. Low median nerve palsy, a devastating situation. Not too long ago, Paige told himself, Lassiter would have kissed his medical career goodbye with injuries like these.

"You're going to need some time in ReGen on those, Doctor," he predicted, testing for skin sensitivity as he spoke. "Meantime, we'll see if some splinting won't help, until we get full nerve return." He hit the wall com. "Elaine, could you step in here a minute, please?"

A moment later, a pretty young Earthling in white trousers and lab coat came in and was introduced.

"Elaine Hoey, one of our better OT's, Dr. Lassiter." He picked up Lassiter's left hand and deftly manipulated the thumb and fingers. "Elaine, we need some kind of a thermoplastex splint for this hand, to maintain a functional abduction of the thumb, okay?" Her hands were quick and expert as she, too, examined the deformities.

"Yep. And how about a full abduction splint for nighttime?"

"Sounds good. Work up some kind of a dorsal blocker for the right hand, too. We've got both motor and sensory problems, bilaterally."

"Got it." She paused at the door. "You want a smaller splint for later on?"

"We'll check that out as we go along. Thanks, Elaine." He began to unwrap Lassiter's bandaged feet as the OT left. "Let's take a look at those feet now, Doctor."

The feet were a different story. The wounds were healed and the reflexes good. Paige ran through a quick exam and came up gratified with his progress.

"Your feet are healing surprisingly well. Why don't we try getting you up this afternoon on the bars, start you ambulating again?" Lassiter shook his head fearfully.

"I can't," he said. "I'm sure I can't. Not yet."

"Sure you can—" Paige began, and Ulrika interrupted with:

"He can *not*, doctor! Let alone to him!" Paige turned slowly, not terribly pleased.

"Excuse me, Miss Drac?"

"The poor man is correct. He suffers greatly. We have been trying to walk for the last two days, and we are still unable. The pain is too intense." Paige scowled as he consulted the chart, flipped a few pages.

"Up two days ago? Whose bright idea was that? I don't find any orders here to get Dr. Lassiter up. Certainly not mine." He waited, and after a moment, she inhaled deeply.

"He has been here over a week, Doctor. He had two travel

days more on *Skipjack*, coming here. The feet are obvious healed. I thought he would benefit from some exercise."

"*You* thought." Paige said nothing more, simply narrowed his eyes and kept staring hard at her.

"It's my fault, Dr. Paige," Lassiter apologized, over the silence. "I insisted on trying. Miss Drac had nothing to do with it." Paige smiled tightly.

"No problem, Doctor. Miss Drac and I can discuss this later." To Ulrika, he said. "In my office." She turned on her heel and left as Paige began a routine neurological workup.

Halfway through the examination, Lassiter inquired after Marik.

"Oh, we're taking good care of him," Paige assured him. "Why do you ask?"

"I want to be sure he's all right. He saved my life, you know," Lassiter said.

"So I've heard," Paige said, pulling out his penlight. He doused the overhead lights. "Look straight ahead, please." He checked Charles's optical reflexes, nodded, and brought up the lights again.

"See, I was pretty much out of it when he brought me in, talking wild. I don't know what-all I must have said. I understand he had to impose a telepathic Ban just to sneak me through the Nazi lines, coming back."

"That's understandable," Paige agreed absently, pocketing the penlight. "Shut your eyes and let's see you touch your nose with alternate fingers. Please. Good." He made a few more notes. "Pain can make people say and do some pretty strange things. I wouldn't worry too much about it."

"He rescued my wife, too, but that's to be expected. He's probably in love with her." Paige looked at him sharply, and Lassiter smiled whimsically through his thick pale lashes. "*Everyone*'s in love with Miss Audrey, Doctor. She's a very beautiful, charming young woman."

"I'm sure she is," Paige agreed professionally. "Can I see that left foot one more time, please?" Lassiter gave him the wounded foot, continuing sincerely:

"Well, what I mean is, I can see why Marik saved Miss

Audrey, but, by doggies, I'm not even *pretty!*" Their shared laughter was healthy and spontaneous, and Paige felt reassured. He had dealt with a great many psychopathic patients in his time, and none of them had ever joked with such easy grace. He began to feel good about red-coding the psych flag on Charles Lassiter's record. He would probably turn out to be perfectly all right. He stood up and leaned against the foot of the bed.

"Let's see: you've been here a week. We'll give you the rest of today to get settled, Doctor—"

"Charles, if you please."

"Charles. And tomorrow we'll get you started on your way back up. How's that sound?"

"That's fine, Doctor, just fine."

And even after Paige left, Lassiter still thought it sounded fine, because it meant that, very soon, he could look in on Marik and see for himself that he was alive and well. All things considered, it was paramount that no harm should come to Dao Marik, to whom he owed a solemn debt of honor he must somehow manage to repay.

Tommy Paige leaned against the wall of his small office, his arms folded, regarding Ulrika Drac with something akin to distaste.

"What do you want, Doctor?" she asked. "I have meds to draw and a very busy schedule I have keeping."

"I'd like to know where you get the right to make decisions about my patients, Miss Drac," Paige began, as Big Artie Michaels walked in, looked from Paige's angry glare to Ulrika's complacent superiority, and lounged lazily against the edge of Paige's desk.

"This looks promising, guys," he offered cheerfully, pushing his old-fashioned spectacles up the bridge of his nose. "I hope it isn't something private—"

"Before you become too agitated, Doctor," Ulrika announced in a lofty tone, "you should know that I obtained Priyam Sharobi's permission to get Dr. Lassiter out of bed."

"—because if it is, I can always leave," Michaels finished.

"Just say the word." They continued to ignore him, so he shrugged, shoved his hands into his pockets, and stayed.

"You got—" Paige stopped and began again. "You went to Sharobi—over my head—without even speaking to me first? And why is that?"

Ulrika smoothed the front of her uniform. "Erthlikli are frequently overemotional. I did not wish to precipitate a disgusting scene."

"Well, you precipitated a doozy this time, lady," Paige flared. "For a stunt like this, I could have you booted out of here so fast it would make your head swim!"

"Boot me out, is it? I think not. Sharobi is Chief of Staff. Why should I speak to an—an *ex-slave* when I can speak to a man of honor?" Artie's head came up quickly in surprise. Paige, stunned, colored darkly, and she continued, sensing victory.

"Perhaps I am the only one aboard who recognizes the shock-collar scars on your throat, Paige. Didn't you tell them you had been a Krail slave? I wonder what would the staff are thinking if they knew you came from such—" she smiled thinly, "such humble station, eh? I wonder who then gets 'booted'? They maybe don't know, but *I* know. And I will tell, if I must! No one puts me off of *Hope*! No one! I know enough—about everyone—to keep me here forever!"

"Your trouble is, you know too damn much, Miss Drac!" Paige broke in. "And that could get you into a whole lot of trouble! Now, I'm going to say this only once, so listen up: slavery aside, shock-collar aside, when you want to have anything to do with one of *my* patients, you talk to me, understand? No nursing supervisor, no Sharobi, no Captain Kris, no Federation High Council. *Me—and nobody* but *me!* You got that?"

"*I* don't have any problem with that," Michaels said to the room in general. Ulrika, however, was not to be moved.

"Look up it in the staff handbook, Doctor: I am to always obey orders of the *senior* physician—in this case, Sharobi— over the orders of *lesser men*. And so I shall!" Ulrika patted her braid. "Do *you* got *that?*" She gave him a superior smile and, obviously feeling she had scored a point, marched past Artie Michaels and out of the cramped office. Paige watched her exit with hot and angry eyes, absently rubbing the twin white scars at the base of his throat.

"Someday, Big Artie," he muttered, "somebody's going to do us all a favor and break that broad's scrawny lily-white neck." Michaels raised his eyebrows, but made no answer. There was really nothing he could have said.

Audrey Lassiter, Charles's wife, sank down luxuriously into the deep warm bubble bath, feeling her knotted muscles already beginning to relax. The past week had gone by so quickly she'd hardly had time for a quick shower and snatches of sleep, much less time to think; but now, settled at last in her comfortable apartment in Hope House, where patients' onboard relatives were routinely quartered, she could afford to take time for herself. She splashed lazily at the creamy bubbles, watching a miniature rainbow shimmer in each one, her thoughts rambling idly.

She was glad that the Timeslide was over, although she wouldn't have missed it for the world.

That she and Charles had been privileged to participate in the Timeslide was in itself a small miracle.

That they had gotten back relatively safely from the Past, with its many unexpected dangers, was another.

And that, despite his terrible injuries, Charles would live, after all, was yet a third, and by far the most important.

Priyam Sharobi had promised her that Charles would survive. Like any good wife, she should be delighted, she thought; but she had mixed feelings about it, which made her feel disloyal and sullied. After all, Charles was her husband. Not perfect, any more than anyone else (Dao Marik, for instance) was perfect; but her husband, nonetheless.

She should be (and was) proud of his rescue of those poor little Jewish children; but her pride had turned to horror in *Skipjack*'s Sickbay, where she found Charles in restraints, screaming and ranting insanely about what he would do to Dao Marik, for taking him down, and to her, for infidelity with

Marik. He'd called her dreadful names, accused her of nonexistent sins. Had promised vengeance on them both, for betraying him.

Infidelity! What a dreadful accusation to make in front of everyone, even if it were true! They had all been understanding, of course. Had commiserated with her, explaining that Charles didn't mean what he was saying—didn't even *know* what he was saying!—and that she mustn't fret about it.

But she did fret, because she knew what they did not, that although there was nothing between herself and Dao Marik but one lone dance, one lingering kiss, she had been unfaithful in her heart. Had relived the scene with Marik in her mind, time and again, remembering his strong arms and the scent of his skin—

She cut off the thought and covered her erring heart with a handful of frothy scented bubbles, as if to hide it even from herself.

It was not as if she had sought the encounter, she told herself defensively. She had been at a tremendous emotional disadvantage, just then. For Charles was a busy, practical, distant man, with no time for the small graces a woman like Audrey lived upon. She had been so starved for a kind word, for comradely laughter, for a gentle touch, that when Marik stopped dancing and held her close with such tenderness in his eyes, with the storm beating at the window, and the two of them alone—

For an instant, she could feel his arms around her, her inconstant heart fluttering, her face lifting to his. . . .

"Enough of *that*, Audrey, my girl," she muttered savagely, sitting bolt upright and flipping the drain lever with her toes. The delicious warmth sluiced quickly away, even as she turned on the cold shower full force and stood under it until she was thoroughly chilled. Then, snugged into the oversized robe that had been provided her, her wet hair turbaned in a thick towel, she padded barefoot and shivering into the sitting room for a cup of hot coffee.

The door chime sounded, and she found a well-dressed middle-aged woman standing there, basket in hand.

"Mrs. Lassiter?" She extended her free hand, which Audrey took briefly. "I'm Lorraine Beasely, from the Welcome Committee. May I come in? Thank you." She marched in without waiting for an answer, and Audrey closed the door behind her.

"You'll have to excuse me," she apologized, holding her robe together at the throat. "I'm just out of the shower. Would you like some coffee?"

"Oh, no thanks. Just had some. You go ahead. Well! Welcome to *Hope*, dear. I have a few gifts here for you, from local merchants and well-wishers, don't you know, to help you get used to the City." She plumped down on the sofa with her basket in her lap. "That's what we call the Earthling Level, the City. It's real name is Earthscape, but actually it *is* a city, it really is. We have everything! A park with a zoo, and a big pond that Environmental Control keeps frozen in winter, so people can skate. Do you skate? Oh, good! In the summer we have ducks on it, and swans and rowboats and whatnot."

"I had no idea," Audrey said. She took a seat across from the friendly blue-haired Earthling lady, who handed her several church bulletins.

"We have all the amenities. If you're religious, there are two churches on this level, Protestant and Catholic, that serve all levels. The synagogue and mosque are on the Einai and Krau levels, respectively, and the kiva is on the Senn level. You can get a religious pass if you need one; just ask Christine, in Social Services." She handed Audrey another brochure.

"If you're a shopper, and who isn't, we have an incredible Mall, not to mention the Alleys: we have a really good florist, seven or eight restaurants, four art galleries, two theaters, a dozen or more boutiques, and a real *museum*, don't you know? And the hotel has a ballroom you wouldn't believe! In fact, they're having the big Christmas Ball on the twenty-third, so you won't want to miss it! It's formal, and just everyone comes, don't you know! Even Priyam Sharobi shows up every year, all gussied up fit to kill! There's a live orchestra and everything!" She reached into the bottom of the basket and pulled out an envelope.

"Here's a bid for you and your husband, if he's well enough.

Otherwise, feel free to bring a friend. You mustn't miss it! It's
the social event of the season!" She began rummaging in her
capacious basket, pulling out gifts at random.

"Thank you very much," Audrey said. "I never expec—" But
Lorraine forged ahead happily, not hearing a word.

"Well, now we have some more presents for you, dear. I just
love this part, and I know you will, too! Here's a pak of credit
chits, don't lose it, good for ten percent off on anything in the
Mall. And this here is a free ticket to the fashion show at Maison
Blanche this Wednesday—the luncheon is included—in the Rose
Room on the second floor. It starts at eleven-thirty sharp, so don't
be late." She unloaded several small, decorative containers of
herbal teas and various cosmetic samples, as well as a plastex
packet map, which she unfolded for Audrey, pointing out areas of
interest while she plunged on:

"Now, here's a map of the whole ship, at least all twelve
residential levels of it. You're not allowed on Engineering or
the Bridge or places like that, of course. That's here and here.
And no one goes to the empty levels—there's three of
them—because there's nothing there yet, don't you know?

"Now, you know, don't you, that the Power Core and the
hospital cut through all levels? Well, they do, but they're
restricted. You need a visitor's pass for the hospital, unless you
work there; and the Power Core is off-limits to everyone but
crew. You can go anywhere you like in the City, but you'll need
a visa for all the other levels.

"See," she confided, folding up the map and handing it to
Audrey, "people can get pretty confined on a ship, even a big
ship like this one, after a while; so by using visas and so on, it
makes you feel like you've really *gone* somewhere. And each
level is designed to be exactly like that race's planet, the Krau
and the Xhole, and so on, so it's like going abroad, don't you
know.

"And people don't overdo the foreign travel one bit, because
the big mega-lifts between levels are awfully expensive. Not to
mention planetfalls! Why, going planetside costs an absolute
mint, even if you can get clearance! But, then, you're really on
another actual planet, so that's something, isn't it?"

"I suppose it is," Audrey agreed quietly, feeling a little bit overwhelmed. Lorraine fixed her with a speculative eye.

"What do you do, Mrs. Lassiter? Isn't your name Audrey? Can I call you Audrey? Thanks, just call me Lorraine. Plain Lorraine. So, like I said, what do you do? I mean, for work and all? Or do you have small children? The report said no children."

"I have no children," Audrey admitted. "My husband has one grown son by his previous marriage. Hector. Captain Hector Lassiter, Special Forces."

"Oh, that's real nice. Special Forces. Um-hm. Well, you know, Audrey, everyone works on *Hope*. Keeps us from getting bored, don't you know? The report says you'll probably be here for a few weeks, so what would you like to do? I mean, it's not *obligatory*, but most people choose to do something."

"I'm an artist," Audrey offered, sipping her coffee. "And I've done some photography."

"Why, my goodness," Lorraine said, poking an index finger into the wrinkle that had once been a dimple, "the nurses in Pediatrics were just saying the other day that they needed an art therapist to work with the children. Would you be interested in doing that, do you think?"

"Oh—I'd love it." Audrey smiled, and Lorraine heaved a deep breath of satisfaction.

"I knew it! I had you pegged for a go-getter the minute I saw you! She's no sit-and-moan-er, I said! Not this one! I'll just run right over and tell them, and they can get in touch with you here, all right?"

"T-that will be fine," Audrey stammered, as Lorraine gathered up her basket, checked her ticket and levered herself out of the deep sofa.

"Oh, my, it's getting late. I've got to go, don't you know." She shook Audrey's hand briskly and trotted through the door, still chattering. "It was so nice talking with you. We're real happy to have you aboard. Call me anytime, we'll have tea. And I hope your husband gets well soon, dear.

"You have a nice night," she called over her shoulder, as she hurried away down the hall.

"Thank you," Audrey murmured, shutting the door behind her. The room seemed much larger and very quiet, now that Lorraine had gone, she thought, smiling to herself. And yet, how nice of her to have come. She freshened her cup, strolled to the window, and stood looking down at the park.

It was cold and windy out, and all the trees were bare. Dry leaves skittered across the street, blew against buildings and whirled in fretful eddies. The evening sky was heavily overcast, and two warmly cloaked nurses hurried along the sidewalk past the Medical School toward the warm lights of Park Place East. Environmental Control had planned freezing rain and snow for later tonight, and the thought gave her a delicious shiver.

Her heart leaped involuntarily as a dark-haired Einai in hospital greens crossed the street into the park. She couldn't see his face, nor whether he walked with a limp, for he was too far away, but for a moment he had seemed poignantly familiar. Silly of me, she thought. He could be no one she knew. There must have been dozens of Einai aboard. Marik was still in the hospital, recuperating. Still, she watched him until he was lost to sight among the skeletal gray branches; then she finished her coffee and pulled the drapes firmly shut. Time to get her emotions back on their collective leash, she scolded herself. Enough of these useless fantasies.

As soon as she dried her hair, she decided, and got into something Charles would approve of, she would pay him a nice long visit.

The door chimes sounded their pleasant two notes once more, and Audrey opened the door again, this time to a pretty young woman in flawless makeup, who gave her a bright smile.

"Avon calling!" she announced.

CHAPTER

IV

DAO MARIK OPENED his eyes from a restful sleep and focused on the pale oval of light beside his bed that resolved itself slowly into Audrey Lassiter's face. He drew a deep breath and reached out slowly, his fingers lightly tracing brow and cheekbone and heavy mass of silky chestnut hair. There was a hint of her flowerlike scent on the air, and he almost smiled.

"I thought I had wakened," he whispered, "but here I am, still dreaming." His thumb caressed her lips. She took his hand away from her face, gently but firmly, and placed it on the side of the bed.

"We have to talk, Priyam Marik."

"All right." He snapped off the ReGen unit, pushed it aside and sat up, giving her respectful attention. She moistened her lips with the tip of a pink tongue.

"I've just come from visiting Charles again—"

"How is he coming along?" Marik was genuinely concerned. "Will they be able to repair his hands?"

She shut her eyes momentarily against the thought of his hands.

"They say so. It will take time, but—yes, he'll be fine."

He breathed a relieved sigh. "Thank T'ath. There was no time to take him down carefully, but I've been worried about it ever since."

She nodded. "He's worried about you, too. That's the problem: he insists I look after you. It's like an obsession with him. He's even convinced Priyam Sharobi that it's a good idea."

The steady gray gaze never left her face. "That bothers you."

She looked away, blushing. "Of course it does. Doesn't it bother you?"

"I'd be a liar if I said no. Charles is my friend; we have a bond of honor between us. And yet"—he smiled—"one *is* permitted to dream." She realigned the books in her lap.

"I think I have a solution, Priyam." He waited. "You asked me once if we could be friends."

His gray eyes warmed. "At the Summer Palace. Yes." They both remembered the Summer Palace only too well.

"Well . . . since we're going to be seeing so much of each other—and things can't possibly go on the way they have been—what if we were to make a-a pact, you and I?"

"A pact."

"A verbal contract, just between us. One that we would both honor, agreeing to be very good and dear friends, forever." She looked him full in the face. "And to, please God, let that be the end of it!"

"Do you think it would work?" he asked soberly.

"It must work!" she burst out. "It has got to work."

"And, more importantly," he continued, "would it make you happy?"

"I—I think so. It should, shouldn't it? Yes," she decided, "it would make me happy. And better yet, it would make Charles happy."

He regarded her tenderly, then: "Done," he said. It was Audrey's turn to be surprised.

"Just like that?"

"Just like that." He extended his right hand, which she took, and, holding her hand (not palm to palm, as Erthlikli were wont to do, but thumb to thumb, Einai fashion) closely against his chest over his right heart, he held her eyes with his own.

"This will be our contract: I, Priyam Hanshilobahr *Dom* Dao Marik, agree to be the dear, good, faithful friend of Owdri Lassiter for the entire length of forever, and one day more. Upon that day, our contract will become null and void. It will be, as you say, the end of it.

"Now, you repeat, after me: I, Owdri Lassiter—"

"I, Audrey Garsaud Lassiter—" She startled inwardly, stumbling on the next words, for, gazing into Marik's eyes at such close range, she had almost said *take you, Dao Marik*. She counterfeited a cough, and repeated the contract after Marik through to the words 'forever, and one day more.' "That should be long enough for anyone," she murmured, her eyes soft.

For an extended, electric moment Marik contemplated kissing her one last time; then, considering his friend Charles, and the question of his own and Audrey's honor, he released her hand reluctantly and leaned back against the pillows, his jaw tight. Audrey seemed very much relieved, whether by his decision or by their pact, he could not tell.

"Things will be ever so much better this way," she said. "Now we're free to go everywhere we like together and have a wonderful time." She favored him with a lovely smile. "We'll make Charles happy, and we'll both be safe, won't we?" *Will we?* Marik thought. He smiled, but made no reply.

"One last thing," he said, after a long pause. "If we're to be friends, we should use our given names. Therefore, I will call you Owdri, from now on, and you will call me "

"Dao!" Mykar Sharobi came striding into the room. "You look better every time I see you!" An entourage of medical people that included Tom Paige and Artie Michaels crowded into the room behind him.

Sharobi was obviously making Grand Rounds, and in one no-nonsense moment, while Paige pulled the MAXpak and Michaels checked out the ReGen unit, he gave Marik a quick *chom-ala* and greeted Audrey with a string of instructions.

"Mrs. Lassiter. Nice to see you. I see you've been reading to our fallen hero, here," he continued, glancing at her books. "Well, he's to be up and about today. I'm putting him to work, so I'd like you to do two things for me: first, I want you to see that Marik gets moderate exercise daily. Not too much, maybe a couple of hours a day, but regular, understand? I'm putting you in charge of that.

"Then perhaps you'd read to another patient I've got down the hall. Name is Garrett. He was injured out on Seddaj, and he's been pretty low. He could use some pleasant female companionship."

"I'm happy to do both, Priyam. If you all will excuse me?" She smiled at them collectively and, taking her books, made a graceful exit.

Sharobi peeled off Marik's plastex conformer and examined the healing gunshot wounds with quick, expert fingers. "Fine-looking young woman," he commented, feeling for the callus on the clavicle and going carefully over the bright green, newly regenerated tissue around it.

"Yes, she is," Marik agreed noncommittally. Paige lifted his brows and whistled soundlessly, snapping his fingers.

"Let ol' tall, dark and feline hit the wards," he muttered, resurrecting an old joke between them, and Marik grinned.

"She's also Charles Lassiter's wife," he pointed out, then sucked air sharply between his teeth, as Sharobi hit a sore spot.

"Sorry." Sharobi finished his exam, replaced the conformer and straightened. "You're coming along surprisingly well. You'll still need ReGen two hours every morning, of course; but it's just a matter of time now, unless you do something stupid and open it all up again. Need some exercise to strengthen the muscles. The hearts-scan looks fine. How're the blood gases, Doctor?" This to Paige, who replaced the pak on the MAX's flat stern.

"Everything well within limits, sir. Looking good."

"Good. We'll get you up and out of here before you die of boredom. What's next on the agenda, Paige?"

"That would be Brian's new patient, sir. Bry?" Brian Bakunas, a tall, rangy youngster with cool blue eyes, a humorous mouth and cropped blond hair, stepped forward confidently. The burn scars that marked his hands and half his face, rather than marring his appearance, gave him a reckless, devil-may-care aspect that half the nurses on the floor found irresistible. He consulted the folder.

"Sir, I admitted an Ildeforan woman from planetside presenting with classic SLE. Pink butterfly across the face, hair loss, joint pain, chronic fatigue, Reynaud's Syndrome and all. The local medic wanted us to prescribe uppers to get her up and working again, but I decided to beam her up instead." A few of the medics exchanged astonished grins.

"Up and working? *Working?* He's lucky she didn't fall on her face just from *up*! Didn't she list her symptoms?" Sharobi demanded. "I gather the man has a white tip on his stethoscope!"

Bakunas grinned engagingly. "Well, no, sir, he's not blind, exactly, and yes, she did list her complaints, but his lab tests were inconclusive, so he told her it was all in her mind. Sent her to us for malingering. And he really wants her to have those amphetamines!" Everyone but Sharobi laughed aloud.

"When are these half-eared medicine men going to learn that the patient is their best diagnostic tool?" he growled. "Where'd he get his diploma, out of a can of Baffin? Poor woman! All right, all right, you people go on ahead, I'll be right with you." Paige led the medics away as Sharobi blew out a tired breath and dragged his hand down his face.

"Get better fast, Dao," he advised. "We've got some really interesting things going on. I've got a full-body transplant you'll want to have a look at. Oh-eight hundred tomorrow morning. I'll expect you to scrub in. Paige is reattaching an arm afterward, too—the last arm we have in stock, I might add! If the Senn don't get here pretty soon with the new supplies, we'll all be in deep *pift*! Anyway, you'll want to be there for the arm surgery, too."

"I'd like that," Marik agreed warily. He was interested in learning the new techniques, but Sharobi had been trying to coax him away from *Skipjack* and onto his *Hope* staff for several years. Obviously he had not given up, but Marik had no intention of making the switch just now, if ever.

"Then there's an Einai family," Sharobi continued, "whose child is dying of Ensi-vo; but they won't let us use the Droso Solution. Dead set against it. I'll want you to talk to them. Get us that permission while we can still save the child. There are a few other matters, nothing much. Get your sea legs. Take all the time you need; I'll talk to you later." He glanced at his ticket and up again. "Say, about four, in my office." He nodded shortly by way of a farewell and was gone as abruptly as he had arrived.

Since it was noon, Audrey decided to have lunch before she met Garrett. Following signs written in Ertheng, Kraun and Eisernai, she found the cafeteria already busy with the luncheon crowd. Medical people of all species, trays in hand, were queued up in the food line, where everyday victuals from several planets steamed fragrantly. Audrey took a tray, eating utensils and her place in line, sharing a smile with the tall Kraun doctor two places ahead of her. *I wish they would hurry*, she thought hungrily, watching the server scoop a dollop of creamy blue louvi onto a diner's plate and cover it with a pale peach-colored sauce. She caught the smell of shrimp and pecans as the Einai next in line ordered tchorimondo, and several crispy objects were put on her plate, along with a bowl of mint-green tarangi.

"Excuse me?" Someone jabbed at her back. "Aren't you Mrs. Lassiter?" She turned to see an Earthling crewman about her own age, with *Hope*'s familiar anchor symbol embroidered on the left breast of her uniform. Her face was friendly, with bright blue eyes and a freckled snub nose, and her compact build went well with her open, forthright manner.

"Why, yes, I am," Audrey answered, and the girl shoved a small, square hand at her with an engaging grin.

"Hi! I'm Barbara Mutowski. Call me Mutt. Everybody does, and I'm kind of used to it."

Audrey shook the proffered hand warmly. "What do you do, Bar—Mutt?"

"I load cargo. I'm the lading officer around here. Pretty important job, too. See, if the cargo hold isn't packed just right, with no spaces between containers, we can run into some tough inertia problems in decelera—" She read Audrey's uncomprehending gaze. "Anyway, that's not important. I heard you were aboard, and since you were standing right there, I just wanted to say 'Hi!' "

"I'm so happy to meet you, Barbara, but—how on earth would you know *I* was here?" The line moved up and she indicated to the Minsonai server a small garden salad, a cup of tea, and bowl of clam chowder.

"Oh, we know everything on Earthscape. It's like a small town; everybody knows everyone else's business." She pointed out a cheeseburger, fries, and a chocolate malted, and ticked off people on her fingers. "Four of you came in on military skimmer from *Skipjack*; you and your husband, Mister Donovan, who was your Timeslide Controller, and"—she clutched her throat dramatically, rolled her eyes, and sighed—"Mister Marik."

"I take it you find Mister Marik attractive," Audrey said, paying the cashier.

"I'll say!" Mutt agreed, grabbing her own tray and leading the way between the crowded tables to an empty out-of-the-way booth. "Of course," she continued as they sat, "not like Artie Michaels. There's a guy to die for! But he can't see me for dust!"

"Why do you say tha— Oh, my dear!" Audrey dropped the spoon she had just dipped into her chowder, for it was populated by two small donzes, which had crawled up the warm spoon handle and clung there with every tentacle. Several Einai at the next table laughed, and Mutt jumped up hastily.

"Oops, they did it again!" She grabbed the soup bowl and said cheerfully, "Every Friday they get the chowder and the donze soup mixed up. The Minsonai, what do they know from clams, right? To them, fish is fish. Hang on, I'll straighten it out." She was back shortly with a bowl of chowder, and Audrey spooned through it cautiously, making the Einai laugh again. She thanked Mutt profusely.

"Oh, no problem. It happens all the time. One time, an old lady from Federation Central, some kind of high mucky-muck, got hold of a donze, jumped up on a chair and began screaming, and half a dozen Droso fainted dead away."

"Why would they—?"

"See, the Droso are real sensitive to sound. The wrong pitch, even over a short period of time, could kill them; so we have to be awful careful about machinery and such. Don't want to lose any Droso, right?" She dug into her cheeseburger with evident relish. "So I hear you've been working in Peds. How do you like it?"

Audrey told her how much she had come to love it, even in the few days she'd been there.

"I don't know how you do it," Mutt commented, shoving several fries into her mouth. "Just hearing about sick kids gives me the willies."

"Yes, well, I don't know how you lading people manage to get all that cargo into the bay, either," Audrey countered. "It must be terribly stressful, trying to fit it all in."

"I don't know about *stressful*," Mutt said. "It just takes a kind of three-dimensional thinking, sort of. Kind of a special mindset. I mean, I'm not much good at words, or, like, dressing up and being social and all? But I have this knack—you know—for stacking things tight. So—" she tipped up her shake to get the last of it, and licked the foam off her top lip, "I got the job. So far, I'm rated a hundred per cent!"

"I'd love to see how it works," Audrey ventured. "Could you show me sometime?"

"Sure!" Mutt glanced at her ticket. "In fact, we're shut down until 1600; if you want, I can show you right now." Audrey smiled.

"No time like the present," she said.

It was almost 1500 when Audrey stopped at the floor station for West Wing, where several nurses were busy about their various duties.

"I beg your pardon," she asked generally, "could someone please tell me where I can find a patient named Garrett?" A tall Krail nurse who was filling a row of hypodermic injectors ordered, without looking up from her work:

"Wtorkow, take this woman to Sergeant Garrett's room. I have no time to waste playing tour guide, I have to finish drawing meds. I'm late-running now, thank you to idiot Paige!"

"Sure." A middle-aged Sauvagi nurse came out from behind the desk. "Right this way, *Fom*." As they proceeded down the corridor, he confided, "I see you've brought some books. Good. He needs somebody to read to him. He's been really depressed, and we don't want to— Ah, here we are. Sergeant? *Hom* Garrett? You have a visitor."

The young man in the bed had a shock of sandy hair and strong, square shoulders, and the stump of his right arm, up to the shoulder, was immobilized in a cryogenic splint.

"I don't want any visitors. Get rid of 'em." He covered his bandaged eyes with his left arm and turned his face toward the wall.

"Oh, trust me, *Hom* Garrett, you'll want *this* visitor," Wtorkow assured him cheerfully. Audrey shook her head quickly, wordlessly, but he indicated the chair next to the bed with a placating gesture and left her there.

"*I don't want any company, all right?*" Garrett snapped. "Wtorkow? Dammit, *Wtorkow!*" He struck the bed with his free fist in impotent rage and his face turned blindly toward her. "Look, I don't know who you are, but you've got the wrong room, okay? No offense, but I don't want to see anybody." He made a brief, bitter chuckle. "*See* anybody. That's pretty good, eh?"

Audrey walked a few feet closer, and he sniffed. A wry smile twitched the corner of his mouth. "A lady, right?" he asked. "You're a lady."

"Umm-hmm."

"What're you, some kind of social worker? A psychologist, maybe?"

"Uh-uh."

His face scanned the air like a radar dish and he sniffed again, exaggeratedly. "You're not wearing old-lady perfume. So you're nobody's grandma, right?"

"Right. I'm Mrs. Lassiter. Priyam Sharobi asked me to come and read to you."

He shook his head ruefully. "Oh, boy. They never give up, do they?" He shifted in the bed, careful of his bad arm, and extended his left hand in her general direction. "Alfred J. Garrett, Sergeant, GFArmy, ma'am. Just call me Joe." They shook hands. "You smell great. What is it? Smells like Rhea." She shook her head; then, remembering, said aloud:

"No. Frangipani. Do you like it?"

"Yeah. I like your voice, too. I knew a girl once, on Eisernon, with a voice like that. Her name was Ilen. She was beautiful." His face colored under the unkempt blond bristles. "Tell me what you look like." She hesitated, and he hastened to add, "I'm not trying to be fresh, Mrs. Lassiter. It's just that, if you tell me how you look, I can picture you in my head. Then when they give me back my eyes, I can see if it matches the real thing."

There was a little silence, for Audrey knew, as Garrett must, that human eyes were very hard to come by, even for a ship like *Hope*. Too many bereaved relatives, intent on their own grief, missed the opportunity for some part of their beloved dead—in this case, their eyes—to live on. *Hope* had exhausted her supply of available human eyes on Seddaj, Audrey knew, and was even now negotiating with the Senn for a fresh supply. Meanwhile, Joe Garrett, and all the others like him, would have to go on living in the dark.

Audrey sat down. "Well. Let's see: I'm five feet five inches tall—"

"Good, so far," Garrett interjected. "I'm five *nine*. Go on."

"And I have dark chestnut hair and dark eyes—"

"You sound really beautiful, Mrs. L. Are you beautiful?" He could hear the smile in her voice even in his private darkness.

"Better than that, Sergeant, I'm married. And I love to read aloud. I have here, let's see, a collection of Frost, the Bible, Kuzpa's *Meerut Tantara*, and the *Makaha*, by Kaz Chivalek. What would you like to hear?"

"No love stuff right now." He twitched his vinegar smile again. "Maybe next year."

"That lets out the *Makaha*."

"Maybe we'd better try the Bible," Garrett said.

"Anything in particular?"

"Anything you'd like to read, ma'am," he countered, and she opened the book at random.

"Here," she said. "Psalm Twenty-seven:

"The Lord is my light and my salvation; whom should I fear?
The Lord is my life's refuge; of whom should I be afraid?
When—"

"Try number eighty-eight, Mrs. L," Garrett interrupted. "It's maybe eighty-seven in your version. It's more appropriate." She turned the pages and began:

"Oh, Lord, my God, by day I cry out—"

"Not there. The third verse." His lips twitched again. "My uncle was a Methodist minister, so I kinda know this stuff."

"My eyes—" she glanced quickly at the intent face under the bandages, and started again:

"My eyes have grown dim through affliction;
Daily I call upon you, O Lord; To you I stretch out my hands.
Will you work your wonders for the dead?
Will the shades arise to give you thanks?
Do they declare your kindness in the grave,
Your faithfulness among those who have perished?
Are your wonders made known in the darkness,
Or your justice in the land of oblivion?

"But I, O Lord, cry out to you;
With my morning prayer I wait upon you.
Why, O Lord, do you reject me; Why hide from me your face?
I am afflicted and in agony from my youth;
I am dazed with the burden of your dread.
Your furies have swept over me, Your terrors have cut me off;
They encompass me like water all the day;
On all sides they close in upon me.
Companion and neighbor you have taken away from me;
My only friend is darkness."

"This is awfully somber," she said, breaking off briskly. "Come on. You're a military man. How about the *Meerut Tantara* instead?"

Garrett looked doubtful. "How does it go?"

"I haven't read it. I've heard it's a military *sufi*, about the Seige of Meerut."

"Out on Shandra."

"That's right. A handful of local Federation troops died to the last man defending their unprotected city-state. They held off ten thousand Krafcikun until reinforcements came, half a day too late. They saved the city, but they never knew it. It's supposed to be read to a rataplan of drums, but if you'll bear with me, I'll try it *a capella*."

"Sure," Garrett said. "Go for it."

"It begins like this:

"We fought them in the desert and we flanked them in the rain;
   We beat them down at Saxé and on Bangla's sodden plain.
   We wasted them at Varva and we zilched 'em at Ravel,
   But they turned on us at Meerut and they really gave us hell!

And the trumpets blew tantara! Ah! the trumpets blew so clear,
   As we fought for our great city-state, and all we hold so dear.
   Brave the trumpets blew tantara as we sweated in the sun,
   While each mother's son was slaughtering another mother's son.

We badly needed water. As for food, it was the same.
   And the yells went up for 'Medic!' but the medics never came.
   So we died there at the gateway, and we killed 'em as we died.
   Lads, we never won the battle, but we tried, by God, we tried!

Then bury us at Dvina, lay us soft to rest at Shai.
   And when the Mass is ended, with our families standing by,

Let the trumpet sound tantara. Make them play it sweet and
    clear
So we'll hear it where we're lying. But let no one shed a
    tear

For the men who died at Meerut. On some vast Elysian
    plain,
We've counted our last cadences and rally round again
To take our final, joyful rest on heaven's tropic shore,
While the names of Meerut's heroes are remembered ever-
    more.

*And the trumpets blow tantara. Ah! The trumpets blowing
    clear
Shout it's worth your life for truth and right,
And all we hold so dear."*

Rather rough piece of doggerel, Audrey thought, and raised
her head to say so, but Garrett evidently felt differently about
it.

He lay very still, making no sound, but his ragged breath,
like a child's quiet sobs, made his chest shake. He had no tears,
nor anything to weep with, but his grief touched Audrey's
heart, and she reached over and took his hand. He responded
with such a fierce grip that she thought her own hand would go
numb; but after a while he let her go, found his water glass
unerringly on the side table, and drank.

"Sorry," he muttered, holding the empty glass as if he could
see it. "It's not that I'm antisocial or anything," he explained
after a moment. "I mean, about not wanting company, before.
It's just everybody keeps trying to cheer me up. Trouble is, I
don't feel like cheering up. I lost two of my men on Seddaj.
Two buddies."

"Want to tell me?" she invited, and he took a deep breath.

"Sure. Why not? It was the day between the Cohosh Siv and
the Feast of the Unborn Martyrs. Yearly festival day on Seddaj.
There was this big parade, bands and floats, and politicians

making speeches. They had skimmered in this whole contingent of Federation military, phalanx after phalanx, just for show. Took a whole day, just to get us all planetside.

"Before the parade, they made us exhaust our needlers. No loaded weapons allowed, they said. I guess the Grand Moritz remembered how easy it was when *he* took over, with the Army behind him. Maybe he didn't want a repeat of recent history." He settled himself more comfortably and continued.

His squad, he said—Connors, Sanders, Ross, LaFarge, Doc and Garrett himself—were marching in crisp formation along the boulevard with the rest of the battalion in the mellow autumn sunlight. Brass bands were playing stirring military themes. The wind was cool and the sky was a bright blue-green, with the occasional flock of flying frogs swooping low over the parade. Crowds of shouting Seddaji in colorful festival attire waved bright pennants at them and cheered, and vendors hurried through the crowds selling sweetmeats and banners.

The men were executing a few of their better military drills in front of the Grand Moritz's palace, when suddenly the whole ornate marble edifice blew apart with a huge roar, drowning out the music. There was wholesale panic as screaming spectators scattered wildly, tripping on discarded band instruments, and officers shouted hoarse and futile commands over the melee. A massive column segment, whirling through the air, landed in the middle of a shrieking crowd, and another huge shard struck down Connors and Ross, right beside him.

Garrett found himself staring blankly at a dismembered arm in a Federation uniform sleeve, lying there on the pavement, still holding a weapon. It was only when he recognized the needler as his own that he realized he had lost the lower half of his right arm. A second blast exploded garishly nearby, and there was a third and a sixth and even a tenth blast; but Garrett did not see them, for the second explosion had taken his eyes.

"They told us later it was terrorists," he finished quietly. "That made it worse. I could've understood, maybe, if it was a coup or something like that. Somebody trying to make things better. I couldn't agree with the way they did it, but I could've maybe understood.

"But this was just terror for the fun of it. Because they knew they could get away with it—*and* with the five million *loé* that was stashed in the palace vault." He twitched the bitter smile again. "I'd like to kill the guys who did this, Mrs. L. I really would. I hope I get the chance, someday."

"You don't mean that, Joe."

"Yes, ma'am, I do. If I had 'em here, right now, I'd kill 'em with my bare hands—hand—without thinking twice."

"But how—?"

"I'd pop their necks, ma'am. You can do it easy with one hand. They taught us in basic training. I'd kill those guys in a minute, given half a chance. I think about it all the time."

A small silence grew, while Audrey rearranged the books. There seemed nothing left to say, so after a few minutes of desultory conversation, she left, promising to come again soon. And for the rest of the evening, she found she could not shake the memory of Garrett's blind, still face, and his powerful clenched left hand, and the cold, grim determination in his voice.

It was full noon, with the predators far behind them, when Nalinle started up the stony trail that led upward through the foothills at G'ham. A monotonous whisper of wind blew dust among the barren rocks, where thin, dry vegetation eked out a meager existence. Nalinle's mouth was dry. The ache in his shoulders had become a constant companion. It seemed by now that he had never had any other life, only this eternal jogging upwards toward some unreachable goal, with Mikai's dead weight across his hearts.

There was nothing to eat at midday, nor anything to drink, so Nalinle rolled a small smooth stone about in his mouth, to assuage his terrible thirst. He pitied Mikai, whose tongue could not manage a stone, whose throat must remain parched until they found water. He resettled the boy and jogged on, his feet raw where the stone had skinned calluses down to live flesh.

By mid-afternoon, the wind died. The path was steeper, with trees, twisted as his son was twisted, clinging to life by scant toeholds in the sheer rock. There was an oppressive silence, as if the desolate peaks were listening, and Nalinle stopped and listened, too; but he heard only his own breath, dragging into his lungs and out again, and an occasional whimper from Mikai, who slept and sweated against his chest. Nalinle jogged on, saying "Hope . . . Hope . . . Hope . . ." to himself as he ran. It gave him some measure of courage.

The sun had dipped behind a taller peak by the time Lal, sprawled on a flat boulder above the trail, caught sight of him. He was sentinel today, and he saw Nalinle halt before the fallen tree that blocked the trail, looking for a way around it. Saw him peer over the dizzy drop-off and finally spot, halfway up the tumbled rock face, the narrow cleft leading to the bandits' hideaway. As he started toward it, Lal backed off his perch and ran to the bandit chief, who was sharpening his knife nearby under an acacia tree.

"Two come, Auken," Lal reported. "One man, one boy." The leader halted in mid-stroke, and Sturz, who had been napping, hitched up on one elbow.

"Where?"

"Through the crevice." Auken made for the near end of the passageway with Lal following close behind.

Nalinle came out of the dark cleft, squinting against the light. As his vision cleared, he made out two men standing before him, one of them with a long, curved knife in his hand. He stopped uncertainly.

"Peace . . . to you," he said. "Do you have water to share?"

They made no answer and he tried again. "Water," he explained, making a drinking gesture. Nothing. He made the gesture again. "Water?" he persisted. The bandits stood there, wordless and malicious, and Nalinle began to back away, right into Sturz's spear point. His sudden startle amused them.

"Did you see him jump, Auken?" Lal laughed. "What a face he made!"

"And see what he is carrying!" Sturz pointed. "An idiot!"

Nalinle held Mikai closer. "Please . . . he is my son."

"Master, do you hear? His son is an idiot!" *But I am not*, Mikai protested silently. *I can understand, and think and wonder. If you don't see this, stranger, then which of us is the idiot?* Sturz thrust his dirty, unshaven face close at Mikai. "What can you do, boy? Can you sing, eh? Can you do tricks?" They laughed again and Nalinle backed up a bit.

"He cannot speak. . . ."

"Then what good is he?" Lal asked, losing interest. "What good are *you?*" He whipped out his knife and laid the edge at Nalinle's throat. "Why shouldn't I cut off your head?"

"Leave him alone," Auken said. Lal put away the knife and Auken studied man and boy objectively. Took Mikai's face and turned it from side to side. "Where are you from?"

Nalinle tipped his head toward the flat, wet, green place that could barely be seen from the mountain. "Beyond the hills, and beyond the forest before the hills . . . wetlands, and the River . . ."

Auken gazed in that direction, calculating quickly. "And the boy?"

"I carried him. I ran, and I carried him. He is my son."

"That is a long way to carry such a boy. What will you do with him?"

Nalinle, feeling easier about their safety, put Mikai down gently on the path and rubbed his sore arms. "There is a starship . . . they call it *Hope* . . . they will make him well. . . ." He smiled innocently at Auken. "The people on *Hope* . . . the star people? . . . they *know* how to make him well . . . the runner said so."

Auken's face and voice were expressionless, and utterly without mercy. "There is no ship."

It took Nalinle a few seconds to process this blasphemy. His face was stricken. "*Yes!* Yes, its name is *Hope*, and they . . . they will make Mikai straight!" *All this way, all this suffering, for nothing? Can it be that it is not true?* Growing fear and despair made his voice quaver. "The runner said twenty-four days, swiftfoot, to the mountains at G'ham, there is a ship called *Hope*. . . ."

"He lied." Nalinle shook his head, mutely pleading against his crumbling hope, as Auken beat him down with his monotonous voice. "*He lied.*"

"No!" Nalinle burst out, grabbing Auken's tunic and shaking him in desperation. "I have only one day left to run! There *is* a ship, there *must be* a ship! All this way, oh, gods, all this way—!" He never saw Sturz's blow coming, but only opened his eyes, a long while later, and found himself lying face down on the rock. He could smell Mikai's familiar scent behind him, and there were dust and pebbles in his mouth. Someone kicked him onto his back with a rough foot and he saw the bandits standing above him, silhouetted against the glaring sky. Sturz's spear point came to rest at the base of his throat. He lay very still, breathing lightly, his eyes wide with fear.

"I could let him kill you for that, swamplander, father-of-a-fool," Auken said, stooping to slip a noose around his neck. He tugged him to his feet. "But you are strong. They will pay well for you in the city."

"But—" Nalinle protested numbly. "But—my son . . ." No one moved or spoke but Lal, who was absently hacking a dry twig to bits with his knife. He leered suddenly, showing stained teeth, and Nalinle, realizing what they had in mind, fell on his knees and grabbed a double fistful of Auken's robe. "Lord, do whatever you wish with me, but spare my son!"

"I will not put my hand on him. Neither will my men touch him." Nalinle, his eyes welling with relief, started quickly for Mikai but was brought up short by the tether, which nearly strangled him. Auken began to walk away, dragging Nalinle after him, with Sturz prodding him along from behind.

"I can't leave him," he gurgled against the tight rope. "I—"

"Auken!" They turned to see Lal standing by Mikai, knife in hand. "What of this one?"

"Leave him!" Auken ordered. "I gave my word. Besides—" he gazed up at the sky where large carrion eaters circled slowly, "it will soon be feeding time." Nalinle turned to him in mute horror, struggling ferociously to get back to his son as the bandits started down the mountain. Nalinle resisted as long as he could, but they continued as if he were not there. He was forced to stumble along with them, constantly looking back and pulling with both hands on the noose to keep from choking.

Mikai, helpless on the ledge where they had left him, tried to call to his father, but the cry that emerged from his throat was like that of some primitive beast, and the bandits mocked it repeatedly among themselves as they dragged Nalinle after them down the mountain.

CHAPTER

V

AFTER AN HOUR, they came upon a cave set high in the rock face over a precarious ramp of talus. Picking their way gingerly to the entrance, they fastened Nalinle's hands behind him and rolled a heavy boulder over the free end of his tether, leaving him standing in the broiling sun. Auken came out of the cave with several small bundles of dried meat, two of which he threw to his men. They caught them on the fly and fell to at once. When they were finished, Lal brought out a skin of water, beaded with moisture, and shared it around, while Nalinle, the rope chafing his neck, strained to see the ledge where Mikai still lay.

Above them, and to the right, he could see birds of prey stark against the sky, circling the ledge. Quietly and desperately, he kept tugging at the rope, gagging and strangling, until it seemed that he and Mikai were one, and the dark wings crisscrossing Mikai's body were crossing his own. It was like a waking dream, like a vision brought on by the headman in a sacred ceremony. He knew the terror Mikai felt, tasted the hunger in each of the birds.

When Auken's shadow fell across his face, he did not flinch, so real was the dream. Auken squatted down by him and offered him a bundle of meat, but Nalinle simply stared at it and then at Auken. His yearning for his son superseded even hatred.

"Are you hungry, swamplander? Eat." He bounced the bundle lightly in his hand and tossed it into the dust between Nalinle's feet. "Eat. I will untie your hands." He loosed the

tether, and Nalinle stared up at Mikai's ledge, absently rubbing
his wrists.

"Forget him," Auken advised. "Such a one is better off
dead."

Nalinle ignored him, and he persisted, tempting, "In the city
are things you have never seen, even in dreams. Houses three
and four levels in the air, and boxes that talk and sing." He
gestured at the ledge. You will be glad that one is not there to
get in the way." *Five birds now*, Nalinle thought. *How will I get
back to him in time?* "You could not see all this, with such a
son! Who would buy you?—with *him!*"

Nalinle drew in the dust with an absent forefinger as he
spoke "Before Mikai, there were others . . . strong, not like
Mikai . . . and while they lived, Nalinle ate—and slept—and
saw . . . and did not see.

"And then came Mikai, and I became another Nalinle . . .
who had to find new ways . . . and *see* in new ways . . . and
think in new ways . . . nothing was the same as before. . . ."

"The boy is better off dead."

Nalinle nodded at the ground. "You are right. Everyone says
Mikai is better off dead." He looked up at Auken at last. "But
Nalinle is better because he lives."

Auken, all business again, tucked the bundle of dried meat
into the waistband of Nalinle's dhoti. "Keep it. Later, you will
be glad." He got up and rejoined the others, leaving Nalinle
gazing upward at the ledge. They were getting ready to go: bare
feet whispering on rock, a muttered comment, the small human
sounds of people stirring about. He glanced down at his crude
dust-drawing of the three bandits, the magic picture he had
made, spat on it, and rubbed it out with his foot.

Auken gestured to the others. "Roll away the stone." They
put their backs into the work, and the massive stone slowly
rolled back, freeing the end of Nalinle's tether. For a long
moment, he stayed immobile, even submissive; then he sprang
into violent action, catching them by surprise. He leaped
suddenly atop the boulder like a monkey, climbing up the talus
and over the few stable outcrops as fast as he could go, his
tether trailing behind. Auken was beside himself with fury.

"Get him! Sturz! Lal!" he shouted as they began to climb after Nalinle. "Your spear, fool! Use your spear! But don't kill him!" The spear whispered over Nalinle's head as he dropped flat against the searing talus, but he was gaining no ground, for the rocks kept slipping under him, threatening to bring him down and over the edge of the scarp. He had to crawl upward on all fours now, the angle was so steep. Rocks kept sliding under him. Any moment now, he would slide to his death off the edge of the cliff.

The rope went taut, cutting off his breath.

"I've got him!" Lal shouted, panting hard from his exertion. "Auken! I've got him!" Nalinle made a last, desperate effort to free himself; wrapped both hands around the tether and jerked with all his might. Lal did not let go the rope, but the movement overbalanced him, and he began to slide, making a hoarse, animal sound of panic. Nalinle tried to retain his footing, but the whole talus ramp let go with a mounting roar, taking the three bandits and Nalinle with it. The ground began to tremble. Nalinle grabbed a jutting rock and hung on for dear life, but it pulled free and smacked his forehead as he came tumbling down toward the scarp. The bandits slid, screaming, off the edge, Nalinle with them, and just as he was about to plunge into the abyss below, he was brought up short by his left ankle. His head and shoulders hung over nothingness as he looked down at the sky above him, up at the far-off rocks below, where three irregular patches of color marked the demise of his captors.

He shut his eyes and concentrated on gaining the scarp. Slowly pulling himself around, careful to make no sudden moves, he managed to get his shoulders back on solid ground. His ankle was still tangled in the chance loop of the rope which had snubbed him fast to a sharp jag of rock. He eased himself around, shale skidding under him as he moved, and untied his foot; freed his neck and started to throw the rope after the bandits, when he reconsidered. Might he not need this rope sometime in the future? Could it not help him to get Mikai to the *Hope* ship? *Mikai!* Coiling the rope quickly, he slung it around his shoulder and he began climbing back across the sliding tumulus toward the ledge and Mikai.

He regained the trail and climbed as fast as he could, but the rockslide had dislodged a boulder farther on, and he had to go over or around it. He chose to go upward and began to climb, scraping elbows and knees raw against the pitiless rock face. He strained toward Mikai with all his will, and was encouraged, and yet dismayed, when an occasional shadow swept his face, and he heard the cry of a bird of prey. He had almost reached the ledge when he missed a vital toehold. He felt blindly with his foot for another, but it gave way as he put his full weight on it, and he went tumbling back down the scarp in a cloud of rock and dust, fetching up hard against a boulder far down the slope. He lay there stunned for a moment, then began to climb again, bleeding from several wide abrasions, but determined as never before in his life.

He made the climb by the hardest, dreading what he might find, pulled himself painfully over the top of the ledge, then got to his feet and stumbled toward his son.

The air was full of large birds who circled and swooped at Mikai, not deadly serious yet, but playing at it. Nalinle came up at a staggering run, waving his arms wildly and shouting over Mikai's incoherent noises of relief and joy. *I knew you would come, Father! I knew you would never leave me to die alone! I knew it, I knew it!* "Fa'!" Mikai mouthed, unable to articulate the rest. "Fa' com'!" Mikai laughed the laugh he detested, as he had no other, and he must laugh aloud. For his father, his savior, his very spirit, had come to his rescue, and he was glad.

The birds began to swoop angrily on Nalinle, tearing at him with beaks and talons, and he grabbed up large rocks and pitched them with deadly accuracy. One bird, its wing slightly out of kilter from a well-placed throw, spiraled downward sharply until it was out of sight. After a few more passes, the birds flew away, screaming in frustration. Their calls echoed back from the rock walls, growing fainter and fainter until they were gone.

Nalinle scooped Mikai up and hugged him, laughing and crying at the same time. Mikai tried excitedly to respond, flailing wildly at the innocent air.

"Yes! Yes!" Nalinle exulted. He rocked the boy in his arms,

and this gave way to dancing, a stamping of feet and a whirling, which took them off the rock ledge and over the other, clear, side of the trail all the way to the top of the mountain, where, they had been told, *Hope* was waiting for them.

Captain Donelang Kris, sitting perfectly still at the conn on *Hope*'s bridge, was first to hear the music. It was a distant, staccato, many-voiced chant, an ancient fluctuating song more easily recognizable, even in this age of technology, than terse signs and digital readouts. Kris lifted his head, smiling in satisfaction.

"Here they come," he said.

The ship, a small fast scout, appeared as a fleck on the forward screen, followed at some distance by a much larger Senn freighter.

"She's making signal, sir," his com ops reported. "Senn scout *Ojibwa*, escorting the FMS *Geronimo*. Permission to dock?"

"Granted. Give them formal welcome, and inform Sachem Gallatin that the potlatch is scheduled for fourteen hundred sharp, in Reception Area Eight. And Coto," he added, "inform Priyam Sharobi that his spare parts have arrived."

"*Alai*, sir."

"Second vessel approaching on the port bow, sir," First Officer Tong reported, and the Captain took one look and heaved a profound sigh.

The ship in question was a familiar, gaudily decorated craft that had seen better days but was still eminently spaceworthy. Emblazoned on its ample flank was the legend USO ENTERTAINMENT and in (not much) smaller lettering under that, 'Stars Serving the Star Service!' There were airbrushed color graphics of someone's impression of the cosmos. There were enlarged autographs of the various entertainers who had done tours with the United Star Organization in the past. There were bevies of pretty girls posing in swimsuits at the expanded viewport. Beyond them, in the seedy interior, a band could be seen tuning up.

The ship dropped into position on *Hope*'s port quarter, and Tong looked up from her station.

"It's USS *Broadway*, sir. She's making signal." Kris indicated the forward screen with a gesture. It came up quickly, flooding the bridge with light and sound, and the face of Sid Behrman, MC *extraordinaire*, beamed down at them. In the near background, the band played show tunes at full blare, and starlets waved at the camera.

"Captain Kris! Good to see you, good to see you! Here we are again, right on time, with a wonderful brand new show that's gonna knock you right on your bonanza! Yes, sir, never let it be said that Sid Behrman's kids would leave you people high and dry over the holidays! From Montezuma's Halls to Xholemeache's Walls, we're always there for your calls! No, sir, nothing's too good for our people in the Star Service!" The band sounded a final chord and fell silent and Behrman lifted his brows well into his balding scalp and peered over his glasses like a superannuated cherub.

"Permission to come aboard, Captain?" And Kris, with a weary sigh, gave his gracious permission for the show folk to proceed.

Tong handed Kris a manifest which included all personnel aboard *Broadway*, and indicated with a well manicured finger tip one particular name, that of one Waylan Stubbs.

"Waylan Stubbs, country singer, guitarist—"

"You dislike the guitar?" Kris queried blandly, and his First Officer's patient gaze was both answer and reprimand. She handed him a personnel report.

"I enjoy guitar music, Captain; what I don't enjoy is the idea of a convicted murderer coming aboard." Kris frowned and studied the report carefully. 'Stubbs, Waylan,' it read. 'Height: 1.79 meters; weight: 76.4 kilos; hair: blond; eyes: blue; occupation: musician; Special notes: arrested murder 18 November, '61, Droso City, Zerev, 3 counts; incarcerated five years at Penal Station, Moon 9, IAGO Tracking Facility; declared rehabilitated by medical court, 5 March, '87.' There followed a list of pertinent family information, details of his crime, his medical record and his security code. Kris rested his nose on his steepled fingers and shut his eyes.

"Inform Security about our guest, Miss Tong. Mister Wimet

will no doubt appreciate the prior warning." He opened his eyes with an apologetic smile. "On the outside chance that Mr. Stubbs's rehabilitation proves to be a temporary one."

"Right away, sir."

"And contact Mr. Behrman for me, Coto, if you please."

"*Alai*, sir." The screen blazed with light and the camera discovered Sid Behrman unpacking his suitcases in his stateroom. Cases, room and occupant were in equal stages of disarray.

"Mr. Behrman," said Donelang Kris. Behrman straightened abruptly, squinting at the screen. Held up a hand.

"Who's there? Hang on. Wait." He groped for his glasses, put them on, and his face cleared. "Oh, Captain Kris. Hey, great stateroom, Captain, it's beautiful, I really love it. And I want you to know that my—"

"Waylan. Stubbs."

Behrman faltered to a stop and then regained his stride. "Uhhh— Wonderful entertainer, wonderful. Great kid. Loves dogs and kids, loves 'em. Played for the crowned heads of seventeen planets, and he won the Country Music Award four years run—"

"And killed three people on Zerev with his bare hands," Kris assisted. "Can you vouch for this Stubbs? Do you have documented proof of his rehabilitation?"

"Sure, sure, no problem!" Behrman started patting his pockets and digging through his cases for documentation both men knew was not there. "Now, where is that . . . I *know* I have it here somewhere. . . . Look, Captain, the kid needed a break, okay? He's a good kid, he messed up, but now he's over it, and we needed a country act in a hurry, all right? I guarantee he won't cause any trouble."

"You can assure me of this?" Kris asked, and Behrman grabbed his heart with both hands.

"Captain! Sweetie! You know me. We're old friends! Would I lie to you?"

Kris blinked his depthless black eyes. "Thank you, Mr. Behrman," he replied and rang off.

Would I lie to you, Captain, sweetie? Behrman had asked.

Kris almost smiled. *I don't know, Mr. Behrman; is the Dowager Empress large? Is the sea damp? Is the Pope Einai?* He stifled an inclination toward laughter, and, making a conscious act of the will, gave the whole matter into the hands of Nepht, god of the Deeps.

The situation thus resolved, Donelang Kris leaned back in his command chair and resumed his introspective study of the endless starry void.

"We're pretty nearly out of everything," Sharobi confided to Marik. "We have three kidneys left, all Minsonai; half a *doss* Erthlik heart-lung sets, none of them child-sized; no long bones of any species; and no eyes of any kind. We're really down to the bottom of the cistern.

"Sometimes you can go months without needed spare parts, and then you come up against a deluge of patients, like this Ildefor thing, and all of a sudden you're a day late and a credit short." He pushed open the doors to Surgery One and stepped into the adjacent scrub room, Marik following close in his wake.

"I'm surprised we have a suitable body for this brain transplant today." He kicked the lever, 'washed' his hands under the scrub lights, and shoved them into synthon gloves, then waited for Marik to do the same. Both men thus prepared, Sharobi led the way once more into the operating room.

Inside a large plastic cubicle dead center of the floor there lay in a MAX a thin, frail old man who was neither a politician nor an entertainer, but who was widely known on his world both for his astute philosophy and for his kindness. In return for those gifts to others, his planet had unexpectedly raised the funds for a brain transplant, which funds had come at a welcome moment, as the philosopher's original body had begun to deteriorate rapidly.

Several nurses and interns, as well as Jenner, Sharobi's favorite surgical nurse, and Sebastian Meng, the Chief of Anesthesia, were waiting at their stations around the plastex cubicle, and their murmured conversations died down as he seated himself at the main controls. Marik took his place at the secondary station, and Sharobi barked:

"Anesthesia?"

Dr. Meng bowed slightly. "Ready, Priyam."

"All set?" He looked around at his team, and nodded.

"Let's get on it, then. Com." The nurse switched on communications with the patient. "Mr. Stuart? Mr. Stuart, this is Priyam Sharobi. Can you hear me?"

The patient, heavily sedated in his MAX, turned his head and nodded slowly.

"Now, in just a minute, Dr. Meng here, will put you to sleep. There'll be a little sensation of falling, and then nothing—until you wake up with a brand-new body. All right?" The old man nodded drowsily again, and Sharobi asked Brian Bakunas, "How's that host?"

"Host body prepared and ready, sir," Brian replied, from his station. "Host is a male Caucasian Earthling, twenty-six years old at the time of death, Beta biochemical setup, blood type AB positive, codon full complement."

Sharobi gave Meng a slight nod and Meng's fingers moved over his keypad. Stuart dropped off to sleep at once.

"He's under."

"Keep him light," Sharobi instructed. "Let's have the host." Jenner depressed a knife switch and a second MAX entered the sealed environment. In it was the athletic body of a young Earthling male, recently deceased. Marik was not surprised. It was customary to brain-transplant only into like species, the prevailing medical opinion holding that a change of venue from one aspect to another was hard enough on a patient; a crossover from one species to another—say, Earthling to Kraun or Einai—would have been too much for anyone's psyche to bear.

"What'd he die of?" Sharobi wanted to know.

"According to Records," Jenner volunteered, "he and his skimmer-buddies were hot-dogging over McArthur Base, got a little too low, and he bounced." She shook her head indulgently. "Kids!"

Sharobi jerked upright as if someone had jabbed him with a

pin. "A *retread?* I promised Mr. Stuart a new body, and you people are trying to slip a *retread* in on me?"

"Priyam, it isn't as if—" Jenner began, but Sharobi cut her off with an offended air.

"This body is a damn *retread*. I'll bet he's been rebuilt from the ground up a half a dozen times!"

"Sir," one of the interns defended, "he's a first-timer, and he's in top shape. He was in ReGen for over a week, and you can see for yourself, we put him together good as new. Better!" Sharobi swung his massive head toward the audacious youngster and heaved a deep breath, saying nothing, a gesture Marik usually described as having been breathed upon by a bison. The foolhardy intern swallowed hard and stood his ground.

"We really worked hard on him, Priyam. Tuned him up. Reamed all the arteries clean, even the real little stuff. Fused the broken bones with plasmic. Flushed his soft tissue until there's not even a hematoma left. All three of us got straight A's on this jobbie from Old Man Claiborne, and you know how tough *he* is!" He cleared his throat. "We did a helluva reconstruction, here, Priyam, if you ask me."

"Nobody asked you, young man," Sharobi countered. "But if they asked *me*, I'd have to admit that for a rebuilt body, I suppose it's not too bad. And it isn't as if we have much of a choice." He gestured at Jenner. "Hoods."

The hoods rolled back on each MAX and Sharobi slipped his gloved hands into the manipulator sleeves and slowly began to move the right one downward.

"Scalpel, please," Sharobi murmured.

"Scalpel coming down," Jenner replied.

From the overhead, a manipulator equipped with a scalpel began to descend in exact replicaton of the motion of Sharobi's hands. One smooth dancer's movement, and the scalpel drew a thin red line around the old man's shaven skull. Marik, moving his manipulators in to sponge the bleeding, noted that the head with its network of blue veins, looked fragile as an eggshell.

Jenner brought down a small drill, already whirring. Sharobi took it over and drilled several small holes around the perimeter of the skull, preparatory to removing the brainpan.

"Suction." Marik suctioned away blood and fluid as Jenner sponged up. "Readout on the host body?" Bakunas checked his board.

"Heart rate sixty-eight, pressure one twenty-five over seventy-eight, respiration twelve. All veins patent—"

"*Tre*phine," Sharobi muttered, and, echoing the order, Jenner brought the whirling, circular instrument. There was the sound as of a saw cutting softwood as Sharobi wielded the trephine.

"—fluorocarbon preparation holding up nicely," Bakunas continued. "As healthy a dead body as I've ever seen, sir."

"That may be," Sharobi answered glumly, "but when push comes to shove, it's still a damn *retread*."

Precisely at 1400 hours, the Senn party swept through the corridors like a pride of lions, looking neither to the left nor to the right. They were an impressive people, a race composed of Abomaircuns (who had emigrated *en masse* to a newfound planet to re-create the world their ancestors had enjoyed on Old Earth) superimposed on an indigenous alien race of sapient humans descended from oversized cats.

The resultant hybrid easily topped two meters, and, along with proportionate bulk, impressive manes and prominent canines (not to mention the ceremonial regalia of the Abomaircuns), the individual Senn tended to be daunting indeed. In a group such as the one sweeping into Reecep Eight at the moment, they were downright intimidating.

In the lead, wearing eagle feathers and a magnificent buffalo robe, came the sachem, Joskwa Gallatin, followed by his shaman, Eddie Wolf Eye, and three trusted lieutenants. Sharobi, Marik, and Father Santino, along with Dalton Truax, who was an Abomaircun crewman, rose to greet them. Earlier, on an impervious ceramalloy disc in the center of the room, Truax had built a fire, which had now burned down to banked flames and breathing embers. Gallatin stopped before it and lifted a hand.

"We come in peace," he greeted them, and Sharobi responded in kind:

"We welcome the Senn in peace for as long as the waters flow or the grass shall grow."

"The shaman says, 'We've heard that one before,'" Truax translated Eddie Wolf Eye's surreptitious Sign language.

Gallatin grunted, sat down with his people on one side of the fire and shrugged off the ceremonial buffalo robe. "You don't mind if I get rid of this thing, do you, Mike? It's hot as hell," he said conversationally, earning himself a dirty glare from Eddie Wolf Eye, who was unwrapping the red stone peace pipe. Thus chastised, not only the sachem but the entire group fell silent while the old man made his preparations.

Wolf Eye's attention to his task discouraged conversation, riveted their attention, focused them as one. It was his gravity, Marik thought, that elevated the meeting to a higher plane. You didn't have to understand what he was doing to sense its intrinsic importance, its mysticism, and its centuries of tradition; Wolf Eye knew, and believed in it, and he made you believe, too.

He murmured over the tobacco, filled the bowl, lit it with an ember, and solemnly pointed the pipe stem at the heavens, at the earth, and at each of the Four Directions, while Truax said softly, "Eagle . . . and shrew . . . cougar . . . and badger . . . bear . . . and wolf . . ."

Marik whispered to himself, "Ordinate . . . and abscissa . . ." at the same time as Father Santino, beside him, murmured:

"In nomine Patris . . . et Filius . . . et Spiritu Sancto . . ."

They passed the pipe, each man, even Marik, taking his share of the rich, fragrant tobacco smoke. When it was done, the shaman, looking upwards, raised his hands, Signing as he prayed, and Truax interpreted:

"Grandfather, look at our brokenness. We know that in all Creation only the human family has strayed from the Sacred Way. We know that we are the ones who are divided and we are the ones who must come back together to walk in the Sacred Way.

"Grandfather, Sacred One, teach us love, compassion and honor that we may heal the earth and heal each other." Wolf

Eye made the sign for 'I am finished speaking,' and Sharobi nodded curtly to the priest, who responded with:

"O God of our common stories, may the ages upon ages of your faithful presence fill our mouths with witness upon witness of your love. Let our unique and diverse memories call us to a common gratitude, a common praise, and a common life in your gracious creation."

After a respectful moment, the sachem lifted his head, the eagle feathers in his scalp lock stirring gently, and regarded Sharobi for a long moment. The harsh planes of his face were set off by the humor in his intelligent black eyes, and even seated cross-legged there on the floor, his posture was impeccable. He might have been a sculpture carved from some ruddy stone. Then he grinned.

"I hope you have some top-drawer trade goods, Mike," he began chummily, "because when you see the spare parts I brought you this time, your face is going to fall off." He made a sign to his men.

"Okay, boys," he said. "Bring in the merchandise."

Angelo's barbershop was located off Main Street in a narrow, cobblestoned alley in the Italian Quarter. Never a large establishment, it was rendered even smaller by the fact that Angelo had something for everyone. It was generally understood among staff, crew and population alike that whatever you couldn't find anywhere else, you could find at Angelo's—and promptly, too!

There were piles of outdated magazines, for perusal by waiting customers and invaluable for illustrating school reports; a box of sturdy, battered toys 'for the kids'; an aquarium with one fat, remaining fish named Il Duce (its having eliminated the smaller competition by the ancient and time-honored method of its namesake); a period coat rack; hand-colored pictures of the Blessed Virgin and the Sacred Heart, bought these many years ago in Rome, Old Earth; and a large covered glass container of Italian egg cookies (in case someone came in with a sweet tooth), that stood check by jowl with the all-species currycomb-comb-and-brush display beside the old-fashioned cash register.

In celebration of the season, a big Santa Claus decorated the front door. A crèche occupied one cramped corner, leaving standing room only for a pair of oversized plastex reindeer, and someone had painted thick white snowflakes all over the inside of the windows, which boasted a pair of ratty wreaths linked by dusty scarlet ribbon.

Every available wall was lined with mirror, which served only to multiply the affable confusion, until patrons felt as though they were having their hair cut in the middle of some comfortable, rummaged-through steamer trunk. It was a wonder, though perhaps it should not have been, that the shop was always crowded with customers.

Today, the first day of Christmas/Hanukkah vacation, it was full of children, all talking at once. Angelo, carefully trimming Tom Paige's hair, was, as always, the soul of patience.

"But, Angelo," said the boy called David, "what if he says no?"

"He's not gonna say no," Angelo assured him. "Priyam Sharobi gonna like the music. Everybody gonna like the music."

A crewman stuck his head in the door. "Hey, Angelo, you wouldn't happen to have an extra can of terminal cleaner on you, would you? I'd go down to Central Supply, but it's way the heck—"

"Sure. Sure. Hang on, Doctor—" this to Tom Paige, who was sitting half-shorn in the chair, "I'm'a be right back." He started digging through drawers. "I got it right in here someplace."

"Take your time, Angelo," Paige advised. "So what are you kids up to now?"

"We wanted to put on a show!" Gino, who was the oldest, explained disgustedly. "You know—like a warm-up act, for when the USO ship comes? With singin' and dancin' and—and a pageant! For Christmas like!"

"And Onam!" little Jayshree interjected, nodding wide-eyed.

"Cohosh Siv!" Dof exulted.

"Kwanzaa!" Ahmad contributed.

"And Hanukkah, too, we were hoping," David finished. "But Priyam Sharobi probably won't let us."

"Well, sure he will!" Paige tried to be encouraging. "Why wouldn't he?"

"I'll lay you ten to one he says no, Doc," Gino offered, pulling out a ten-credit note. "Put up or shut up."

"He's not gonna say no, *babbaluche*," Angelo flung over his shoulder to his nephew. "He's gonna like it. So *you* shut up, eh? Show some respect! Ah. Here she is." He straightened and kicked the drawer shut in one motion. "Here's your cleaner, Mister Standing-up-y Bear." George Standing Bear grinned. He had long since accepted Angelo's version of his name.

"Thanks, Angelo. Catch you later." He disappeared down the alley, and Alison, one of the older girls, said primly:

"He may very well let us do the singing, Angelo, and he might even permit the entire programme, but I'm certain he jolly well *doesn't* like *children!*"

"He prob'ly doesn't even like programs," WonKi said glumly. Dolf nodded agreement and thrust his hands into his pockets.

"He don't like *any*thing!"

"I don't like it," Sharobi grumped to Joskwa Gallatin. "All of a sudden, you're not interested in anything we have to trade, except—"

"Ah! Except!" Gallatin interjected. "Except what we really need." Sharobi shook his head like an angry bison.

"Not a chance, Joskwa. If we concede you all gambling rights aboard *Hope—great T'ath, all gambling rights, across the board!*—then what do we have to bargain with, next time you bring us a load of spare parts?"

"You'll think of something. You always do! Smart man like you? I'm not worried a bit. Look at it this way, Mike," Gallatin suggested. "I hate to say it, but if you don't buy from us, where will you get parts? We're the only game in town.

"Without us, where's your limb reattachment clinic? Your whole-eye replacement program? Your anatomy labs at the Med School? Plus—" he sat forward, gesturing with both hands for emphasis, "we're not even asking for Point Of Purchase payment; we're just negotiating the opportunity—the *opportunity*, mind you!—to recoup our losses through the *voluntary participation* of the very folks who benefit from our merchandise! Now, tell the truth, Mike, is that fair, or what?"

Sharobi massaged his bulldog jaw. "How about we give you just the bingo concession in trade for this load?"

Joskwa Gallatin gave him a long, sorrowful look and got to his feet. "Come on, boys," he told his men, "let's hit the trail. We're not getting anywhere here." Eddie Wolf Eye got up stiffly, along with the other Senn, and Sharobi waved them down again.

"Now, wait a minute, just a minute, here. Sit down, Joskwa, sit down. I'm not refusing, I'm just talking about terms." They sat easily, all but Wolf Eye, who made it down to the floor again with some difficulty.

"If you're willing to make any kind of a reasonable offer at all, we can talk all day," Gallatin said, and Sharobi responded gruffly with:

"If you think I'm unreasonable, dammit, why are we having a powwow?"

"Say the word, Mike, and I'm out of here." Sharobi said nothing, and the sachem stood up, his men obediently rising with him. Eddie Wolf Eye glared balefully at Sharobi and creaked painfully to his feet once again.

"I'm not asking you to leave," Sharobi countered, "but I'm asking you to reconsider: the *entire gambling concession*? You people would make so much money, we'd never get you out scouting again!"

And that was the point. They desperately needed the scouts. For a ship like *Hope* to function, emergent races on various planets must be found; contacted; prepared. Pandemics must be reported. New biologicals must be identified and gathered for testing and processing aboard ship. Someone had to go trekking into raw bush country and hunt them all up.

That was the job of the Senn, inveterate merchants who traded the width and breadth of the galaxy, keeping their eyes open all the while for the opportunity to advance the cause of galactic health and longevity, and turn a few quick credits in the process.

In return for this consideration, *Hope* paid the Senn a substantial bonus on a *per planetas* basis, and furnished them a full terraformed level of the ship as a base of operations.

Mykar Sharobi needed his Senn scouts. *Hope* would cease to function without them. But they needed him, too, for since their planet had been destroyed, *Hope* was the only home they had. He summoned all the patience he could muster and gestured them down again.

Gallatin sat, and it was the space of many breaths before Eddie Wolf Eye, face impassive to the point of stone, managed to fold up his stiff joints and sit heavily yet again, almost concealing the muffled grunt of pain that escaped him.

"You know that I am your friend," Gallatin said formally. "And I know that you are mine, and that you have respect and compassion for the last remnant of a race whose very planet was battered to dust—"

"Aw, hell, Joskwa, don't start that hearts-and-flowers routine again!" Sharobi interrupted. "Every damn time you start to lose an argument, you give me that pathetic old 'last remnant of a once noble race' *pift*!"

"*Pift?* I share my heart with my friend, and you call it *pift?* I am wounded, Mike." Gallatin gained his feet with an offended air and folded his arms across his chest, under his magnificent mane. The others rose, too, all but Eddie Wolf Eye. Instead, he Signed a brief message to Truax, who mumbled back, "Maybe I better not say that here."

Gallatin began to Sign silently and Truax interpreted for him:

"I, Joskwa Gallatin, Sachem, have been insulted by these short, rude *awanoots*. I will take my people back the way we came, until the white-eyes make a proper apology. My warriors will take eight-hour shifts guarding our merchandise in your refrigerated cargo bay until you pay the rightful price or we decide to remove it. I have spoken." The fringes of his buckskin shirt moved slightly in the breeze from the ventilators, and his eagle feathers spun idly. He cut an impressive figure, standing there, until he glanced down at the old man on the floor.

"Frank," he muttered to the man on his right, "help Uncle Eddie up, will you?" As the stalwart young man hauled the shaman to his feet, Gallatin raised his right hand, palm forward, at the group, and intoned:

"We leave you now. We will be aboard *Ojibwa*. Naturally, we expect restitution, in the form of a cash settlement, and a believable apology." They strode majestically out, Frank still supporting Eddie Wolf Eye, but Joskwa Gallatin turned at the door and pointed at Sharobi.

"If you change your mind about the gambling concession, Mike, give me a call on my private number." He winked. "We'll do lunch."

CHAPTER

VI

JOE GARRETT WAS lying there, squeezing a hard rubber ball in his left fist, listening to some stupid game show on the tri-D. He had taken to exercising his left hand with the ball, trying to keep his arm muscles in top shape; for no matter what they said, he knew he might never get a new right arm, much less new eyes. He had a hard time trying to make his peace with that, and was wrestling with it yet again when there was a knock at the door. A vaguely familiar male voice said, "Joe Garrett?"

"Yeah," Garrett replied. "Who is it?"

"You sure you're the authentic Joe Garrett, now," the voice persisted in an amused drawl. There was the rattle of a bag and the faint, muted *thrum* of a stringed instrument bumping something.

"What is this, some kind of joke? Yeah, I'm Joe Garrett, Sergeant, GFA. So what's going on? Who are you and what do you want?"

But the visitor was not to be put off. "You *sure* you're the famous Alfred *J.* Garrett? The man who threw that magic block in the Old Miss-LSU game of '65 that let ol' Waylan Stubbs run seventy-five yards for the winning six points? *That* Joe Garrett?"

Garrett sat up suddenly. "*Waylan?* Waylan Stubbs? Dammit-to-hell, *is that my buddy Waylan Stubbs from Gulfport, Mississ-eye-yippee?*"

"You bet your butt it is, hoss!" Waylan laughed, crossing the room to envelop Garrett in a bear hug and whack him across his good shoulder. "What the hell you doin' in here? Hidin' out from a irate husband?"

Garrett laughed aloud. "Sure. Half a dozen of 'em. Sit down, Wayle, sit down. My God, it's good to see you! Pull up a chair. How's life been treating you?"

There was a small hesitation. "That's a whole long story, Joe. I can't even begin tell you the half of it, right now."

"You were out on Zerev, weren't you, last time I heard?"

Another pause. "Yeah, well, you know how it goes. Zerev just didn't work out. I'm here with the USO now. Playin' gittar. But, hey, let's talk about you! Where you been keeping yourself?"

And Garrett told him where he had been, and what had been happening since the last big football game, several lifetimes ago. And after a while Waylan unlimbered his guitar and played some old tunes they could sing to, and told him stories about USS *Broadway*, and her showgirls, and what had happened to Sid that time on Dvanti, when the locals were so pleased with the show that they presented Sid with a native wife.

"So, here she was," Waylan chortled, "standing there by this preacher-creature, with all the relatives behind her, and all her grabbers and legs and manipulators just wiggling fit to kill. And here's poor Sid—his eyes was about to pop out of his little ol' bald head—and he couldn't say nothin' to offend 'em, because they were meat eaters, see, and she was the headman's only daughter!" He cackled. "One wrong word and he was Sunday dinner!"

Garrett, who'd had little reason to laugh recently, slapped his thigh and howled. "So how'd he get out of it?" he choked, after a while. "Come on, man, don't keep me in suspense!"

"Well, Sid's pretty smart! What he did was, he—"

Ulrika Drac swept through the door like an arctic chill. Garrett could sense her disapproving presence even before she spoke, and it sobered him.

"Did you men not hear the visiting hours announcement, a while ago, they are over?" she asked in an acid tone.

"I'm sorry, I guess we missed it, Nurse," Waylan put in. "I

haven't seen my buddy Garrett, here, since back in college, and since I'm always travelin' with the USO, I thought—"

"I know what you thought. Why do you think you can overstay your visiting hours, only because you are some *entertainer?* I am not impressed with foolish USO. Adults play-acting like children. It does not wash up with me, *Mister Entertainer.* You will leave, right now."

Garrett, absently squeezing the ball in his left hand, broke in. "Leave him alone, Ms. Drac. He's okay."

"Thank you. I do not need you, Garrett, to tell me how to run my ward. Or my patients. You will quiet your mouth and this—*person*—will go home."

Garrett's fist clenched and remained that way. "He'll leave when I get damn good and ready to let him leave. Now bug off."

She walked up to his bed, patting her braids. "Is that correct, Sergeant? And if I put him out, what is a patient with one arm and no eyes going to do about—" His left hand shot out and gripped her throat in a powerful fist, cutting her off in mid-word. He sat up in one smooth move, his thumb positioned accurately on her larynx, and obviously applying much too much pressure. She was wheezing loudly and her eyes were wild with fear. Waylan got to his feet slowly, putting down the guitar with exaggerated care.

"Now, take it easy, Joe. You don't wanna do something stupid, here, man," he soothed, as Ulrika, her face a dirty shade of blue, began clawing desperately at Garrett's hand. It might have been made of iron. "Let me take care of it."

Garrett ignored him. "Try to remember something, you vicious, know-it-all bitch," he ground out between his teeth, pulling Ulrika's face close to his own. "Even a man with one arm and no eyes *still has another arm.*" He gave her a last savage shake and shoved her halfway across the room, then picked up the hard rubber ball and began squeezing it rhythmically again, as if nothing had happened. His forearm muscles, Waylan noted, rippled like thick snakes.

"Listen, I got to go pretty soon anyway," Waylan said mildly, but Garrett shook his head.

"How about another tune first?" he suggested, ignoring Ulrika as she fled the room with the few shreds of dignity she could salvage.

"You got it, champ." Waylan Stubbs sat down on the end of Garrett's bed and, taking up his guitar, played a continuous medley that lasted over an hour.

When he left at last, Ulrika Drac was nowhere to be seen.

It was after closing hours, and the City Museum was closed and dark. The lone guard, Heber, sat at his desk eating banana chips, deeply engrossed in an old Kraun adventure novel called *Seven Ways to Die*. Heber liked his job as museum guard, but he had no illusions about it. The term 'guard' was one of title alone, for there had never been a break-in, and there would probably never be one. But Heber or one of the other guards was always there, just the same, because the Regs book insisted upon it.

Heber didn't mind. It was a soft situation, easy money. He usually spent his lazy nights reading and snacking, getting up only to relieve himself and to make the customary two rounds of the place. He was careful about that part. Took his time, made sure everything was all right. No candy wrappers or fruit cores lying around. Nothing missing. You never could tell when kids or primitives would make a little mischief, mess up a display. Like the time the high school kids had stolen the Dowager Empress's coronation gown and dressed Maisie, the feeble old gorilla, in it, down at the zoo. There had been hell to pay for that, he remembered. The kids had been publicly chastised, and the guard involved had been docked a month's pay.

But that was right and proper, he thought. After all, like the rule book said, valuable artifacts from several worlds were stored on the premises, not only for the enjoyment of the inhabitants of *Hope*, but for the edification of the many planetside visitors as well, and should be protected. Besides, the book continued, people were accustomed to seeing armed guards in a museum. There was the psychological factor to consider. His presence there was a subliminal comfort, a signal that all was well.

So here he sat, night after night, like a long-unused shore cannon, providing security to an empty building by the mere fact of his presence.

He turned another page of *Seven Ways to Die*. The action was beginning to heat up, and he bent forward over the book, stuffing chips into his mouth and munching furiously, really getting into it. The hero, Bwill Moffatt, had made his way into the cruel warlord's palace, darting past doorways and skulking through a mirrored plastex maze, when unexpectedly a cross-bow quarrel missed him by scant millimeters, striking the maze wall beside him instead, and shattering it with a muffled crash.

Heber sat bolt upright, suddenly alert. There had been another, real crash of plastex breaking—hadn't there?—right here in the Museum. He looked back at the book and up again, momentarily fuddled, but then, from one of the rooms down the corridor, there was a soft, uneven footfall, a brush as if someone were carefully feeling for a way through the darkness—

Heber was galvanized into action. He hit the alarm button, alerting ship's security, jumped to his feet, and started snapping on lights.

"Halt!" he shouted, his heart thumping. "Who goes there?"

There was the sound, several rooms away, of uneven, hurrying footsteps, and the metallic rasp of a door refusing to open. He raced for the source of the sound. The Egg Displays. No one there. The Costume Room. No one. The Bone Room, with skeletons of over a hundred galactic species.

Yes!

The cloaked intruder, there at the far wall, was struggling with the push bar on a manual portal, and Heber rushed over and grabbed the abnormally high, hunched shoulder, whirled the figure around—and shrank back, crying out involuntarily.

The face that turned to him in such close quarters was a huge, monstrous four-horned caricature, a hideous grimace in wild coruscations of color, a frightening specter out of his worst nightmares. In that paralyzing instant, the intruder struck Heber off his feet with a hand that felt like iron, and resumed struggling with the heavy bar. Heber, belatedly remembering his holstered weapon, snatched it free in a burst of courage and aimed it shakily from where he knelt on the floor.

"Halt!" he shouted again, his voice breaking into the upper register. "Stop where you are!" He fired once, missing by several meters, but by then the monster had pushed through the portal into the multicolored glare of night lights from the busy street outside, before which the awful apparition became only a silhouette that disappeared instantly into the crowd.

It was late that night when Waylan Stubbs let himself, his girl and his package quietly into the stateroom he shared with Sid Behrman. He was surprised to find the lights on, and Sid and the juggler, Mancini, waiting up for him. Mancini was drinking a beer, and Sid looked worried.

"Hey, what's goin' on?" Waylon greeted them, glancing at his ticket. "How come y'all're up? This late, I thought everybody'd be sawin' logs."

"Where have you been, Waylan?" Sid asked. "We looked everywhere for you. No one knew where you were." Mancini drained the beer can and dropped it in the waste receptacle across the room, pointedly not looking at him. Waylan smiled and shrugged.

"Oh— I don't know. Out. You know. Lookin' at the Christmas lights, huh, babe? Did some visitin'. Some shoppin' for the folks back home." He hoisted the bulky, oversized plastex bag, and smiled his fallen-angel smile. "Just shoppin', that's all."

Mancini jerked a thumb at Stubbs's companion, one of the new girls from the chorus, he thought. "So who's the lady, Waylan?"

Stubbs circled her satin waist possessively with his free arm. "This here is Miss Lilyjean McClure, all the way from Kansas, USA, Earth. I thought, if you wouldn't mind, Sid, we'd sit around for a while tonight and, uh, talk about country life, and all." He smiled innocently again, and Sid got the picture.

"Okay, okay. You can have the room. I'll find somewhere else to bunk. Meantime, try to get some sleep," he advised, looking uncomfortable. "We'll talk tomorrow morning."

●   ●   ●

It was afternoon when they rode into the city. After a hot, dry, interminable day on the desert, the sight of its lush green palms and citrus trees stirring above its stone walls was, Voldi thought, like a welcome splash of clear cold water.

"There it is!" he exulted, his arm around Esme tightening a trifle. "Fatima, City of the Caliph. Named for the daughter of the Prophet. As the poet has wisely written, 'Each of its bricks is as valuable as treasure, its jasmine gardens dawning in the heart of the night.'"

Esme had been riding all night, too, and listening to poetry made her feel like spitting up. Her throat was dry, and her head hurt and her rump was sore. Every jarring gallop brought her more closely to what was at least an awkward situation, if not a downright dangerous one, and her determination grew stronger by the minute that, come what may, she would have nothing to do with this alien Prince.

They rode past the sentinels into the walled city, shady and cooler under the towering date palms. There was the sharp, sweet smell of orange blossoms, and fountains splashed behind grilled courtyard gates. Vendors carrying baskets of ripe melons staggered by on their way to market, and a man passed them balancing a tall pole strung with dozens of round breads baked with holes in their middles. The heady smells of jasmine and fried confections assaulted their nostrils, and Esme's stomach writhed hungrily. She'd had nothing to eat since noon yesterday, and suddenly the city, the palms, and even Voldi's face began to swim before her eyes. She tried to speak, but slumped forward into a deep faint.

She did not know when they drew up at the palace gates, nor was she aware that Voldi picked her up bodily and, striding down the polished corridors, closely followed by Sethi and Kedar, kicked open the door to his old friend's quarters and deposited Esme unceremoniously onto his couch.

"Here she is, Your Highness," Voldi announced. "Esme Cuf, the most beautiful woman we could find on the continent; young, healthy, intelligent, and she's an R.N., so you two have something to talk about together."

"No talk," Kedar admonished under his breath. "We don't want talk. They have plenty of time for talk later; now let them think of love, of moonlight, of marriage. As Abu Nuwas's poem says,

> 'How can you but enjoy yourself,
> When the world is in blossom,
> And wine is at hand?' "

The Prince raised his head from the large volume he was perusing and peered over his glasses at Esme. Voldi looked, too, and swallowed hard. She lay there, disheveled and just now coming awake, looking vulnerable and beautiful and— He looked away.

"Let's get out of here, Sethi," he muttered, but his friend made an absent, overhand gesture, watching the Prince.

"In a minute. I want to see the Bookworm's reaction."

Prince Salman rose with some interest and adjusted his eyesglasses, staring at Esme with an expression of eager curiosity. Kedar gripped Voldi's arm

"He's going over to the couch," he whispered excitedly. "He's seen her! He's *noticed* her!" Salman knelt down beside the couch and patted Esme's hand. She opened her eyes and sat up abruptly, pushing her dark curls off her face and pulling her shirt together at the throat.

"You are Esme Cuf, R.N.?" he asked huskily, and she nodded cautiously. A broad smile wreathed his face, making it almost attractive. He edged closer. "You don't—I mean, you wouldn't, ah—" He passed a hand across his brow, then blurted:

"You wouldn't happen to have a copy of *Gray's Anatomy*, would you?"

Kedar slapped the heel of his hand against his forehead, and Scthi turned away with a groan, but Voldi said nothing, for in his heart of hearts, he was glad. Against his better judgment, and certainly against his will, he realized that he had fallen hopelessly in love with Esme Cuf.

"Sorry," she said. "I'm fresh out. Is there somewhere around here I can get a quick shower?" The Prince helped her to her feet, escorted her to an inner door and ordered Dawan, the eunuch in charge, to see that Esme got a bath and a change of clothing; then he regarded the other men mildly as he sat again.

"Thanks for the present. She seems like a nice girl. Too bad about the *Gray's*."

"This is unforgivable behavior, Your Highness, this preoccupation with books!" Kedar protested. "You are ruining our collective reputation!"

"He's right, sir," Sethi agreed. "We have an image to uphold. We're known all over this sector as dangerous, daring, romantic buccaneers of the desert, sweeping down the dunes and carrying off—"

"Carrying *on* is more like it," the Prince mumbled into his book. "Pull that lamp closer, will you, Sethi, there's a good fellow. I want you all to hear this concept from Aristotle." Sethi adjusted the light obediently as Salman read aloud, " 'For friendship asks a man to do what he can, not what is proportional to the merits of the case; since that cannot always be done, e.g., in honours paid to the gods or to parents; for no one could ever return to them the equivalent of what he gets, but the man who serves them to the utmost of his power is thought to be a good man.' "

Kedar snatched off his kaffiyeh, threw it down and stamped on it. "Outrageous!" he shouted, and the Prince, without looking up, held up one didactic forefinger.

"Not actually *outrageous*," he corrected, in a preoccupied tone, "but fascinating, nonetheless. Don't you agree? Kedar? Voldi?" He looked up and, finding no one there, sighed and returned to his books.

Esme stood at the latticed window of the harem, looking out into the twilight garden. A nightingale was singing to the moon, and delightful scents wafted on the cool air. She had spent hours in the bath, with the servant-girls vying with each other to wash her hair and marveling at her green skin. The voluminous clothes they brought her were smooth and silky, with plenty of places to hide her Life-Glow and compak. They hurried, giggling, to bring her trays of *gaz* and countless little cups of sweet tea, coffee, and tea once again. After a while, she was served an entire meal of pilaf, shish kebab, olives and melon, and she fell to with a healthy appetite.

Now, fed, bathed, rested and perfumed, she paced restlessly before the window, wondering idly where Voldi was, and how she could convince him to take her back to the hospital.

She had no idea that someone was watching her in turn.

The Grand Vizier, sitting on his cool rooftop across the way, sipped at his water pipe as he regarded the girl with a speculative eye.

"Are you quite sure that she is intended for Prince Salman?" he asked Dawan, who was standing beside him.

"Certain, Excellency," he answered. "I was present when Voldi, Kedar and Sethi brought her to him this afternoon."

"And—"

"And he asked her for a book." The eunuch smiled.

"A woman like that one," the Vizier mused contemptuously, "and all he wants is a *book!* Yet, this is good for us. It is important that he make no marriage except to my daughter, Bibi Ramlah. Then the throne is mine." He puffed at the pipe and narrowed his eyes as Esme stretched luxuriously behind the lattices. After a pause, he continued:

"The Caliph grows worse by the moment. I think one more week should kill him. So far, I've been able to convince the court that he is under stress because of Salman's unwillingness to marry and assume the throne; but you can see, Dawan, why Salman must not marry this female." He blew smoke rings. "Little chance of that, of course. The fool wishes to waste his life studying *medicine*."

"She is very different from our women, Excellency," Dawan pursued. "What if her beauty changes his mind?" The Vizier, watching Esme curl up gracefully on the window seat, smoked moodily for a while before removing the tube from his mouth.

"That is a possibility we cannot entertain. Much as it pains me," he sighed, "I think we had better kill her now, just in case." The eunuch bowed low, pulling out a long wavy *kris* from his wide sash.

"My thoughts exactly, Excellency," he murmured, and was gone without a sound.

She had made a place for herself in her few short weeks on *Hope*, Audrey thought, lugging her art supplies down the corridor to Pediatrics. Charles was going to be here for a while and, as Lorraine had pointed out, it was only reasonable that she make good use of her time. Everyone on *Hope* worked, except for the mothers of young children, who had their hands full enough. And, thanks to the Grans, a volunteer association of older people who played with the ship's youngsters and took them on field trips to parks, zoos, and the Arcade, even the busiest mothers had two afternoons a week to themselves.

Audrey, who was a gifted artist, found herself much in demand in Pediatrics, where ailing youngsters could often express their fears and concerns more easily in pictures than in words. She enjoyed the work, and was getting to know some of the patients rather well.

One was an adolescent Droso who had taken a fancy to her. Whenever she came into the ward, it would snuggle close and stroke her face with its manipulators, humming in its own language. Watch out for it, everyone had said. Be on your guard. But Audrey could only see, behind the multifaceted red eyes and deadly proboscis, a lonely child that needed attention.

"Be careful, Mrs. Lassiter," Bassett, one of the senior nurses, warned, as it came running up as usual, cocking its right foreleg to its face every several steps. "Poor tyke, it's badly retarded. You can never tell what it'll do."

"Oh, I think I'll be all right," Audrey protested gently, giving the Droso a close, warm hug. "It just likes the attention."

"I don't know. A couple of weeks ago, it was petting its Gran's face, the way it's petting yours right now, and two minutes later it had sunk that sharp little proboscis right into his jugular and drunk a liter and a half of nice fresh AB positive." Audrey laid a hand at her throat.

"Oh, my. Whatever did you do?"

The nurse grinned. "First we gave the Gran a fast transfusion and then we gave sweetie here an hour in Time Out, with no tri-D for two days. It hates that, don't you, hotshot?" It nodded vigorously and she scratched its coarse, hairy cranium between the bulging eyes. "You've behaved yourself pretty well since then, though, haven't you, sweetie?"

"Yesss," fluttered the Droso's wings. "Aaaiii goood, naaaooo. Drrrnnnknnnggg ooohnnnlllll *appp*le juuuzzz." It lurched off suddenly to join the other children, constantly bringing up its right foreleg in an abrupt ataxic jerk.

"What happened to it?" Audrey wondered. "Why is it like that?" The older woman lifted her brows and lowered her voice.

"Birth defect. The parent was hooked on black-market insecticide. She was inhaling it for weeks before she laid her egg-raft. MedLog says she was high as a kite even when she laid, so, of course, this poor kid and its sibs were all messed up. The parent ingested most of the eggs—to get rid of the evidence—before the authorities rescued them, and we brought the survivors up here, but"—she shook her head—"this is the only one that survived." She folded her arms on the desk in righteous indignation, her lips tight.

"Can you imagine? The selfish beast sold out her own children *for a chemical high*! And they want us to believe they're a civilized race!"

Audrey's face was a study in compassion. "The poor little tyke," she sympathized. "What's its name?"

"We don't know." Bassett pulled some files and began thumbing through them. "It can't communicate very well, and the parent, of course, didn't bother to name it. And since they only have gender during mating and laying season, we just call it 'sweetie' or 'honey,' or 'Suzie' or 'Johnny,' or whatever. It doesn't seem to mind what you call it."

"But it ought to have a name of its own," Audrey persisted, and Bassett, having found the file she was looking for, looked up pleasantly.

"Go for it," she invited. "It would help to have something to call it besides Droso Adolescent." Audrey watched the Droso as it staggered clumsily across the floor on its six starkly striped black-and-white legs, its foreleg popping up intermittently, and a synapse closed inside her head.

"Semaphore," she decided. "We'll call it Semaphore. Semmy, for short."

"Semmy," Bassett said to its file, writing it in. "That's cute."

"Yes." Audrey smiled to herself. "It is, isn't it?"

Semaphore.

Last week, she and Dao Marik had spent an evening Christmas shopping. Audrey wanted to send gifts home for her uncle's family, and Marik was looking for something special for his daughter, Misi, who was all of two years old. Audrey bought the ideal gifts for everyone on her list, and Marik found a fuzzy baby barong, crafted by the Gund toy people, and bought it on the spot. Swathed in tissue and appropriately boxed, it rode in one of the many bags and bundles he balanced on his arm.

"Oh! Dao—look!" Audrey tugged him to a stop among a crowd of youngsters in front of a shop, and he paused obligingly, very conscious of her hand warm on his arm, his name warm on her lips.

The shop window was a miniature Erthlik village. There were houses and a steepled church, lit from within, dozens of stiff little trees, and a twin metal track running around and down and through the cottony hills, over a tiny wooden bridge and past a red station house that read 'Albertville.' On the track was a clumsy machine that puffed smoke out of a funnel at the top and drew a whole train of cars behind it along the track. Every time it approached the roadway crossing, a black-and-white-striped wooden arm on a pole beside the road shot up stiffly and remained at attention until the train passed by. Marik was mystified. Audrey was enchanted.

"Oh, don't you love the little semaphores!" she exclaimed.

"I'm very fond of semaphores," he offered gravely, "whatever they might be."

"The little black-and-white things," she explained, pointing through the shop window. "They pop up and let people know that a train is coming." He leaned close.

"People can see those little—*semaphores*, is it?" She nodded. "But they can't see and hear the train itself?" He suppressed a smile. "That's remarkable. Rather like having a small alarm ring to tell you a bomb's just gone off." She laughed and squeezed his arm as they walked on.

"I'm sorry. You get to thinking everyone in the galaxy knows about railroad trains and—and depots—"

"And semaphores," Marik assisted, wryly. "Don't forget the semaphores."

She would not, she knew, standing there in Peds days later, ever forget the semaphores. She tugged herself back to the present, and the children.

Another of her favorites was Semmy's friend, Liat Jevic, the Einai child stricken with Ensi-vo. Though wan and weak, she had the face of an angel, with large golden eyes, pale jade skin and a wealth of thick black hair. She had to be handled like a china doll, for her illness had progressed to the point where any random bruise might spell her death, but her fingers were nimble with pen and brush, and her renderings were delicate and precise.

She had finished yet another painting when Audrey came in this morning.

"See, Owdri?" she exulted shyly, offering the paper to Audrey as she sat beside her bed. "See? Aun." Audrey slipped an arm around the pitifully thin shoulders and took the picture.

It was a watercolor of the Einai fern forest, with a big papery aun hive half hidden in a tangle of blooming coreliae vines. The top of the hive was shaped like a lens, and from openings in its sides flew swarms of brilliant green insects, speckled with purple and gold splotches. Their wings were indicated simply as blurs, and along with the lush green foliage, the riot of golden flowers and the hot blue sky itself, the picture made the viewer feel he was standing in the wet, oppressive stillness of Eisernon's torrid noon.

"Why, Liat! It's beautiful!"

Liat nodded solemnly. "I know. We have lots of beautiful places at home."

"I mean your drawing, honey," Audrey explained, "and

besides, before you know it, you'll be able to go home and see it again for yourself." Liat met her eyes and slowly shook her head in the negative.

"I've got Ensi-vo, Owdri," she explained patiently. "I'm never going home again." Before Audrey could answer, Gäth, a Sauvagi boy wearing an Alizirov device on one shaven leg, came running with a skippity-hop, flung himself boisterously against her and shouted:

"Hi! Audri! When're we gonna draw some war stuff, huh? Skimmers and pulser cannons and stuff!" He made both hands into needlers and fired at Liat point-blank. "Ssst! Ssst! You're dead, Liat! You're good as dead!" Liat turned that level golden gaze on him and nodded again.

"I know," she whispered. "I know."

Basset came up briskly and began straightening Liat's bed. "My gracious, Liat, we've got to get you ready. Did you tell Mrs. Lassiter what's happening this afternoon?" The child gave her head a faint negative shake, and Bassett explained, "We're having our big Christmas party this afternoon. Games and races and lots of goodies and presents. Look, here come all the Grans now." She wheeled Liat, bed and all, into the play area.

A crowd of older people carrying Christmas presents came into Peds, each seeking out his or her particular child. Following behind them was Dao Marik, and Audrey felt her heart stop as he started her way.

"Hello, Owdri."

"Hello yourself. What are you doing here?"

"I came to help judge the games, as well as to look in on one of the patients. Liat Jevic." He sat beside her in one of the folding chairs lined up against the playroom wall. "Sharobi thinks she needs some special attention."

"So do I. Other than her drawing, she just sits here waiting to die. She needs some kind of a diversion."

"Such as—?" Audrey caught her lower lip between her teeth.

"Her drawings are always pictures of fern forests, and aun—and jat herds hidden in the copses. I think she's terribly homesick." She faced him quickly at such close range, he could see the idea dawning in her eyes. "What about a visit to the Einai level? Mightn't she feel reassured?"

"She might indeed," he agreed. "Unfortunately, she's too weak to be moved." He checked his ticket and got to his feet. "I have to speak to her parents, right about now, but I'll look in on her afterward. See what we can do. Thanks, Owdri." He started away but retraced his steps. "By the way . . . I have a few more gifts to buy for Misi, as well as some for my steward and his family. Could you come along—please—and help me choose something appropriate?"

"When?"

"This evening?" She considered that, then nodded, and he continued, "I'll meet you under the clock at Holmes'. About 1730?"

"Seventeen-thirty it is." He took her smile with him when he left, for he did not look forward to his meeting with the Jevics.

Liat's parents came into the office cubby, diffident but determined. Marik, seated behind the desk, took quick stock of them. Good folk, hard-working middle-class people, the neri-osh of the earth, so to speak.

"Chom-ala, Chom-shan Jevic, Chom-ben Jevic," Marik began in Eisernai, "Zo-ili Priyam Hanshilobahr *Dom* Dao Marik. Mekka som-iki—"

"If you please, Priyam Marik," Noln Jevic interrupted, "we would rather converse in Ertheng. Wouldn't we, Ferri?"

"Please. You wanted to talk to us about Liat, Priyam? Has there been a change? Something is wrong?" Marik shook his head.

"No, no change. Nothing new is wrong. Just the slow decline that's so typical of the disease. So far we've been able to keep her relatively pain-free, but you understand, it will become progressively worse until it goes beyond our control." Ferri Jevic's eyes were wet and green-rimmed, and she pressed three fingers to her lips to keep them from trembling.

"They told us," she said softly.

"There is a cure," Marik offered. "A total and complete cure, that would give your daughter back to you in perfect health."

Jevic's jaw was tight. "You're talking about the Droso Solution," he said shortly. "Forget it. There's no way one of those cursed bugs is getting anywhere near my baby. If there's no other way, if Tadae wants Liat that badly, then she—" his voice broke and he cleared his throat quickly to cover it, "she'll just have to die, that's all." His voice broke again. "Others have died before her." Both parents were clearly grieving, and Marik tapped his thumbs against his lips for a long moment, eyes narrowed, thinking fast.

The Droso Solution was the problem. The Earthling and Einai settlers of the pioneer planet Zerev had first discovered the Droso, an indigenous, insectile life form, and promptly ignored them. They concentrated instead on rounding up *kundu* by the thousands and shipping them off for beef and fur. In the rush of settling in, rounding up, hewing down and building, no one gave the Droso much thought, until all at once, along the forest's edge and in the harvest fields, people began turning up dead. Drained. Bloodless.

Investigators quickly determined that the Droso, which were harmless nectar-drinkers during most of the year, required sizable quantities of mammalian blood during their fall mating season. They had always depended upon the *kundu* for blood. Without it, they could not produce viable young. Their race would become extinct. But the *kundu* had been decimated. There was only one blood-source remaining—the settlers themselves—and the Droso had tapped into it with a vengeance.

When the realization dawned, the settlers panicked. Reasonable suggestions of using cattle to fill the Droso's blood demand fell on deaf ears. Mobs, led by relatives of the slain, burned down Droso living-canopies and slashed their delicate egg-rafts to bits, along with the fetuses inside. The Droso retaliated in kind, leaving drained human husks all over the settlements.

The situation had escalated to concerted genocide on both sides until one woman, a pariah among her neighbors and family, made contact with the Droso; taught them human speech; negotiated an uneasy peace. Quite by accident, she also discovered that human blood, ingested and regurgitated by a Droso, was returned to its owner purged of all viral and bacterial agents. No matter how sick you were before the Droso ingested your blood supply, you would be cured when it was returned you. The tricky part was convincing the Droso to return it.

Scientists, ignoring the discoverer, pounced enthusiastically upon her discovery. Someone even got a Nobel prize for medicine on the strength of it. Leukemia, AIDS, Scup, Ensi-vo and a host of other illnesses were quickly eradicated from the planet by means of the Droso Solution, and the blessing of the Solution had been spreading slowly from Zerev to the near galaxy ever since.

But even yet, there were always those who hesitated, who feared; those who had lost a loved one to the Droso, and continued to hate. Marik wondered which category Noln Jevic fell into.

"Can we do this, then?" he offered, after a moment. "We can't create a new blood supply for Liat, for the Ensi-vo's already attacked the DNA in the strategic cells we'd need; but a very old-fashioned protocol, a special blood transfusion of packed red cells, can buy her another month or so. Will you let us at least give Liat some new blood cells, to help extend her life until we can find some compromise between your wishes and her survival?"

"How long has she got without it?" Jevic demanded hoarsely, and Marik's eyes were compassionate as he answered:

"A few more days, maybe. A week at the most." Ferri moaned softly and buried her head against her husband's shoulder, and Jevic passed a quick hand across his eyes. Looked away. Nodded shortly.

"All right. All right, you can give her the transfusion—but I don't want to hear any more about the Droso. Ever again! And that's final!"

The couple had hardly signed the consents and left the room before Marik rang the Medicomp.

Medicomp by, it responded.

"Marik, Dao." There was a quick skitter of voiceprint match.

Go ahead, Priyam Marik, the Medicomp replied metallically.

"I'd like a full report on an Einai family named Jevic," he requested. "Parents Noln and Ferri, patient's name is Liat. Special attention to anything having to do with the Droso, or with visits to Zerev. Have it sent to my quarters, please."

Understood. Medicomp out.

Marik sat tapping his fingers on the desk. There was more here than met the eye. What possible reason could these decent and loving parents have for allowing their only child to die rather than subject her to the Droso Solution? *Find that answer, Dao my lad*, he told himself, *and you can save Liat's life*. He only hoped he could find it in time.

Meantime, she had to begin eating, smiling, trying to stay alive. Owdri was right. What Liat needed, as much as she needed the transfusion, was a change of venue. An outing. A picnic.

The party was in full swing as he stepped out of the office. Loops of red and green crepe paper all but obscured the overhead, and a pile of presents waited invitingly under the Christmas tree. People from Dietetics were laying out a staggering spread of edibles from several worlds, and the children were noisily playing games under the watchful eyes of Grans and staff alike. Just now, they were in the middle of a footrace, and one of the Grans, standing beside Audrey on the sidelines, was cheering as if his child were running an Olympic marathon.

It would be a close race, Audrey thought. Semmy and Gäth were running, along with a badly burned Earthling child on crutches, two more wearing Alizirov devices, and several—including Semmy—with cerebral palsy. Each Gran was cheering his or her child on, and the noise level was deafening. Semmy stumbled, recovered and took the lead. His Gran was fairly frothing with excitement.

"That's the ticket, Semmy!" the old man enthused. "Make them hunt their holes! Let 'em know there's a God in Israel!"

He pounded his mottled, palsied fist against the air, as Semaphore made the peculiar buzzing sound in its thorax that was the Droso equivalent of laughter, crossed the finish line first, and promptly fell on its face.

"Wwonn!" it hummed loudly, spinning furiously on the floor. "Wwonn!"

The Gran hobbled over, hauled the Droso to its feet and hugged it fervently; then, remembering himself, dusted it and himself off and stood very straight.

"You did a fine job, Semmy, a fine job," he said soberly, laying an impressive hand on its prickly cranium. "I'm proud of you, son." Semmy enclosed him in its manipulators, stroking his face, but the old man worked his way free.

"Here! Here, now, enough of that. Quite enough. Go get yourself some juice, now, run along."

"Juuzz! Thnnkzz, Mmajrr!" Semmy hummed, its foreleg jerking up to its face excitedly, and it lurched away at top speed toward the refreshment table.

The Gran came back and sat down next to Audrey. They exchanged smiles and she extended her hand. "I don't believe we've met. I'm Audrey Lassiter." The old man got to his feet and took her hand with a courtly bow.

"Calvin Rutherford Hayes, Major, GFArmy, retired, ma'am. Pleased to make your acquaintance." He sat gratefully again. "I guess I got a mite overexcited. Did you see my boy win, out there just now?"

"I surely did, and I was so glad. Semmy and I are great friends." Semaphore staggered up with a cup of hot tea for its Gran, sloshing it all over his manipulators.

"Dddammm," it hummed, and Calvin took the plastex cup.

"Thank you, son. And Semmy: remember to don't swear in front of the womenfolk from now on, all right?" It bobbed its knees and the foreleg jerked up again.

"Zzzorrriii, Mmmajrrr." It was off again to speak to Liat, and Calvin watched it go with gentle eyes.

"I've been his Gran since he was a day old, falling all over the nursery floor," he said reminiscently. "I picked him out right away. We had a choice, you know. They offered me three youngsters to pick from: Semmy, here, a blind Seddaji girl, and an Earthling kid born with half an arm, who was in ReGen."

"What made you choose Semmy?" she asked, and the old man sipped noisily at his steaming tea and patted his mouth with a crumpled handkerchief.

"Well, I'll tell you, ma'am. First, he was so poor, he didn't even have a name—and he never did, till today! I just always called him 'son.' Then again, the others didn't need me like he did. He was a real mess when we started out, his CP and all. They've done wonders for him, and they tell me he'll be perfectly normal, given a little more time.

"But what decided me most was the boy's spirit. Did you ever really watch him?" he demanded, his eyes growing suspiciously moist. "He never gives up! And he never gets discouraged! And he cares about everyone else!" He turned to Audrey, scowling comically. "Besides, he calls me 'Major!' Only one who does, anymore." He paused, obviously deeply moved.

"And there's one more thing, young woman. It may sound foolish to you, but"—he wagged his head admiringly, wiped the handkerchief across his nose and jumping chin, took a deep breath and braced up—"that little devil snaps the smartest salute I've seen in many a year!"

CHAPTER

VII

IT WAS GETTING dark and the City was covered with heavy, wet snow. It limned each bare branch in the park across the way and drifted whitely in the gutters. Evergreen garlands, spangled with lights and fastened with fat red bows, were looped between lampposts, and bustling trams, packed with passengers and festooned with silver tinsel, splashed through the crowded streets. Christmas carols floated clearly on the cold air, which smelled of fresh coffee, spices, and pine.

Bundled up appropriately for the weather, Marik stood expectantly under the old-fashioned holly-draped clock at Holmes', where he and Audrey Lassiter had agreed to meet. He was excited at the prospect of spending another evening with Audrey, even though they had solemnly agreed to be merely friends from now until forever! Viewed in the light of Audrey's friendship, he mused, forever was a happy prospect.

People in heavy coats and mufflers hurried in and out of shops along the way, and strangers of all species exchanged holiday greetings as they jostled past each other on the crowded sidewalks. Little children with bright eyes and shiny cheeks tugged package-laden parents this way and that, and a group of fresh-faced teens poured noisily into the Arcade down the way, wearing identical copies of the latest fad footgear. A patently phony Santa stood by a plastex kettle ringing his hand bell, collecting money for the poor, which would be translated into the appropriate currency and donated to the planets currently receiving *Hope*'s assistance; while on a farther corner, a small group of uniformed Salvation Army people played heartfelt carols and collected for the same cause.

A gust of chill wind smote the back of Marik's neck, and he hunched his shoulders and tugged his muffler close. The snow was coming down in earnest now. Environmental Control had predicted three inches overnight, and evidently meant to keep its promise. Dusk was falling quickly, brightening the reflections of colored lights swimming in the street. A passing tram splashed the shimmering picture into fragments, which regrouped wetly for the next assault. Across the park, the bells of both Our Lady Help of the Sick and St. Luke's-on-the-Green rang out for evening prayer. Eighteen hundred, then, Marik thought. A quick check of his ticket confirmed the time. Audrey was half an hour late. Probably the crowd, he thought. She'd be here any minute.

An antique horse-drawn carriage, its cloaked driver and blanketed horse busily munching their various suppers, stood by the entrance to the park, where through the trees he could glimpse ice-skaters on the lamplit pond.

It looked and sounded for all the world, Marik mused, like any busy Erthlik city at the height of its holiday season. It was hard to imagine that everything—the park, the luxury apartments, the shopping mall—was a carefully constructed artificial environment, a live-in theatrical setting enclosed by an immense duralloy hull, and that outside the illusion of normalcy was the cold black vacuum of space.

The Erthlikli were fortunate to be provided such a perfect environmental replica, he reflected. Nor were the Erthlikli the only race aboard to be so privileged. There were eight more residential levels, each designed and landscaped to give its occupant race the truest flavor of its homeworld.

Botanists could trek among Minsoner's cool, misty rain forest, and photo-hunters might shoot Kraun fauna in their natural habitat. Snorkelers explored the small Xhole 'sea,' enjoying balmy turquoise water, coral grottoes (cleverly designed to function as anti-slosh baffles during acceleration and deceleration), and idyllic tropical weather.

The infrequent visitor to the new Droso level found himself

using a back-strapped flitter to hover like the Droso among the silk webs and flowery canopies high above the forest floor.

It was a galaxy in a bottle, Marik thought. Life in a gilded cage. Existence in a goldfish bowl. *Well*, he told himself, stepping back to avoid a harried Einai matron with an armload of packages, *at least it's clean and safe. We have that.* Hope *is probably the safest place in the galaxy.*

He checked his ticket yet again. A quarter past. Audrey really *was* late. Where could she be?

At last he caught sight of her coming toward him in the crowd, bright as a finik in her red coat and fur muff. He lifted a hand in greeting, willing his hearts to steady, and Audrey waved gaily back at him. She tucked her hand through his arm companionably as they made their way along the sidewalk through the milling throng.

"I'm so sorry," she apologized. "I was visiting Charles and I lost track of the time."

"Quite so," he approved. "How is he coming along?"

"Oh—fine." She seemed reluctant to discuss Charles, so he steered the conversation to a safer tack.

"Where do you suppose all these people come from?" he wondered aloud, sidestepping an imposing group of oncoming Kraun.

"Isn't it wonderful? Barbara told me the hotel is brimful. Seems people from other levels all want to share the Christmas celebration, so they get their permits early and make it a real vacation."

It seemed reasonable. In a restrictive environment—and no matter how large the ship, it must at some time become a restrictive environment—people needed somewhere to go to 'get away.' The difference in levels, climates and festivities (not to mention the occasional planetfall) provided a never-ending change that tended to keep *Hope*'s people not only happy, but mentally healthy as well.

A Sauvagi woman in blue earmuffs, accompanied by three small ear-muffed children, squeezed past them and into a crowded toy store, murmuring apologies in her own language. Marik answered in kind and earned himself a smile. Audrey hugged his arm so close he could feel her warm contours, and he covered her gloved hand proprietorially with his own. From a rooftop, a cold gust of wind blew a glittering veil of snow between them and the street lamp, and they caught the scent of expensive perfume and Chinese food in the crystal air. Bits of snow spangled Audrey's hair, and her eyes were shining. It was, Marik felt, a perfectly beautiful night.

"You are comfortable, Charles Lassiter?" Ulrika asked, smoothing the warm oil languorously into the fair, freckled back under her hands. "You like the nursing care I give you, do you not?"

"Yes, ma'am, I do," he assented. "You give back rubs like Mama used to make." Her hands froze in place.

"Your mama used to—?"

"It's a joke, Miss Drac," he explained. "It means you do real well."

"Ah." She resumed the treatment. "These attentions . . . they make me feel I am helping you. That I am somehow so close to you. Your . . . very good friend."

"I feel the same way. Could you please get up by my neck? It's real stiff in there." Her hands slid obligingly to his neck, kneading the knots out of the taut muscles.

"I share with you, Charles Lassiter, something I do not share with other patients. Besides the special care . . . a secret!" She leaned close and whispered, "I told you I know everything—about everyone! I even know about the psych flag in your file." He became unnaturally still, his splinted hands lying loose on the table beside him.

"I've been flagged?" he repeated in a strange voice. "But who—?" *Anderson! It had to be Neal Anderson . . . or Marik!* "Who—who else knows about this?"

"It was red-coded. Only Paige knows. He was admitting physician. And me. No one else." She leaned close and murmured huskily into his ear. "And I will never tell, Charles Lassiter. You mean to me too much. You can trust to me, to keep your secret." He turned and sat up then, the light reflecting oddly in his pale blue eyes, and gave her the slow, puckery smile that always made her heart race.

"And you know you can always trust me, Ulrika." Incredibly, he reached out and took her in his arms, the splints stiff against her back, and kissed her until she was breathless. "Where can we get together, darling," he whispered against her cheek, "and discuss this like civilized people?"

She swallowed past a dry throat and stammered, "My—my quarters. My room. I am off at 2400. We can meet there. For as long as you like." He kissed her once again, for good measure.

"I'll be there. Twenty-four hundred. Wait for me."

"I will," she promised, already planning the candlelight, the wine, the negligee she would have to buy. "Oh, certainly I will."

His name was Te-o-kun-hko, the Runner, son of a Hopi father and a Sioux mother, and he was a Senn warrior-in-training. Not yet twenty, he had so distinguished himself, academically as well as in the Lore of the People, that he had been chosen to accompany Sachem Gallatin and the others on this last trade mission. His buddies had thought it exciting; had envied him and joshed him about his good luck, teased him for being the only Hopi selected.

If they could see him now, at the crack of dawn, Runner thought, standing a lone eight-hour guard in the frozen-commodities section of *Hope*'s cargo bay, perhaps they would think twice about his good luck. Who could have known that the negotiations would come up against a stone wall? Sharobi, for all his bluster, was usually reasonable. Gallatin had expected no problems, but then, perhaps he should have, Runner told himself, licking his long canines absently. We were, after all, dealing with aliens. Dealing with another species was always unpredictable.

He began to think about aliens, and inevitably, his thoughts ran to the kachinas, the gods who came up from under the earth to dance with the People during the rain dances. When he was a boy, he had thought that the kachinas were actually the gods themselves.

Now, he knew better. Now that he had been initiated into the kiva society, he realized a deeper, more impressive truth: that the masks worn by the kachinas, while they did not hide the faces of gods, but of men, made the mere men behind them godlike, so that they emptied themselves completely of self and for a while, became the god they represented. It was a spiritual performance, mystically elevated from the ordinary, and he revered it. It was part of the life of the People.

He was squatting on his heels, leaning comfortably against the bulkhead, when the strange kachina appeared. It was unlike any he had ever seen, yet what else could this hideous horned face represent but some affronted god? What else could it be, if not a kachina? It made no move, but simply stood there before him, waiting, and he rose in respect, astonished that it had heard his thoughts and come. He knew it could not be a god, and yet—

The kachina lifted a hand in greeting, and, instinctively, Runner answered in kind. It regarded the cartons solemnly, and after a moment of silence, pointed stiffly at one of them.

"Open this crate." The voice was scarcely above a hoarse whisper, and was that of neither a man nor a woman. Runner hesitated.

"I am ordered to guard the merchandise, kachina, and not to open it to anyone."

"I am not 'anyone.' You know who and what I am. I have been with the People always. I was there in the corn pollen; in the sand painting when you were born; in the cornmeal that blessed you on your naming day. I command you, open the crate."

Runner, mystified, hesitated between his orders and his heritage, but in the end, his heritage won out. He broke the seals on the self-refrigerated container the kachina had indicated and opened the enclosed plastex bag. Inside, in a perfect state of preservation, was a complete human arm, species H. Sapiens Eisernonica, male. The masked creature stared at it for a long moment.

"Remove it. Give it to me."

"But—"

"Give it to me. Now."

Runner put on his gloves and pried at the arm, but it was flash-frozen to the sidewall of the carton. "It will not come."

"Take off the gloves," the kachina croaked, "and use your nails. Dig them in deeply, and the arm will come. There is much medicine in what I am doing." *Much medicine?* Runner asked himself. *What does this masked thing think I am, some breechclout savage?* He dug in his nails angrily and jerked at the arm, but succeeded only in raking several raw furrows in the skin. He pulled away in disgust at the bloody skin under his nails, even as the kachina leaned forward to see the result.

"Ugh! I've got—"

But he never lived to say what he had got, for the masked creature hit him viciously behind the left ear, dropping him to the floor. Then it felt for the throat pulses and, satisfied that Runner was dead, rewrapped the frozen arm, resealed the carton, removed the mask and—PprumBurr, the Droso physician, was standing in the portal, watching with its great red faceted eyes. "You havv killd himm," it noted. "Aii know who you arr." The murderer turned toward it and in one hand held out a small object which the Droso recognized. Despite itself, its legs bent slightly, reflexively, in dismay.

"Do you know what this is?" the murderer asked. PprumBurr knew all too well. It was a small metal whistle of specific manufacture, outlawed in most of the known galaxy. When blown, it emitted a sound known as the fatal note. Because of the Droso's unique physiological makeup, that sound immediately rendered unconscious any one of their species who heard it; persistence of the fatal note became exactly that: fatal. "One word about this," the murderer continued, not waiting for an answer, "and every Droso on the ship dies, understand?"

"Aii nnderstnnd." PprumBurr's wings were a silver blur as it answered the deadly creature before it. *I could sting it to death before it blew the whistle on me*, it thought, *but I am a physician, dedicated to saving lives, not taking them*. It turned dejectedly and left.

The murderer, having made sure that everything was in order, placed the mask in a large shopping bag, stepped over

Runner's prone body and, leaving the cargo bay, crossed the crowded corridor. There, exchanging amiable smiles and holiday greetings with others who were waiting for the lift, the murderer pressed the lift button for Earthscape.

Charles Lassiter watched Ulrika set down his tardy lunch tray, her manner distant and cold.

"Good afternoon," he ventured, but she ignored him; snatched the cover off his meal; stabbed at his fish and held up a morsel to his mouth.

"Eat," she said. He pushed her hand away with his splinted one and met her eyes squarely.

"You seem to be mad at me, Ms. Drac, and I find that most peculiar, since *I'm* the one who waited outside *your locked door* for three hours last—"

"*You* waited? You did not even show out! I wasted my whole of the evening! I bought wine! Flowers, even, and you never came! *I* am who waited, Charles Lassiter, not you!"

"I was there. Where were you? And what were you up to?"

She tapped the edge of her flattened hand against her bottom lip. "Up to here! Fed up! Finished to believe an Erthlik again! Here, eat your meal, I have *important* things to be doing, after."

"I don't understand," Charles pursued. "You say *you* were there—and I know damn well *I* was there—so what happened?"

She shoved a forkful of pan-fried tilapia at him. "I do not care what happened. Eat!"

He took the bite and chewed thoughtfully. "I sat there for three hours outside Room 1108, West Park Place, and—"

"*East* Park Place," she corrected coldly.

"East!" He made an embarrassed face. "Woops! Right church, wrong pew." Her puzzled scowl prompted him to explain. "That means I went to the right room, but in the wrong building."

"You went to—"

"Yes, ma'am. I sat out there waiting for you in *West* Park, and you live in *East* Park. What an idiot I am!"

"No, no," she corrected him. "People often are making

mistakes." She looked relieved, and the tension in the room lessened perceptibly. "But you did try to come. You did not forget." She fed him the next bite much more gently. "I was in my room all evening, waiting," she insisted. "You are my witness of truth, I never left. I was there all night."

He smiled. "I'm sure you were. I wish I had been with you. Shall we try again?"

"Not tonight. I have . . . something important to do."

"As it happens," Charles said, "I'm busy tonight, too, so it works out. Shall we say 2300 tomorrow night?" She nodded and he added, "And now *that's* settled, can we do something about another serving of peaches for a poor ol' sick man?"

She bent over to kiss his forehead before she left. Smiling.

Security Chief Alan Wimet zipped the closure over Runner's stiffening features and signaled the medics away. "We won't know anything until after the autopsy," he told the concerned group of men around him. "Naturally, Priyam"—this to Sharobi—"this area is off-limits to any but Security personnel, until further notice." Behind him, his men were stringing warning tapes around the sensitive perimeter, while others 'scoped for prints and took DNA code samples from every available surface. The medics strapped Runner's body into a Tube case and coded it down to the morgue, and the extended hiss of compressed air sounded like a last breath. Wimet turned to Bublec, the guard who had been on duty. "So now, you were allegedly behind the security shield when this person came up to the booth."

The Minsonai readjusted his ice-pak and lifted his chin in affirmation. "I told you twice before: I *was* behind the shield when this alien—"

"Excuse me, 'alien' is a pejorative term. I believe you mean, this *non-Minsonai* came up—"

"—with a package and told me the stasis monitor was all fixed and could I help him bring it in." He shrugged. "It was the right size and all. How was I to know?"

"Was it a man or a woman?"

"With ali—uh, non-Minosnai personnel, sir, how can you tell? And I certainly didn't want to ask."

"Well, did he—or she—thumbprint the register? Did you make a voiceprint match? What about ID?"

Bublec looked embarrassed. "Well, *bom ichi ni frange*, sir," he exploded defensively, "the little, uh, *person* just asked me to help carry the package! And I came out and lent it a hand. I didn't think about ID's and stuff! I mean, this is *Hope*, not some Rim station where you're watching for bandits!"

"So, go on, you helped the person with the package . . ."

"And when I turned around, *fong!* Right across the back of my neck!" He massaged the area in question. "I went out like a *shiin*. That's all I remember until you people woke me up a while ago."

"Would you know the person if you met him again?"

Bublec shook his heavy head. "No. They all look alike to me."

One of the guards brought Wimet a plastex oblong. "What's this?" he asked.

"Readout on the break-in. Seems the killer stuck Bublec's hand into the ID slot and then hit the manual override from the control station. Walked right in and out again."

Wimet swore softly. "Well, he knew what he was doing, anyway. Thanks, Keely. Stay on it. I'll want to talk some more to Buffalo Calf, here. Now, Mr. Calf, you say you found Runner already dead?"

In-ne-o-co-se, Buffalo Calf, answered, "When I came to take his place, Runner was already dead."

"How did you know?" Wimet asked him. In-ne-o-co-se gave him a contemptuous look, pulled his fur robe higher on his shoulder, and made no answer. "I mean, did you touch him, or speak to him, or what?"

"He was dead. I touched his arm. He was stiff and did not breathe."

"What are the chances he might have fallen, or died of natural causes?" Joskwa Gallatin wanted to know, and Wimet shook his head.

"I don't know. We'll just have to wait for the autopsy report."

"Well, we may as well wait in comfort," Sharobi said, shivering. "There's a lounge just down the hall. Nothing fancy, but it does have hot coffee and sandwiches—and a place to sit."

Wimet glanced at his ticket. "I'll be right with you." He hurried away as the others followed Sharobi to the lounge and settled down to wait.

Charles Lassiter was surprised when the tall man in the Security uniform came into the room, shut the door behind him and, dragging up a chair, sat backward on it beside Lassiter's bed. He'd caught a glimpse of a second Security man outside. *Something's up*, he thought, and felt his stomach tighten with apprehension and excitement.

"Lassiter, right?" the visitor asked without preamble. "I'm Al Wimet, Security Chief. I understand you're an NOC for Interpol."

"That's right."

"There's been a murder. No apparent motive, but a few good clues. We have a suspect, Waylan Stubbs, snagged for three murder one convictions out on Zerev, but we don't have enough on him to make a move yet. We'd like your help verifying data, if you're willing to lend a hand."

Lassiter regarded his splinted hands with a quizzical smile. "I haven't been able to do much with them lately, but I'll do what I can," he agreed.

Wimet stood abruptly. "It's medical stuff, you can handle that. Sharobi's letting us use the morgue lab. You'll work there. We'll bring you what we have. If you need anything else, ask. Sergeant Lu-wen will be just outside." He glanced at his ticket. "We'd like you to get started right away." He shook Charles's hand briefly and left. Charles, amazed at his good luck, was still smiling when Ulrika came back at last with his peaches.

CHAPTER
VIII

PRINCE SALMAN WAS concerned as he left the Caliph's chambers. His royal father, who had always been active and vital, had become a virtual invalid, suffering constant headaches and severe vision problems. Specially ground spectacles had done no good, and now he had trouble even walking. He looked as if he were at death's door. One didn't have to be an alchemist, Salman told himself, to realize that something was terribly wrong.

Abdul Hamid, the Grand Vizier, kept reassuring Salman that his own preoccupation with books was the source of his father's malaise, and dismissed those physicians who disagreed with him. Several had utterly disappeared, and Salman suspected foul play, but he had no proof. Hamid disclaimed any knowledge of their fate, and chose to advise Salman himself.

Take a wife, he insisted, and your father will cease worrying and get well. He never mentioned the subject of his own unattractive daughter; but she loomed in the background of every conversation like an evil *djinn*. Through it all, Prince Salman remained unconvinced. He was certain that the cure for his father's malady lay somewhere in the books he constantly perused.

Now, making his way down the cool corridors toward the harem, he had a possible solution. This Esme, this nurse, must know a great deal, coming as she did from the very stars his people navigated by. She could examine his father and know what was wrong. She would tell him the truth. He would ask.

He brushed past the two guards and inquired of several

ladies splashing in the bath where Esme could be found. In her room at the end of the hall, they told him, and giggled, misunderstanding his interest. He thanked them, and went on.

He pushed aside the gauzy curtain that served as a door and entered the unlit vestibule. He could see her clearly through her mirror, sitting at the window seat, intent upon a small hand-held object. She appeared to be speaking to it, or into it, which mystified him.

A flicker of motion at the edge of the mirror caught his attention, and he peered closer. The eunuch Dawan, a drawn *kris* in his hand, was stealing up behind Esme. There was no mistaking his intent. Salman stepped boldly into the room and Dawan's face registered a nice mixture of chagrin and frustration as he quickly sheathed the poised *kris*.

"Master!" he exclaimed, dissembling quickly. "How—how good it is that you are here! I heard a sound, and came to the aid—"

"Begone, dog," Salman commanded, "and stay well away from this woman, or your head will go the way of your other members!" Smiling through clenched teeth, Dawan bowed himself out.

"Be careful of him," the Prince warned, watching Dawan's retreat with angry eyes. "It is always better to be with the other women than alone."

"It's even better," she told him firmly, "to go back to my job at the hospital! The sooner, the better! I have work to do."

"There is work for you here, Nurse Esme. My father is ill, and no one will help him. That's why I am always studying books, to somehow find a cure. I thought perhaps you—" She patted the seat beside her and prompted:

"Now, calm down. Start from the beginning and tell me all about it." And so he did, right up to the fact that his father had been having minor seizures of late. By the time he finished, her face was grave.

"Do you want it straight, Your Highness?" He nodded once. "I think your father has a really serious problem. He needs to be seen on *Hope*, right away. Can you get him ready? We'll bring him up."

"Impossible, Nurse Esme. The Vizier and the physicians loyal to him would refuse. And even if we convinced them to let him go, and something bad should happen to him while he is there"—he shook his head—"there would be a bloodbath. Starting with the two of us."

"Well," she said briskly, picking up the small object she had been speaking into earlier, "if you can't bring Mohammed to the mountain, you've got to bring the mountain to Mohammed!"

She flipped the communicator as Salman demanded joyfully, "You know of the Prophet? Are you a *Believer*?"

She waved him to silence as the communicator replied, "Emergency Room one. Van Kaalsem here."

"Hi, Aghat'. It's Esme, down on the surface. Get me Dr. Paige, right away. And make it fast, will you? My camel's double-parked."

All of them—Sharobi, Wimet, Gallatin and his Senn—had been waiting in the lounge for what seemed hours, when the wall com rang. Wimet hit it.

"Wimet."

"Al, this is Henning, down at the morgue. We're finished here, and I've got your autopsy report." There was the rattle of a printout, and he cleared his throat. "Subject was a male Senn, aged nineteen years, two months. Weight seventy-five kilos, height one point seven-nine meters. Robust health. Good physical shape. Heart, lungs, internal organs, in prime condition. Negative for neoplasm, occult bleeding, infection, parasites, intraorganic concretions; negative as a disease carrier—"

"Hell, what did he die of, then, boredom?" Wimet demanded. "It wasn't cold enough in there to freeze him to death!"

"He died of a heavy descending blow by a blunt object to the right side of the neck, which fractured the third and fourth cervical vertebrae. From the direction of the blow, I'd guess that your killer is left-handed."

"Killer? You're calling this a murder?"

"I've got the body right in front of me, Al. I can't call it anything else. There's something else, too. Lassiter retrieved scrapings from under the subject's nails. Turned out to be bloody flesh. He's still working on the analysis. We'll get back to you on that. Come down and see for yourself, if you like."

Wimet shook his head. "No, no. Thanks, Henning. Good job." He rang off and turned to the others. "You heard him. It's officially a homicide."

"I can't tell you how sorry I am, Joskwa," Sharobi told the sachem, whose face was set like stone. "It's a shock to us all. We've *never* had a murder on *Hope*. It's unthinkable."

"Unacceptable is a better word, Mike. We trusted your security, and I'm sorry to say, you let us down. And now Te-o-kun-hko the Runner is dead. So we will no longer depend on you. We'll do something about it ourselves. We Senn are quarantining this ship, until the murderer is caught."

"Now, just a minute—" Wimet began, but Sharobi silenced him with a lifted hand.

"Tell me, Joskwa, how do you plan to impose a quarantine without Security's help? This is a big ship."

"We'd like your help—but we'll enforce it ourselves, if need be. You know we can do it, Mike. I'm also ordering our scout ships to surround *Hope* with all weapons enabled. Until the murderer is caught and properly punished, no one will approach or leave this ship for any reason. We can't risk the murderer escaping. I'm sure you appreciate our position."

"What about our work down there at the outposts?" Sharobi argued. "What about the people who will die if they don't get help?"

"What about Runner?" Gallatin retorted.

Sharobi wiped his face and sighed wearily. "All right, you can have your quarantine; and no one leaves, I owe you that much. But I want to be able to bring up anyone planetside who's got a serious problem—with no interference from your people."

"Done. We'll allow incoming—but no one goes off the ship. Make sure you let everyone know we mean what we say. Any boat that tries to leave *Hope* will be blown out of the sky."

The bulletin went out within the hour. Until further notice no one might leave the ship. There would also be a curfew in effect, from midnight until six the following morning, on all levels. Anyone caught out would have to answer to the Senn, backed up by the full weight of Security. Sharobi gave no reason and brooked no argument, and on USS *Hope*, Sharobi's word was law. He had debated with himself whether to make full public disclosure of the murder, but decided against it. When the killer was found (and he had no doubt that he would be) the entire episode could be released to the media, along with the details of the situation. Meanwhile, he decided, there was no use spoiling the Christmas season with misdirected terrors.

The shopping had gone quickly. Audrey chose for Charles a soft, comfortable robe of spun *matriu* fiber that was light and warm, and took colors well. She and Dao had debated about the plaids, and when she decided on the blue after all, they brought several delicate little garments for *Ka*-Misi and an assortment of fishing lures for his steward, Shang, and his sons. They had Marik's gifts wrapped, addressed, and sent by Tube to the Senn level, for the Senn had generously offered (assuming, of course, that they got their exclusive gambling rights in time) to send special scout ships back to the homeworlds with any gifts that required immediate delivery.

After the shopping was done, they strolled arm in arm through the quiet back alleys, passing Scandia Way, Aberdeen Lane and the Via Sorrento in favor of the narrow back street called El Camino Real.

Hardy cactus and succulents, potted in clay jars, stood under warmlights along adobe buildings, and paper luminaria, glowing with candlelight, stood at each doorway. Behind barred wooden shutters, they could hear the sounds of voices and laughter as blindfolded children batted at *piñatas*. Over all hung the delicious scent of chicken, of salsa, and of frying chimichangas.

"It's almost like being in Mexico, isn't it?" Audrey said. The light threw shadows under Marik's high cheekbones and lit his eyes as he answered:

"I don't know, never having been there, but—I do know it's wonderful. Reminds me of the smell of fresh tchorimondo, back home." He inhaled appreciatively. "Are you as hungry as I am?"

She laughed. "Starved."

"Come on, then."

Moments later, they were seated at a serape-covered table inside an establishment called La Posada. Wooden planks ceiled the room behind round *vigas* that extended outside past the red-tiled roof. Handcrafted ceramic tiles, resembling squares of aged leather, formed the floor, and furniture stood dark and somber against the bright paintings lining the walls. The restaurant was full but not crowded, and there was the plaintive sound of guitar music, and of men singing love songs. It was very pleasant indeed. Their waiter, Raimundo, brought chips and salsa, and a margarita for each of them. Marik tasted the frosted rim of the glass.

"Salt!" he said, surprised. "I thought it was ice."

Raimundo laughed. "No, señor. The tequila, it needs the salt to bring the flavor."

Marik sipped again. "Lime juice, isn't it?"

"*Sí*. Lime, salt and tequila, for making you happy. You like to be happy, señor?"

Marik met Audrey's shining eyes across the table. "Yes. I like to be happy."

"Sometimes in my country, the people are so happy," Raimundo continued, "that when they get to the bottom of the bottle, they can eat the worm." Audrey's glass stopped halfway to her mouth and she shut her eyes.

"I don't want to know," she gulped, and Marik, much amused, asked if they could see menus.

Over dinner, which came in huge tortillas fried to look like conch shells, they talked about Liat Jevic. Marik was particularly impressed by her courage. "She's such a frail child," he mused, "and she's been through so much already. We could cure her tomorrow, but the parents refuse to have anything to do with the Droso Solution, so there's the end of that."

"Isn't there any way you can save her? You just can't give up on her."

"Yes and no. No, I won't give up, of course—we gave her a transfusion of packed red cells this afternoon—and yes, I've got some information on her family that may help. Seems her older brother—"

"Oh, has she an older brother? I thought she was an only child."

"She is now. Medicomp had the full story. The Jevics are from Zerev, and Liat's brother, Brenn, who was nine at the time, was killed by a Droso during mating season. It drank most of his blood supply and the Jevics—understandably—never got over it. So, now . . . they will probably lose Liat as well."

"How awful. Those poor people." Marik gazed down into the past and replied quietly:

"It's sad, yes. But you have to grow past things, Owdri. You can't get caught up on one moment in time and make a career of it. Life goes forward—and the living go with it."

"That may be easier for you to say than for some of us," she whispered. He looked up to find her eyes filled with tears.

"I didn't intend to hurt you, my friend."

"No. It's the past that hurts."

"Do you want to tell me?"

She drew a deep, shuddering breath. "If you like. We—" she dashed the tears out of her eyes with an impatient hand, "my family, the Garsauds, were one of those happy families you read about: successful father, loving mother, lovely home on wide acreage. Horses. Gardens. My two older brothers had graduated from the Academy, I had finished at Notre Dame, and our younger sister, Sandra, was everyone's darling.

"Father was a man of strong principles, great passion. But he thought with his heart, and unfortunately, he got involved in local politics. You might remember, the Krail controlled much of New Georgia, back then, and they were very chary of dissidents. But Father felt he must defend those who couldn't help themselves.

"So! He and my brothers—and Steven Brennan, one of their

classmates—joined the Resistance, along with Charles, whose family had a smallholding nearby our plantation. They brought food and medicines to people forbidden them. Printed literature, that sort of thing. It was all very secret, of course, but somehow information always managed to leak out." She paused while Raimundo cleared away the plates, and then continued:

"I don't know what went wrong. I don't think anyone knew, but one beautiful summer morning, shortly after Steven and I announced our engagement, the Krail came and killed everyone in our home—my parents, the servants, Sandra—" She drank from her glass to steady herself.

"There was a mockingbird that kept singing, through it all. I'll never forget that. My brothers and Steven died fighting. At least it was quick." A smile trembled on her lips. "I was the only one who escaped. Can you imagine? I was down in the marshes, that morning, picking wildflowers for the dinner table." Marik covered her cold hand with his own.

"How fortunate for us all that you love flowers."

"They came after me, of course. I spent two horrible days in the swamp, running . . . and hiding . . . Charles rescued me from that. And then he married me, right away, even though he was getting only a wooden wife, for I was numb. There was no one left but me. I felt so guilty for having lived."

"And yet, Charles loved you and married you."

She studied her hands and nodded. "I still don't know how he came up with the bride price my relatives demanded. He was not of our social station, you see. His family was quite poor." Raimundo slipped the check onto the table and melted away.

"But you have gone on with your life, Owdri," Marik assisted gently, "even as the Jevics must go on."

"In a sense, yes," she agreed, her eyes averted. "In a sense, I have gone on."

The guitar music was closer now, and three men in Mexican national dress came round the corner to their table. While Marik and Audrey finished their dessert and coffee, they played songs that harked back beyond their Spanish ancestry to the

Moorish occupation, their black eyes alive and sparkling, their brown hands nimble on the strings. They seemed to be waiting for something, and Marik slipped their leader a five-credit note.

"Only one more song, señor," he apologized, pocketing the note. "It's past the closing time. Even the mariachis have to sleep sometime."

"Mariachis?" Marik was curious. "I thought you were called Mexicans." They laughed, their teeth white in their handsome dark faces. The leader hastened to explain.

"In my country, there was once an Emperor named Maximiliano. A man from France, Napoleon, made him our Emperor. We didn't want an Emperor, but"—he shrugged—"nobody asked us. He didn't do much, but he used to hire guitar players for state weddings—'*pour les mariages*,' he said. So after that, the people, who never learned the French, they called the guitar players *mariachis*. And we have been mariachis ever since."

"That's a wonderful story," Audrey said. They stood there, waiting in embarrassment, until the leader said something in Spanish, and they started yet another romantic song. When it was done, Marik gave him yet another five credits, and noticed with some surprise that they were alone in the restaurant. He checked his ticket. Zero-zero ten Wednesday morning. Ten minutes past the Senn curfew. It was late indeed. Why were the musicians still standing there? What were they waiting for? He decided to take the bull by the horns, as the Erthlikli said. He would be direct.

"I have the feeling that you're waiting for something, and I'm not sure what it is."

"It's the tradition, señor. We don't leave until you give the señorita a kiss." Audrey's expression was a study in dismay.

"Well, since it's so late, perhaps we can forego the custom this once," Marik suggested. The leader shrugged apologetically.

"It is impossible, señor. I am very sorry. You must give her a kiss. It is the tradition, you understand."

"Very well." Audrey's face was white and still as Marik got up, drew her to her feet, cupped her face in both his hands, and kissed her gently on the forehead. She sighed gratefully and they shared a tender smile.

"No offense, señor," the leader said sadly, shaking his head, "but nobody will *ever* mistake you for Espanish." They drifted off toward the nether regions of the restaurant.

"We'd better get going, too," Marik thought aloud. "It's later than I thought." *Yes*, Audrey mused, her heart still pounding, *it's later than either of us thought.* Raimundo was nowhere to be seen. Marik paid the check and left a generous tip on the tray as well, but when they reached the front door they found it locked. One of the cooks, bundled up preparatory to leaving, stuck his head through the swinging doors leading to the kitchen.

"What are you doing here, señor, señorita? It is past the curfew. We are closed."

"Trying to leave. I'm afraid the doors are locked."

The cook gestured over his shoulder. "You can maybe get out through the Mall, I think. The back door, from the kitchen, it leads to the Mall, you know? Anyway, you can try."

The Mall was deserted, the display windows lit and still. Their footsteps echoed back hollowly from the elegant shop fronts with their faceless mannequins, and Audrey had an eerie sense of being watched. Even the animated figures—the elves and the snow maidens, the Santas and the crèche figures— seemed somehow ominous in their stillness. *Probably the margaritas*, she thought, walking a bit closer to Marik. *I'm just being silly.*

The reached the double doors that led to the street, but found them locked as well. Marik tried them several times, to no avail. He knocked on the glass to attract attention, but the snow was coming down heavily, and the streets were empty.

No one heard.

No one came.

"There must be another way out," he said. "After all, the cook got out. Let's have a look around." They retraced their steps, but La Posada was closed and dark.

"Just a minute," Marik murmured. "I think I see someone—" He limped off silently into the shadows, leaving Audrey alone in the darkened Mall. At least it was nice and quiet, she thought. Relaxing, really. Just because there were no people about was no reason to feel uneasy. Lifting her chin, she forced herself to ignore the feeling of being watched, to look around at the lovely Christmas displays. Two little elf-figures were looking at her, and she took several casual steps to get out of their line of 'vision.' Where could Marik be, she wondered. She glanced at her ticket. It had been a good ten minutes already.

She caught a stir of motion out of the tail of her eye and glanced that way, expecting to see him—and screamed, clapping her hands over her mouth.

There was the sound of something falling, and Marik came running back. "What's wrong? What happened?" he demanded, and she pointed at the free-standing display in the corner of the Mall he had come from.

"Over there—! Right near where you were . . . Something *dreadful!* Oh, Dao, it had the most horrible face!"

He frowned. "I didn't see anything, but I'll check again. Stay here." He checked out the display thoroughly but, as he might have expected, if someone had been there, he was gone now, through the small door behind the display that led—out of the Mall! He pushed it cautiously and discovered a passage leading to the cargo bay. Beyond the closely stacked crates, he could see a second door standing open to the outside, admitting cold wind and a wedge of night sky. He rejoined Audrey, who was still pale and trembling.

"Whoever it was found us a way out of here. Come, let's get you home."

They went quickly into the huge, shadowy cargo bay. Some fifteen meters above was the lading control cubicle with its tractor and pressor beams shut down for the night. Several Droso, among them PrrumBurr, the physician, were hanging upside-down from the overhead, sound asleep, as was their custom.

Several meters below them, suspended from the manual crane, one large packing crate hung precariously from the crane over the one remaining floor space among the tight-fitted cargo, swaying ponderously in the draft. Just beyond the empty space the door leading outside stood temptingly ajar. Marik scowled upward.

"That's strange. Lading officers never leave cargo suspended like that. Too much chance of accident. I wonder who left it, and why?"

"Let's just get out of here," Audrey whispered. "When I think of that awful face . . ."

He took her hand. "Think about going home, Owdri. Come on."

They squeezed between cargo, and twice had to climb over crates to reach the open space. 'China, This Side Up,' one of them read in three languages; another read 'Fabric'; and another, on the edge of the open area read 'Gentians, Live Plants,' and had no sides but thin, widely spaced slats.

Audrey gazed at the crate looming above them.

"Did you ever hear of the Sword of Damocles?" she whispered. " 'Heavy, heavy, hangs over thy head . . .' " Marik took her arm reassuringly.

"Don't look up, Owdri. Just follow me straight to the door. We'll be out in a minute." They started across the empty space just as a metallic groan from above warned of the heavy crate that came hurtling down at them at thirty feet per second per second.

Instinctively, Marik whirled and threw a flying tackle at Audrey, slamming them both through the flimsy slats of the gentian container and hard against the back, just as the falling crate hit the deck where they had been standing with a shattering crash. Part of Marik's coat was pinned under its near edge, and he shucked it off and gathered Audrey close, soothing her as he might a child, for she was badly shaken.

"He tried to kill us," she wept into Marik's shoulder, as they huddled there in the dark splintered crate. Whoever it was, Dao—he was trying to kill us both!"

Kee-o-kuk, the Running Fox, was sitting at the conn on his scout ship, *Mandan*, his weapons armed and ready. Only a few hours earlier, Joskwa Gallatin and several elders had come and given him the news that his son, Te-o-kun-hko, the Runner, had been killed. They had sat with him for a long while, sung the songs, and watched while he painted his face for vengeance.

Now, but for his thoughts, he was alone. Before him on the forward screen loomed the incredible bulk of USS *Hope*, the hospital ship from which Te-o-kun-hko had taken the spirit trail.

Kee-o-kuk sat very still, his black eyes endlessly scanning the screen, watching and praying that the murderer would make his move, so that he, Kee-o-kuk, father of Te-o-kun-hko, could blow the bastard out of the sky.

George Crow Dog and Terry Walking-About-Early were standing their watch outside Transport when Angelo's nephew Gino approached and tried to walk right between them. They blocked his way with their considerable bulk.

"No admittance, kid," Walking-About-Early said. "Get lost."

"I don't want admittens," the boy argued. "I'm just takin' a shortcut."

"Nope," Crow Dog said. "Go on home. The curfew goes into effect in"—he consulted his ticket—"twenty minutes."

"Wow, whaddaya know? I can tell time, too!" Gino said, wide-eyed in mock amazement. "We must be twins!" He spread his hands. "You wanna move, now, highpockets, so I can pass? So I can 'go home' like a good little boy?"

"You got a smart-mouth, here, George," Walking-About-Early muttered in Sennimet. "Kid's asking for a fat lip."

Gino gave him a dirty grin. "Yeah, and who's gonna give it to me, you, you outsize pussycat?" He stuck out his fuzzy chin and beckoned toward himself with both hands. "Come on, try it! Take your best shot! I dare you!"

Crow Dog shifted his weight. "Where did a hairless little rat like you learn Sennimet?"

"I pick up languages real good, okay? So what's it to you? You gonna let me pass or not?"

"Not," said Walking-About-Early, shifting his razor-sharp spear to the opposite hand and yawning widely.

Gino shrugged. "Okay. You gotta admit, it was worth the try." He made as if to turn around, then ducked between them and ran lickety-split for Transport. Crow Dog's long arm caught him by the scruff and hoisted him, swearing and flailing, into the air.

"What do you think?" he asked Walking-About-Early, who lifted his brows.

"The Rat? He's got some promise. Maybe we ought to take him with us, as a replacement for Runner. Think he looks anything like a warrior?" They studied him thoughtfully for a moment; then Crow Dog shook his maned head.

"Nah. Looks more like lunch," he drawled. Gino redoubled his efforts to free himself.

"Lemme down, dammit!" he grunted. "Lemme down, my uncle Angelo's waiting for me! Leggo!"

"Listen, Rat," Crow Dog told him, shaking him hard. "You get off the streets and haul tail back to wherever you came from, understand? If I see you again before 0600, I'll peel off your pelt and tan it for moccasins!" He dropped Gino, who bounced back off the floor undefeated.

"Oh, yeah, pussycat? You and what army? Eight to five you can't get a hand on me again! No, better than that! I'll give you ten to one!"

Both men brightened with interest. "You're laying *odds?*" Walking-About-Early asked. "You're a *gambler?*"

"*Par excel awnts,*" Gino retorted. "I'm a *real* gambler, not like you guys! I'm so tough, I used to deliver pizza to the mob when I was a kid!" He gave them a belligerent scowl. "If I ain't afraid of Santo the Bull, I sure the hell ain't afraid of two overgrown pussycats!" They laughed in derision and he persisted, "Okay. Okay. Let's put our money where our mouth is! You people are supposed to be such high rollers. You ever heard of somethin' called poker?" The two Senn slowly exchanged a baffled glance.

"*Poker?*" Crow Dog frowned. "*Po*ker. I believe it's some kind of a card game, isn't it?" Gino grinned and hitched up his trousers. Licked his lips.

"I've heard of it. Somewhere." Walking-About-Early pulled a well-worn deck of cards out of his pouch. "Maybe you can show us how to play," he suggested. "Starting with a little five-card stud, one-eyed Jacks wild, ten-credit ante, okay?"

Gino scowled at them as they squatted on the deck. "You

sure you don't know about it already?" he asked suspiciously, and Crow Dog gave him an innocent stare.

"He told you we've *heard* of it," he defended. "Deal."

"I don't know what's keepin-y Gino," Angelo fretted, peering out of his front window. "Maybe we better start practicing now, just in case, eh?" There was a chorus of assent from a dozen small voices, and then Alison stepped close.

"I'm not sure I'll be able to be in the programme, after all, Angelo," Alison said. "My parents don't believe in Christmas. And—and I don't think I do, either."

Angelo gave her a tender look. "You and you mama and papa," he asked, "you believe in *singing*?"

"Oh, yes. Surely. We love singing."

He patted her cheek. "Ah, *figlia mia!* So, sing!"

And the children sang, their sweet voices carrying beyond the barbershop into the cold night, while late shoppers hurried home and the silent Senn patrolled the empty streets, searching for a killer.

The hangar deck was hushed and still in *Hope*'s artificial pre-dawn darkness when Tommy Paige came in wearing a disposable plastex flight suit, his helmet in one hand and his medikit in the other. Having agreed to let the homeless Sid Behrman bunk in for the night, he had gone down to the medical library to research a Scup variant. Esme's call, explaining the Caliph's condition, had reached him there. Now he was in a serious hurry to get to the surface. The watch looked up from his robotics magazine.

"Oh, hi, Doc," he greeted him. "Looks like you're all dressed up with no place to go." *Damn!* Paige thought. *I forgot about the Senn flight prohibition.* He decided to punt.

"Hey, come on, this is medical business. Just because the Senn lost a man doesn't mean—"

The watch stood up. Just over two meters tall, Paige guessed, and built like the Xholemeachan Walls. Paige himself was barely more than a meter and a half in height. No chance of taking him in a fair fight, he figured.

"Sorry, Doc. Orders, right from the top. Nobody goes nowhere from here."

"Look, this is different. I'm a doctor! I've got to go planetside! I've got an emergency request for a patient who's seriously ill—"

"Sorry." The big fellow sat back down and opened the magazine again. "Orders say *nobody*. No. Body. This means you." He turned the page. Paige stood there for a long frustrated minute, watching him read; then he turned on his heel and left.

There was always Transport.

The corridor leading to the Transport Sector was short and dark, with airtight portals at each end and a line of pinlights on either side, where deck met bulkhead, to guide nocturnal travelers. Paige, flattened against a jog in the bulkhead, made out two armed Senn guarding the portals but saw no others. If he could somehow slip by these two, he thought, he'd be home free. The problem was 'slipping by.' He needed a place to hide while he figured a plan. Central Supply was just across the corridor, but he could never cross without being seen.

An orderly pushing a floataray came through the portals behind him and went into Central Supply, and then a maintenance man entered and came out a few minutes later with a scrubbervac. Paige took a deep breath and followed them through the door as if he belonged there. No one challenged him. No one demanded ID. He blew a breath of relief and exchanged pleasantries with the orderly as the man left.

Now Paige was alone. He must find a way past the sentinels at Transport, and do it quickly. His patient, according to Esme, was in bad shape and getting worse. He looked around. Every wall was lined with shelves full of medical equipment: IV setups for every known species, surgical trays, monitors of various kinds and sizes. Spare heads for the RIS; gloves of every type, description and number of digits. Adhesive closures. Cylinders of compressed gases. *Gases!*

Hot dog! he thought. *I've got it!* As fast as he could, but very carefully, he stripped off his flight suit, sealed every opening carefully with adhesive closures, and, horsing the gas containers around, found the two he wanted. Connecting the two cylinders with a short, Y-shaped length of synthon tubing, he began filling the suit with a mixture of compressed helium and 5-normal nitrous oxide.

The sentinels, George Crow Dog and Terry Walking-About-Early, had been standing their posts at Transport for almost eight hours, and they were tired. Earlier in the evening, after they had taken Gino for all he had, Crow Dog had amused them both by retelling some of the old stories, and Walking-About-Early had played on his flute the love songs which had won him his wife. They had even exchanged ghost stories from their various tribes. Now they were more than ready for their relief to show up.

There was the barest whisper from down the corridor and a figure—pale, swollen and headless—floated out of a door and slowly ascended to the overhead, bobbing and bumbling slowly away from them. Crow Dog reached for his pulser and muttered, "What's that?"

"Maybe out little gambler friend, come back to lose some more money." Walking-About-Early grinned. "You, there! Halt!"

"Who goes there?" Crow Dog challenged, but the transparent figure continued its slow journey down the corridor. "Halt!" he commanded, but it did not, so he made the obvious move. He shot it in the leg. With a piercing whine, the pale thing began zooming and soaring wildly all over the corridor, and both men ducked as it dove repeatedly between them.

"It's a damn balloon!" Crow Dog tried to shout, but it came out as a murmur. Dizzy and disoriented, he took a few deep breaths to clear his head and found himself sitting on the deck. Walking-About-Early braced himself with a hand against the bulkhead but his knees buckled and he, too, crumpled to the floor.

Holding his breath, Paige took his chance and ran at top speed for the doors of Transport Sector, gained the entry to Trans Four, and, before the increasingly sleepy guards fully realized that their 'ghost' was nothing more than concentrated anesthesia and a flight suit, he had homed in on Theresa

Paladino's Life-Glow and transported down to the surface of Ildefor.

Theresa and Kodi were tired. They had been wandering in the desert for a night and a day, trying to pick up Esme's trail, but they had come up empty. Their rations were gone and they had used the last of their water reserve hours ago.

Now they sat dry-mouthed and grubby on the bare sand, leaning against a warm rock that all too soon would become cold stone, and Theresa gave Kodi a baleful glare.

"Best trackers in the universe, those Senn. Yes, sir, they can track an idea across a dead brain. . . ."

"Knock it off, will you, Tre?" Kodi groaned. "It's bad enough my eyes are fried, much less having you chew my—" There was a whisper; the air shimmered and Tom Paige, cool and clean, his medikit slung over his shoulder, appeared before them. He bowed formally and shook Theresa's hand.

"Dr. Paladino, I presume. And—Kodi, isn't it? *Buflo* Kodi, the famous Senn tracker?"

Kodi held his head in both hairy hands. "Oh, great. Now I get razzed in rounsound. Just go ahead and shoot me, why don't you?"

"Because you still owe me a hundred credits, buddy, that's why," Theresa reminded him, hauling herself upright. "Tom, we've got a problem. We've misplaced Esme, or she wandered off—"

"She was abducted, I tell you!" Kodi interrupted.

"He's right," Paige allowed. "She just rang the ship, from the Caliph's palace no less, and needs a medical assist, on the double. I thought, since Yoghi, back at the outpost, said you two weren't doing anything"—Kodi scrambled to his feet—"and since Kodi, here, seems to have some excess energy, we'd go over and lend her a hand."

"Good with me!" Theresa got to her feet, brushing off sand, and picked up her medikit, while Kodi stood there wearing an air of offended dignity.

"Let's do it, guys," she said, and they shimmered away to

nothing, with only the desert breeze and a lone skulking hyena there to witness the wonder.

As he sat in the luxurious audience room, waiting for the *majlis* to begin, Caliph Ishaq ibn Muhammad al-Ghazi fought to ignore his excruciating headache. In the beginning, the pain and pressure had been only a nagging whisper, a nuisance, a minor distraction; but day by day it worsened until it became the central feature of his life. He woke queasily to its pounding summons, staggered through the day with it sitting astride his shoulders, and rocked himself to a fitful sleep each night, holding his head in both hands and moaning in agony. He was not sure how much longer he could bear it. It occurred to him again, as it had so often recently, that he might very well be dying.

He breathed a prayer for patience. The physicians had done all they could; now the rest was up to Allah. What was ordained would happen. Nothing more, nothing less. In the meantime, he would provide his subjects with whatever encouragement his presence might afford them.

He made a motion to begin the *majlis*, the audience, and the petitioners approached, one by one, and knelt by his elegant chair to speak to him. The first was an old shepherd, his face burned to brown leather by the desert sun.

"Ishaq," he whispered, calling the Caliph by his name, for did not all Islam know that all men were equal under the Koran? "I am Omar al-Bushir Akinli, a shepherd."

"Speak, Omar al-Bushir. I am listening."

"Last year I owned a small flock—one hundred ewes—and only one ram, a prizewinner I had bought in Jiddah. In one year, my flock more than doubled."

"*Al-hamdu lillah!*" the Caliph replied, gritting his teeth against the pain in his head, the shimmering arcs of light in his eyes. "That is a ram, indeed! May your flock be redoubled, and your sons as well!"

Omar shook his head, scowling. "That cannot be! My enemy has stolen my ram, and I cannot afford to purchase another! Without him, my flock will diminish and I will become destitute! He must restore my ram, Ishaq, or my people will die!"

"Sit, my friend, and I will consider this," the Caliph told him. Something black, a shadow, perhaps, or an image of a falcon, swept his vision for a moment and was gone. He motioned to the next petitioner, who came and knelt in Omar's place.

"Ishaq," he murmured, "I am Musa ibn Shaher Khadja. My son is dying of love for a woman, and her mule of a father refuses even to hear his case."

"Love is a difficult case to judge," the Caliph noted. There was a flicker of a dark wing again, just at the tail of his eye. He blinked it away. "Have you spoken to the woman's father?"

Musa waved the suggestion away in mounting frustration. "I tried. He claimed he had no dowry for her; would not listen to reason. So, later . . . my men and I made a *ghazwa*—a raid—on his camp by night. We might have abducted the woman, but in respect for her father, we did not go near her."

"What did you take?"

"I took his prize ram as dowry and—now that his daughter had a dowry worthy of a princess—I demanded that he allow her to marry my son, Akrum. I was so generous to that *spavined camel*," he burst out, "I even offered to share the services of the prize ram with him, as well as those of my own two rams! As brothers! And he refused!"

The Caliph made a placating gesture and Musa, embarrassed, lowered his voice once more. "Come, sweet patience," he muttered, between his teeth, and then continued. "Now this mule, this liar, comes to accuse me before you of discovering his falsehood! While my son pines away in his tent, and the woman weeps alone! I beg you, Ishaq, speak to him! Open the eyes of this blind fool before both our children die of broken hearts."

"Where are these grown-up children now, Musa?" If the falcons behind his eyes would cease beating their wings, he could see more clearly, the Caliph thought. The pressure inside his head was all but unbearable, and the darkness kept obscuring his vision. Some small part of his mind found it amazing that he could still speak and think rationally, if slowly.

Hang on, Ishaq ibn Muhammad, he told himself, *the people need you. Hang on.* Musa was saying something, and the Caliph leaned forward intently.

"My apologies, Musa, I didn't—"

"Akram, my son, is outside. The idiot's daughter is in the anteroom with her servant. They are awaiting your decision." Across the room, Omar al-Bushir fell to his knees on the priceless carpet, hands uplifted in silent petition.

"Be seated," the Caliph told Musa, then turned to the nobleman beside him. "Have them brought in, Mustapha Jehan." The falcons' wings began to beat in rhythm with his heart, making it difficult for the Caliph to see. He blinked rapidly, camouflaging the grasping of his forehead by feigning a pensive pose.

The young man entered diffidently, like the shepherd he was, and gave the Caliph a respectful salaam. From another door, the girl, swathed modestly to the eyes in black veiling, glided into the room followed by her maid. She halted, not sure what to do next, and the young lovers saw each other. The Caliph smiled behind his beard. *Even half-blinded, I can see he loves her*, he thought, and then: *She has the eyes of a gazelle.* He motioned both fathers to approach.

"I have decided the case," he told them quietly. "For the theft of the prize ram, Musa ibn Shaher Khadja is to give Omar al-Bushir Akinli, the woman's father, one of his own rams."

"But Ishaq," Omar protested in a whisper, "what of my own ram, worth more than both his weak-loined pretenders?"

"The prize ram goes to the new couple, Akram ibn Musa Khadja and his first wife—" He hesitated. "Her name?"

"Sara," Omar provided.

"—his first wife, Sara, along with fifty sheep from each father's flock. Make their marriage soon, and may their line increase. May they enjoy health, long life, and an endless river under their garden!" Both fathers, well satisfied, bowed themselves away, and the Caliph held his head in both hands for the space of a breath. Somewhere in the distance, he heard the noble beside him say his name. He felt a peculiar floating sensation; then the pain clamped down and he blinked the darkness away once more. He gestured for the next petitioner. Surprisingly, his son, Salman, knelt at his feet, and the Caliph embraced him and kissed his head.

"What petition does my son make today?"

"Father, I'm very concerned for your health. I want you to be examined by the star people from the *Hope* ship. I've brought them here to the *majlis* to help you." The Caliph could see them, a man, two brazenly unveiled women, and a large creature that appeared to be half-human, half-lion. Was he to let these alien infidels loose upon his person?

"I cannot, Salman. It would insult our own physicians. The finest medical minds in the Empire have done their best. How can anyone, even star people, do better?"

"The finest medical minds in the Empire let my mother die," Salman reminded him, and the Caliph shook his head fractionally.

"That was the will of Allah, my son. Everyone dies, sooner or later, even my beloved Aisha. Perhaps it is now my turn." Off to the right, the sheaf of written petitions in his cousin's hand was a painful glare of white against the intermittent darkness that kept crowding his vision. He felt a wave of nausea, and there was a loud buzzing in his ears.

Salman was saying something about his books, and the expertise of the star doctors, when the dark falcons came back, dozens of them crowding his skull and blinding him completely. He grabbed his head, stiffened, and made a harsh, choking sound in his throat. He tried to rise, to leave the *majlis* before he disgraced himself in view of his subjects, but it was too late.

There in the lavishly decorated audience room, before a score of nobles, guards and petitioners, Caliph Ishaq ibn Muhammad al-Ghazi measured his length on the floor and sustained a massive grand mal seizure.

"Clear the room!" Tommy Paige commanded. "Get those people out of here!" The guards hesitated, but Prince Salman gestured impatiently.

"Do whatever they tell you!" he ordered loudly. The two physicians sitting beside him rose immediately, scowling at the starfolk, but biting back whatever comments they might have made, for was not Salman ibn Ishaq al-Ghazi, the Prince, soon to be the Caliph? And had he not commanded the guards to obey these infidels? The guards herded the crowd out through the double doors as Paige took over.

"Theresa, I want a thousand milligrams of Dilantin, IM, and fifty of Myolax, *per aurem*. Esme, stick something in his mouth so he doesn't bit his tongue off, will you?" She grabbed the sheaf of petitions from the stunned noble's hand, rolled them up and jammed them crosswise with some difficulty between the Caliph's teeth. By now he was foaming at the mouth, his normally bronzed face a dull blue, and his breath came in hoarse, wheezing whoops.

"Gotta intubate him," Paige muttered. "Give me a hand, Esme." She held the jolting Caliph's head as still as possible, while Paige worked to pry open his tensely locked jaws. He had bitten the thick roll of petitions almost completely in half.

Theresa's hypo hissed against the Caliph's bare arm as Paige finally inserted the airway, and she sprayed 50 mg. of Myolax into the patient's left ear. The dreadful breathing was quieter now that the airway was set, and with the unimpeded flow of oxygen, the Caliph's face begin to pink up. He was still convulsing, but the Dilantin and Myolax would control that problem momentarily.

Theresa scanned for vitals, spending on overlong time at his skull, as Paige snapped, "Kodi, ring the ship and tell 'em to lock onto this guy *yesterday!* Where's the damn restraints?" Prince Salman shoved them into his hand and between them, they got the patient, whose convulsions were already beginning to subside, trussed neatly for travel.

Theresa handed Paige the scanner. "Tommy, look at this."

He read it, reset and read it again, then whistled soundlessly. "This guy's got a big-time problem. And I don't mean maybe."

Salman met his eyes. "He is very ill—is he not?"

"Your father is suffering from a growth inside his head, Your Highness. I can't say for sure how serious it is until we get him up to *Hope*, but I'll be honest with you, I'm afraid it's bad news."

"I thought as much." Salman passed a hand across his face. "The physicians have been giving him a tea of boiled red clover, to cool the burning, and extract of opium for the pain, but he only gets worse."

The double doors opened and the Grand Vizier stalked in, followed by Dawan and two well-armed guards. The Vizier made a perfunctory salaam.

"What is the meaning of this?" he demanded. "Who are these people, Your Highness, and what have they done to His Majesty?"

"These are doctors from the starship *Hope*, Hamid Vizier. My father has had a seizure—"

"He has had seizures before," the Vizier interjected. "And he will again. This is nothing new."

"—and I have given them permission to examine him in their hospital."

The Vizier gripped his arm roughly. "Are you mad?" he hissed in his ear. "What if they make a blunder and kill him? Do you know what the army would do—to all of us? What if they take him hostage, and we lose the whole planet in getting him back? What if they are lying?" Prince Salman tugged his arm free of Hamid's grasp and readjusted his glasses.

"I trust them. But since you do not, Vizier, I will permit you to name a hostage, to be held in surety against my father's return."

The Vizier smirked and spread his hands. "What one man can compare to your honored father?" he asked unctuously. "I claim all of them as hostage—including the large hairy creature, whom we already have in custody!—until the Caliph is returned to us in good health."

"He's a very sick man," Paige pointed out. "We may be too late as it is. What happens to us if he dies?" The eunuch behind the Vizier made a quick across-the-throat gesture with his thumb, and bounced his fist a few times in the air.

"I'll agree to stay," Paige offered after a moment, "but you don't need the others. Let them go up with the Caliph, and you've got a deal."

Hamid shook his head. "*All* of you."

"Forget it!"

"Tom." Theresa's eyes were soft behind her horn-rims. "It's okay. We're in this as much as you are. We'll stay." Paige looked around, and each of his companions signified agreement. Reluctantly, he acceded.

"All right. You win. We four agree to—"

"We *five*," Salman corrected.

"We *five* agree to stand hostage for the life of the Caliph. Let me make the arrangements." He walked away a few paces, rang the ship, and got Arty Michaels on the first try.

"Big Arty, I've got a problem. We've got the head honcho down here with what looks to me like a level-four astrocytoma. He's in bad shape, and unless I miss my guess, he needs an RIS procedure yesterday."

"Can do, Tommy. Get him here, give me an hour to set it up with Sharobi and get some tests back, and we're on it."

"There's another thing. The second-in-command here is holding five of us—Tre, Esme, Buflo and me, plus the Caliph's son—as hostages against his life. He dies, our heads roll—literally!"

"Wow! That's massive, it really is."

"Yeah, that's the way we see it, too."

"Look, we can forget about this guy, beam our people up right now and—"

"—and lose the patient, Artie. That's not what we're here for."

"Well, let me beam all of you up!"

"Nope. We need to build confidence in these people for future contact. Dangerous or not, we have to stay. Here's what I want you to do: as soon as you've got the tumor dissolved and the Caliph's out of danger, you've got to set off some kind of huge fireworks display—big enough so they'll see it from the planetary surface—as a signal that he's all right."

"Okay. Maybe we can dig some up somewhere."

His offhanded attitude made Paige uncomfortable. "I mean it, now, Artie. Don't let me down. Our lives are depending on this."

"Yeah, right. I told you, no problem. Relax, will you? We'll send a skimmer for your patient right away, and we'll take care of everything."

"Nix. No skimmers. The Senn promised to blow any departing boats right out of space. You'll have to transport him up."

"Oh, okay. No problem."

"Make sure about those fireworks, Artie."

His laughter sounded callous in Paige's ears. "Sure, sure. We'll look around, see what we can do. See you, Tom."

"I hope so, Artie," Paige said fervently. "I really hope so."

The Mask had tried again.

Sometime in the early morning hours, Sid Behrman told the Security Team from his gurney in the emergency room, someone had sneaked into his room and whacked at his neck with what had felt like a hand axe.

Fortunately, Sid had sustained a whiplash injury some months before, and always slept wearing a cervical collar. The collar had saved his life.

"Why would anyone want to kill a sweet guy like me?" Sid complained, and Waylan, who was there with Mancini, drawled, "Maybe they saw the show last year, Sid." Mancini laughed.

"Very funny," Sid retorted, spreading his hands. "Do I need this? I mean, I'm hurt here, somebody tries to kill me, do I need this abuse on top?"

"Did you see anything of the assailant?" Wimet asked.

"Yeah. Yeah, when the portal opened, I kind of woke up and saw him feeling his way along the all. So I says, what's this, some kind of Crazy got in here? So I snapped on the lamp. He was wearing this ugly mask over his head, but, look, I've seen actresses look a lot worse without their makeup, so I grabbed it and yanked."

"And—?"

"And it pulled off from the top of his head. Whoever it was, he had light-colored hair. And before I could do anything else, he knocked me out cold. Feels like the sonofabitch broke my neck." He fingered his nape gingerly. "That's all I can tell you."

Wimet patted his shoulder. "Good job, Mr. Behrman. You've been a big help. You take it easy, and thank God you're alive to talk to us."

"Yeah, you bet, thank God I'm alive," Sid grumbled. "Dead men can't sue."

CHAPTER

IX

THE TESTS WERE in. Sharobi, shuffling through them this bright cold morning, gave a satisfied grunt. Paige had been right. The Caliph Ishaq ibn Muhammad al-Ghazi was suffering from a fourth-level astrocytoma, a malignancy so diffuse among the brain cells that for centuries, it had been considered scarcely operable.

That is to say, one might surgically weed out the most obvious areas of the dreaded organism, thereby extending the patient's life span significantly; but because of its diffuse nature, it had been virtually impossible to eradicate every last malignant cell, no matter how careful the surgeon nor how great his skill.

Until now, Sharobi thought. This decade, this century.

Until the advent of the Roentgen Intersect Surgery. Even the legendary Gamma Knife of the twentieth-century couldn't hold a candle, he thought, to the precision of the present-day RIS.

They were bringing up the Caliph's MAX now. Marik, who was here primarily to observe, waited at the first assistant's station. Artie Michaels was ready at the Intersect computer. Meng, at Anesthesia, was sustaining the hypothermia, and Jenner already had her hands in the manipulators, just in case the boss ran into trouble. The RIS was not a sterile procedure, so no one had bothered to suit up or wear gloves. Indeed, the actual procedure was so simple, any ordinary team of technicians could run it; Sharobi's presence here was more in deference to the Caliph's planetary status than to the gravity of the procedure.

The patient had been prepared in pre-op. They had given him an injection of isotopes to tag the malignant cells, and started an intravenous infusion of Neriosh 328, which rendered bone radiolucent. Since X-ray couldn't 'see' through bone in any species, the RIS procedure would have been impossible without the Neriosh 328 drip.

They programmed the patient's MAX for hypothermia, dropping his temperature to an even 86.5° Fahrenheit. When he was totally cooled and immobilized, they initiated a full-body scan in case of occult metastasis. Should metastasis have already occurred (if the cancer had spread secretly to other parts of the body), it would be a simple matter to perform a second Intersect procedure on the affected area and knock it right out.

That possibility ruled out, the tagged cancer would then be represented as a three-dimensional holographic cranial image and computer-tomagrammed to a thickness of one cell. That is, the computer would make individual images, as though it were making slices only one-cell thick, of the living brain. These hundreds of thousands of images would then be digitized on the computer monitor (showing up as a sort of a map made of thousands of tiny squares, with the cancerous cells represented as dark pixels), and stored in proper sequence.

The same computer also controlled the actual Intersect device itself, a sophisticated array of twelve X-rays whose extraordinarily fine beams were focused on a single intersection point, known as the I-point, and calibrated to the width of the cell to be destroyed.

Once activated, these tiny individual X-rays could penetrate the living brain without ill effect, for human tissue (even neriosh-treated bone) was transparent to the individual X-rays, which potentiated only at the I-point. The damage caused by attenuation was negligible.

The X-rays, following the pattern on each tomagrammed 'slice,' systematically and rapidly obliterated from the screen every dark pixel (thereby destroying every cancerous cell), but injured no tissue outside it. There was no surgical trade-off in this procedure, Sharobi reflected gratefully, no medical equivalent of 'friendly fire,' no 'acceptable damage.' The intersection pattern that eradicated the malignancy left the healthy brain tissue virtually untouched.

The patient's natural immuno-responses, unmitigated by debility, post-operative stress or invasive trauma, would dispose of the necrotic matter, and the body could begin regaining strength and vitality, with a good prospect of a normal, healthy life. Thanks to the Intersect procedure, Sharobi exulted, the patient brought in this morning dying of a malignant brain tumor could go out to dinner tonight, perfectly cured. It was, Sharobi told himself, a most satisfying way to spend a bright winter morning.

He slipped his hands into the manipulators and jerked his head around at the various members of his operating team.

"Everybody set? Good! Let's give this man another fifty years."

Two hours later, the Caliph, awake, alert, and fully cured, was sitting up in bed heartily enjoying a tray of *gaz*, tea and fruit juice, and discreetly admiring the pretty nurses.

Big Artie Michaels, having completed his shift (and totally forgotten about Paige's fireworks), took the stairs down to the cafeteria for a snack.

Halfway down the first flight, he heard a male voice raised in anger, and curious, followed it. At the far end of the corridor, the Lading Chief was reading the riot act to a female crewman. *The lading officer*, he thought, *the cute kid with the funny name. Murorsky or Mutosy—something like that.* As he came toward them, he could hear the conversation clearly.

"What's the matter with you, Mutowski?" *Ah, Mutowski*, Michaels corrected himself mentally. "You out of your mind, leaving cargo suspended? Those people almost got killed last night! And it would've been *all your fault!*"

Mutowski, braced and formal, snapped back, "No excuse, Chief."

"Well, what about a *reason?*" The Chief pushed his beefy face close to her freckles and growled, "If you don't have an excuse, maybe you can give me a *reason!*"

"Nothing, Chief, except, well—"

"Well?"

"Female problems, Chief. Maybe I was having female problems." She caught a glimpse of Michaels approaching, and he could see her swallow hard as the Chief roared, "Female problems? What *kind* of female problems?"

She glanced at Michaels and muttered confidentially, reddening, "*You* know, Chief. *Fe*male problems."

"Which female problem?" the Chief demanded. "You can't get credit or you can't parallel park?" Artie took it from there; he pushed his glasses up the bridge of his nose and cleared his throat.

"Excuse me, I'm Dr. Michaels. I'm afraid I need to consult with this crewman for a few minutes. Could you excuse us?"

Scowling, the Chief gave in, and with the parting shot of "Ten demerits, Mutowski!" ambled off in the opposite direction. Mutowski's chin was jumping and her cheeks were tear-stained, and when Michaels handed her his handkerchief, she could not meet his eyes.

"So tell me," he inquired politely. "Can you park parallel?"

She burst into unsteady laughter, tears spilling over her freckled cheeks. "You bet I can! And I've got A-1 credit, too!" She blew a mighty blast, dabbed at her eyes, and shoved his handkerchief into her hip pocket. "And I didn't leave that cargo suspended!" He lifted a hand.

"Say no more. I understand. After all, I'm a doctor. And what I prescribe right now is lunch. You game?"

She stared at him for a long moment, realizing that Artie Michaels, the theme of her every daydream, had not only rescued her from humiliation, but had actually asked her to lunch! Not trusting herself to speak, she nodded.

"Okay. Lunch it is." On their way, he asked, "You read a lot?"

"Yep."

"You wouldn't be interested in mysteries, by any chance, would you?"

"Would I? Agatha Christie, Tom Clancy, Amon Benic, Livi Crompian—you name it!"

He paused on the steps. "How about real mysteries, like,

who left that cargo suspended, so they could drop it on Marik and Mrs. Lassiter?"

"Yeah!" She met his eyes. "The real-er they are, the better I like 'em," she said. He pushed up his glasses again and grinned.

"Looks like I'm in luck," he said, and without thinking, she replied cheerfully, "We're both in luck!" and blushed. They had gone all the way to the cafeteria before she dared speak again.

"Where are you going with this child?" Ulrika demanded, stepping in Marik's way. He stopped Liat's hoverchair obligingly.

"We have a pass for the Einai level," he explained, pulling it out of his tunic. "Permission from the charge nurse as well."

Ulrika felt Liat's forehead, studied her critically. "I don't think so. This child is definitely unwell. She should at once return to her bed." Marik met her eyes evenly.

"I don't think so. I think we'll do things just as planned. Pardon us, please?" He made as if to detour around her, but she stepped in his way again.

"I am a nurse here, and you are only a patient! I tell you she will not go!" she insisted, and he interrupted firmly but gently:

"If anyone questions your letting us pass, Nurse, tell them it was on the authority of Priyam Dao Marik. Have them see me."

"You have no authority, no jurisdiction here!" she cried angrily, and Marik lost his battle with a wry grin.

"Ms. Drac, a Priyam has jurisdiction anywhere in the galaxy. I'd think you would have known that." He calmly pushed Liat away, and Ulrika followed quickly, trying to restrain the hoverchair and breathing in short, angry gasps all the way to the lift gate.

"I know who you are! Don't think I don't know! You are that half-caste, that—that pretender to a silly, nonexistent throne!" Marik pressed the stud for the Einai level, inserted the currency requested of him by the ATM, and slowly turned to look at her.

"And how did you come by that fact?"

She patted her tight coronet of yellow-white braids and wiped the thin film of perspiration from her upper lip. "I make it my business to know everything—about everyone! It comes in often very useful." She pressed her thin lips together smugly. "Take your case, for instance: here you are, prating to me about your authority, when even on *Hope*, there are certain prominent people—"

"A Klan full, no doubt," he interjected, having heard it all before. The Purist Klan had been successfully hunting Han almost since the Return of the Erthlikli. She barreled on, spouting her venom as she went.

"—who would be *very interested* in knowing we have a Han on board. All I need is one word in the right ear, and you are gone from the picture! So I would not be making enemies with me, if I were you, Mister *Han*. I would watch my back instead. Remember, *I know who and what you are!*" The lift bell rang and the doors whispered open, and as he and Liat entered, Marik paused and fixed Ulrika with that steady, tiger-eyed gaze.

"The Erthlikli have a saying: 'A little knowledge is a dangerous thing.' Be careful, Ms. Drac. If only a little knowledge is dangerous, too much knowledge could prove—"

The doors hissed shut in her outraged face, cutting off whatever else he might have said.

Lassiter had checked and rechecked his findings, but the verdict remained the same. Under three fingernails of Runner's right hand, he had found unmistakable shreds of Einai tegument, along with traces of Einai blood, type alphaR+. He started to ring Wimet, but thought better of it and logged another in a long list of queries to Medicomp.

Medicomp ready, Dr. Lassiter, it replied.

"Question: scanning *Hope's* entire population, which Einai aboard have type alphaR+ blood?"

Please hold. There was a pause. *Five Einai have blood type alphaR+: Esme Cuf, R.N.; Gerald Versi, M.D.; Noln Jevic; Priyam Dao Marik; and Bram Coto. Further queries?*

Lassiter tapped his stylus absently against the tabletop and chewed his underlip. Marik's blood type was alphaR+, to be sure, but that didn't actually prove anything. The tissue typing had been even less satisfactory. According to Medicomp, any one of the five could be equally suspect. It might be Marik's blood and flesh under the dead man's nails, and then again, it might not. Were a few scrapings strong enough evidence for an actual accusation? He sat tapping his splint thoughtfully against his front teeth for a long minute, then at last, with some reluctance, he hit the wall com.

"Security," it answered metallically. "Wimet."

"Mister Wimet," Lassiter said. "I'm finished examining the nail scrapings, and I'm afraid I have some bad news."

Raintree Street, on the Einai level, was pleasant in the warm summer sun, and Marik pushed Liat's hoverchair carefully along the meandering sidewalk that led through the mini-forest. They were surrounded by lush vegetation on all sides. Bambu reached up for the light, and tall ferns waved in the warm breeze. Flowering shrubs and coreliae vines lent their fragrances to the soft air, and jewel-toned memlikti (surgically deprived of their venom) caterpillared on velvet bellies among the tender green creepers, or hung suspended from webs high in the treetops. Aun murmured in the distance, and there was the plashing of water nearby. Liat heaved a satisfied sigh and adjusted the picnic basket on her narrow lap.

"This is almost as good as real, isn't it, Priyam?"

"It is real, in its own way," he observed. "Look, Liat, a glen with a little waterfall. Shall we stop here, or go on?"

"Here." She looked better since the transfusion; her cheeks had a faint tinge of color, and her spirits were noticeably higher. He spread a sheepskin on the springy forest floor and lifted her carefully onto it. Covering her legs with her favorite afghan, which she had refused to leave behind, he began unpacking the lunch basket.

"I'm not very hungry," she confessed, and he gave her a professorial smile.

"Ah, but you haven't seen what's in here, *Ka*-Liat! We have tchorimondo!"—she started giggling as he pulled out a packet of juicy fried items, still steaming in their wrap—"we have kiwi!"—he handed her several oval, fuzzy green fruits—"we have boiled standi eggs—" He stopped abruptly as she continued to giggle, holding both hands over her mouth. "What is it?"

"You!" She burst into fresh laughter. "Calling me 'princess'! I'm not a *Ka*! I'm just Liat!" Marik touched a gentle finger to the tip of her nose.

"That's strange," he said soberly, thinking of his own baby daughter, safe and well at home on Eisernon. "You remind me very much of a real princess I know, whose name is *Ka*-Misi. Shall we pretend you are a *Ka*, just for today?" She bit her lip and then nodded enthusiastically.

"All right," she decided. "And you must be the servant, and do whatever I tell you." Marik paused in dishing out the food to make a grave bow.

"Alai, *Domne*," he agreed, which sent her into a fit of giggles that lasted intermittently through their long lunch, and through the unaccustomed second helping she asked for.

"I wish Semmy could have come with us," she said shyly.

"You'd like to have it along," Marik repeated her words, hoping for some sort of a breakthrough. It would not do to push.

"Yes. He's my friend. But don't tell Umma and Uppa. They'd be mad. Could I have another donze, please?" Marik obligingly handed her a writhing, many-tentacled morsel, which she bit quickly between the eyes and popped whole into her mouth. "Umm!"

"They wouldn't like for Semmy and you to be friends," Marik probed gently. "Why is that, do you think?"

"Bekowf ub Bwen." Her articulation was unclear and she lifted one finger and chewed patiently until she had at last swallowed the whole donze. "Because of Brenn. Chewing makes me so *tired*," she breathed. There were dark circles of weariness starting under her golden eyes.

"Liat, tell me something," Marik asked. "Who is Brenn?" A shadow crossed her wan face.

"I'm not supposed to talk about it," she mumbled.

"You could tell *me*," Marik invited, and she shook her head.

"I don't want to." Her tone was one of utter finality. She didn't want to talk about Brenn—and that was that! She toyed with a few blades of grass. "Um—Priyam Marik?"

"Yes?" Had she changed her mind? She screwed up her face and smiled.

"Do you want that last jat rib?"

After a while, still gnawing on the rib, she waved a thin jade hand around at the greenery, disturbing a huge cobalt-blue butterfly. "Who do you think made it *really*, Priyam—I mean, servant?" Marik, lounging on the soft moss, followed her gesture.

"The ship designers transplanted everything to make it as homelike as possible, I suppose. Even the memlikti and the flutter-bys. They did a good job, don't you think?"

"No, I mean, the universe and the world and the sun and all. Where do *you* think it started?"

Marik hesitated. "What do your parents say?"

"Well—" She put down the bone, licked her fingers and patted her mouth fastidiously with them, several times, like a scrawny kitten. "My teacher says it happened all by itself. But Umma and Uppa believe Tadae did it—and so do I. Umma taught me the Beginning Story. Do you want to hear it?"

"Please."

She wiggled herself into a more comfortable position on the sheepskin and folded her hands in her skinny lap, fixing him with her great golden eyes. "Once upon a time, before there were any people, Tadae made the suns and the stars and stuff, and He thought it was pretty good. So He needed some people, because He said, what's the use of being a God of love if you don't have anybody to love?"

"That sounds reasonable," Marik allowed, munching another tchorimondo.

"So, He reached down and took some green sand from the bottom of a forest pool, and He made the very first man. And he was so nice, Tadae named him I'achom, 'the best thing.' And He gave him all the birds and fishes and animals to name. And I'achom did. But then he got bored of just animals and fish and birds; he wanted somebody like *him*. So Tadae made him sleep and took one of his hearts out. But, don't worry, he didn't feel it," she hastened to reassure Marik, "because Tadae gave him some kind of anesthesia."

"I see," Marik said.

"Anyway, Tadae made a beautiful golden lady out of the heart and gave her to I'achom. And I'achom named her Kai-ala, because she was the heart of the best thing to come into the world. That made her the *better* best. And naturally he loved her, because she was his own heart." She stopped for a minute to catch her breath. She was tiring quickly now, and her voice was less strong. Marik would like to have taken her back to the Unit, but Liat was so intent on her story, he let her go on.

"Well, Tadae put them on a big beautiful holy mountain to live, the prettiest mountain there ever was, with clear water and lots of deep, comfortable caves. And He said they could catch all the game they wanted, and live in any cave they wanted— except one. This one cave was only for Tadae, and it was called the Cave of Life, and I'achom and Kai-ala were forbidden to ever, ever use it.

"And do you know what went and happened?" Her pinched face flushed with righteous indignation.

"No," Marik lied. "What happened?"

"They did it anyhow!"

"I'm astounded."

"*Really*! They went in it anyhow! The bad old wolf-dog, Waru, sneaked up and told Kai-ala that way back in the Cave of Life was a rock that would make them as smart as Tadae! And all she had to do was go get it, and she would be like a god! 'Cause, see, he wanted them to get in trouble! And so the great big dummy did it!"

"No!"

She was frankly gasping now, but eager to get on with the tale.

"Yep! And she gave it to I'achom to hide, and he did. So after a while, when Tadae looked around for his rock, He couldn't find it. And He knew that I'achom and Kai-ala took it, because who else could take it? There *wasn't* anybody else. So . . . so He made them go away from His holy mountain . . . and said that now they would have to . . . have to be sick and die . . . because . . . because they were bad. . . ." She trailed off as if a new thought had come to her, her head slowly bowing until her face was hidden by the dark fall of her hair. She paused for such a long time that Marik became concerned. He touched her arm.

"Liat?" She raised swimming eyes to meet his.

"I just thought of something," she gulped shyly. "When I was small, I was really naughty sometimes. Do you think that's why Tadae made me be sick and die, too, Priyam, because I was so bad?" Marik gathered her protectively in his arms and felt her emaciated little body shake with silent sobs as he stroked her hair.

"No, no, no, Liat. Absolutely not. Tadae is, above all, loving, and no loving parent would ever kill his child, no matter what she did. He doesn't make it happen, and He doesn't want you to be sick. You don't have Ensi-vo because you were bad. You have it because you accidentally caught a virus, that's all."

"Well," she sniffled, wiping her nose on her wrist, "I wouldn't even *have* it if it wasn't . . . for that stupid old cave and . . . that stupid old rock! Why did *we* have to be the only ones . . . with a cave . . . and a rock? Other people . . . on other planets . . . didn't have to . . . stay out of a cave . . . or die! It's not fair!" Marik wiped her face carefully with his handkerchief, tipped up her chin and looked into her eyes.

"You're right, *Ka*-Liat. Waru never tempted them, as he did us." He rested his chin on her silken crown for a moment, and then continued: "But a serpent named Satan *did* tempt the Erthlikli to eat an apple from the Tree of Life; and the dragon tempted the Krail woman Eija to climb the Pole at Ets-La. All races must suffer if they are to become truly human.

"But remember something else, Liat, and this is very important. For all of us, the end of the story is always the same: hope. All the Beginning Stories end that way, because that's all we have to go on: faith—and courage—and love—and hope." He wanted to say— And he wanted to quote— And he wanted to rationalize—

But instead, he did what he would have done for his own child. He picked up a slice of chocolate cake and handed it to her.

"Would this help, just a little?" He suggested hopefully. She gave him a misty smile and took it.

"Well . . . maybe a *little*," she demurred. She managed to down almost half of the fat wedge before she shook her head at last.

"I'm stuffed," she said, pushing away the remainder; then, remembering her role, she lifted her chin imperiously. "I mean, I'm elegantly full, oh, servant. Now the *Ka* wisheth to seeth the petting zooth."

"I beg your pardon?"

She gave an exasperated sigh and turned her palms up. "I want to see the *petting zoo*, Priyam. Don't you know any royal talk at all?" He tucked the remains of the lunch back into the basket and got to his feet.

"I'm truly sorry, O Glorious," he apologized grandly, scooping her back into the hoverchair with his good arm and depositing the picnic basket in her lap. "Your servant hears and obeys. To the zoo it is!"

Only two other children and their nursemaid, all of them Krail, were visiting the petting zoo, for the day was unusually warm and humid. Beyond the cluster-pavilions, where the onboard Einai were housed, an artificial thunderstorm was building up, indistinguishable from the real thing. In the other direction, Marik could see the hospital above the treetops, and made a mental note to take a direct route there when they were finished here. Liat seemed very tired.

On the edge of the petting zoo was the pen of Liat's favorite animal, the barong, its bathing pool connected to the system of lagoons, ponds and waterfalls throughout all levels of the ship.

Constantly circulating, all the ship's used waters, including gray-and-black water from all levels, were filtered down through a sophisticated system of screens, filters and chemical washes that harvested usable waste materials for composting on the Production Level. The remaining water, now of purest potable quality, was then circulated back up to the habitation levels for reuse.

Just now, the barong's pond was green and still, for the animal was dozing high on its ledge of artificial rock. Everyone loved the barongs. Their devotion to humanity was so intense that their very name was synonymous with loyalty, and they were frequently used on Eisernon as nursemaids for the very young or very old. Gentler than lambs, they were fierce only toward those perceived as threats to their charges, whom they would protect to the death.

As the children circulated among the baby animals, a young dharavi bellowed, making them laugh, and the barong opened its eyes and peered around as if in a daze. Liat was stroking a baby jat and chattering. Marik tried to listen, but his attention was repeatedly drawn to the barong, as it staggered unsteadily to all four feet. Its almost-human nails scratched on the rock as it climbed down and sprang over the fence into the petting zoo enclosure, showing its teeth and growling ominously.

"Liat, it's time to go," Marik said, but she clung to the jatkin.

"Not yet, not yet," she pleaded, as he started to float her away.

"Now, Liat," he insisted firmly. The barong was coming closer, and Marik stepped between it and Liat. Both Krail children approached to pat it, but it eluded them with a nasty snarl and made for Liat with a surprising burst of speed, bowling Marik over and snatching her screaming out of the hoverchair and over the fence. Marik vaulted the fence in hot pursuit and scrambled up the rock where it stood over the sobbing child, glaring at him and showing its teeth. *Can't afford to excite it any further*, Marik thought, forcing away an urge to attack it with his bare hands. *It might take out its rage on Liat.* Instead, he approached slowly, noting the involuntary tremors along the barong's hide, the stiff, stilted gait, the saliva dripping from the massive jaws.

This is not normal, he thought. *Something's wrong with this creature. It's sick, or mad, or worse. I've got to get Liat away from it.* She was sobbing. Only half-conscious, and the wounds on her arm were bleeding freely. "It's all right, Liat," he told her softly. "Just stay still. I'll take care of you." Keeping his eyes on the animal, he called over his shoulder to the Krail nursemaid, "Please! Get us some help, before this animal kills the child!" There was no answer, and he risked a glance her way. She met his eyes with a cold blue stare and, taking each small Krail boy by a hand, led them off.

"Please!" Marik called. "Get help!" The barong snarled and Marik feinted right to attract its attention. *Come on, lady,* Marik thought desperately, *prejudice is one thing, but Liat is just a child—a desperately sick child!* The three Krail disappeared leisurely around the bend of the walk, never looking back.

The barong growled again, and taking Liat's head in its teeth, shook her like a rag doll. Marik threw caution to the winds, and clasping both fists together, rushed in close and swung at its tender, unprotected nose. He missed, his fists striking the animal's hard skull, and the barong swiped at him with a paw, raking three long, bloody furrows across Marik's jaw and neck. Undaunted, Marik swung again. This time his fists struck a hard blow to the sensitive nose and the barong dropped Liat with a pained yelp and dove whining into the deep green water.

Marik quickly examined the unconscious child and found his worst fears realized. She was having a massive bleed and was headed for deep shock. He peeled off his tunic and wrapped it around her, lifted her carefully over the fence, and made for the hospital at a dead run.

The com in the morgue lab chimed, and without looking up from his 'scope, Charles hit it with the side of his splint. "Morgue. Dr. Lassiter speaking."

"Dr. Lassiter, this is Crane in Emergency Room Four, Einai level."

He carefully adjusted the fine focus. "What can I do for you, Ms. Crane?"

"We were told to report anyone coming in with scratches or scrapes. Well, we just got an injured Ensi-vo child in here, and the man who brought her into Emergency has three big bleeding welts across his face and neck."

"Do they look fairly fresh?"

"Yes, sir, they do. Do you want me to keep him here?"

Lassiter thought fast. "No," he decided, "just get his full name and what he does here, and let him go."

"We've already got his name, Doctor," she reported. "It's Dao Marik. Einai male. Claims he's a patient." There was a long silence. "Dr. Lassiter? Dr. Lassiter, are you still there?"

"Yes," Lassiter said. "Yes, I'm here. Thank you for calling. I'll inform Security right away."

Marik paced the waiting room in Emergency Four with mounting impatience. The doctors had refused to let him into the examining room and had shut the door firmly behind them. They had no time for explanations, and answers to his anxious questions were put off until the doctor had finished their business. All he could do was wait.

Noln and Ferri Jevic came into the waiting room, breathless and disheveled.

"Where is she?" Noln demanded, and Marik indicated the cubicle. He started for it, but Marik caught his arm.

"They won't let anyone in until they've evaluated her. Why don't you sit down and have a cup of coffee?"

"I don't want any coffee! And I don't want to sit down! I want to know why my baby was out of the hospital—and running around a zoo—where she could get hurt!"

"My fault, I'm afraid," Marik admitted.

"You!" Ferri breathed. "You took her out?"

"She'd been so emotionally low, I thought she'd benefit from a taste of home. We made a picnic. She was having a wonderful time and doing very well, too, until that barong attacked—"

Noln made a harsh sound of ridicule. "Oh, yes, a barong attacked! Why not a mus? Or a flower? Perhaps a flower attacked the child! What really happened to her, Marik? How did my baby get hurt? What did you do to her?"

It was clear that the discussion would be fraught with more heat than light, and Marik shook his head.

"I'm very sorry," he said, and started to walk away, but Noln spun him around and landed a right to Marik's face that decked him. Ferri clutched at her husband.

"Noln, num! Priyam, he didn't mean it, we're just so terribly upset—" Marik got to his feet, shaking his head to clear it. A painful swelling on his left cheekbone was growing larger by the minute.

"It's all right. I probably deserved it. I wish to T'ath it had been me the barong attacked, instead of Liat."

"So do I!" Noln Jevic growled, jerking away from his wife and crossing to the opposite side of the room. "And I wish it had killed you!"

The cubicle door opened and a woman in Security uniform came out with a clipboard. "Are you the parents? You can go in now. The doctor would like to speak with you." Noln and Ferri Jevic hurried into the cubicle, shutting the door behind them, and the Erthlik Security officer crossed to Marik. "You would be Mister Marik? The man who brought her in?"

"That's right."

"We're having some problems verifying the information you gave us, Mister Marik. Maybe you can help us. You list yourself as Priyam Hanshilobahr *Dom* Dao Marik, but our check with the Medicomp doesn't list you among the galaxy's known Priyamli; and as far as claiming a relationship to the Throne, well—" she laughed lightly, "we won't even discuss that here, will we?"

"My records were—"

"Our check with the zoo vet does not confirm an attack this afternoon. He was away for an hour or two, but considers it highly unlikely that such an event could have occurred. Were there any witnesses to the alleged attack?"

"A Krail woman and two children. I called for help, but they—they evidently didn't hear me."

"Umm-hmm." She made a few notes on her board with her lightpen. "You do know, don't you, that barongs are noted for their gentleness, especially to members of your own species? Tell me, how did you get those scratches and that bruise on your face?" Marik quickly outlined the encounter with the barong, and she made a few more notes. "Are you aware that the Senn guard who was murdered this morning had blood and fragments of Einai skin under three of his nails?"

"No, I didn't know. There was no way I could have. I was

assisting Priyam Sharobi at an Intersect surgery earlier, and
then I was at the park with Liat."

"Sharobi will verify this?"

"Yes."

"Very well. You're free to go, Mister Marik, for the present
at least. We'll contact you if we need anything else." She
snapped the clipboard closed and inserted it into a bulkhead
slot, where its information was logged immediately onto the
Medicomp. "Stay available," she warned over her shoulder.
"We'll be watching."

Marik returned to his quarters weary and sick at both his
hearts. He had planned to give Liat a holiday, and instead here
she was, comatose in ICU, and he was all but accused of
maliciously injuring the child. He had intended to try to sleep
for a while, for today's exertion—jumping, running and carrying, not to mention the stress—had tired him; but he had just
moved out of a regular ward into a private apartment, and
someone had dumped his gear untidily in the middle of his bed.
No rest there.

He dialed for a bottle of tarangi instead, poured himself a
bowl and started for the recliner under the window, when
something furry caught his eye. He crossed to the bed and
pulled it free. Held it up to the light, puzzled. It was a wig! A
blond wig, such as actors used. What was that doing here? He
had never seen it before. Probably got mixed up with his
dunnage. Someone would ask for it, sooner or later. Or not at
all.

He tossed it back with the rest of his dunnage and slumped
gratefully into the recliner. Watched the sky grow dark as he
finished his tarangi. Felt the drowsy warmth of the liquor move
from his belly into his head, and had almost fallen asleep when
the com chimed.

"Marik."

It was Audrey. "Hello, Dao. I heard about Liat. It must have
been awful. Are you all right?"

He smothered a yawn. "Yes. Yes, I suppose I am."

"Good. You and I are going to tour the Museum this evening.

Help take your mind off your troubles. Shall we say, half an hour?"

"Owdri, I—" He hesitated, then relented. What would it gain him to sit brooding all night? "I'd like that," he decided. "I'll meet you under the clock in half an hour."

"'Bye, Dao."

"*Chom-ala*, Owdri."

CHAPTER

X

THE SECURITY GUARD, whose name tag read STEC, WLADISLAU stepped in front of Audrey and Marik as they started up the long ramp that led to the Museum's double doors.

"Sorry, folks. No one's allowed in tonight. Museum's closed."

"Oh, Dao! I'm sorry," Audrey said in dismay. "I thought it was closed on Wednesdays." Stec thumbed back his cap.

"It usually is, ma'am. But there's been a robbery. Somebody stole a valuable artifact, and until the experts round up all the clues, nobody gets in."

"What did they take, Stec?" Marik asked, and the guard shook his head.

"From what I heard, some kind of ceremonial mask or something—" Marik and Audrey shared a quick glance and she covered her mouth with her fingers.

Stec scowled at them. "You two look surprised. You know anything about it?"

"No. Of course not," Marik answered, drawing Audrey's hand through his arm. "How could we?"

"Then you'd better clear out," Stec growled, unconvinced. "Museum's closed until further notice."

They hurried away through the cold night air.

"Now you know I saw something in the Mall," Audrey whispered, shivering. "Whoever it was, was wearing the stolen mask! But why? What was he up to?"

Marik paused on the sidewalk and took her by the shoulders, gazing straight into her eyes. "I don't know, Owdri. And we don't have to know. That's what we have Security people for, so we don't have to worry about these things. I think we should let them do their job and—" He caught a glimpse of the pond and smiled. "And in the meantime, I think you should teach me to ice skate."

She returned his smile with interest.

The pond in the park was well-lit and dozens of skaters were moving to the sound of piped-in music. Audrey, her rented skates slung over one shoulder, led Marik past the bonfire, where a vendor was roasting hot dogs under the watchful eyes of a stocky Security guard, and down to the ice. They shared a wooden bench while she banded her skates and showed him how to band his own.

"I've never done this before," he confessed, as he took one bold step onto the ice and promptly sat down hard.

"Are you sure?" she asked, laughing. "You look like a pro to me." She made a few deft little figures and stopped short, spraying him with ice shavings.

"As soon as I get better at this," he promised with a grin, "you're in trouble. Count on it."

She laughed and skated away swiftly down the length of the pond, turning backward halfway to watch his progress. "First you have to catch me," she called. "If you can find me!"

He got to his feet gingerly, mentally thanking his ancestor cats for basic good balance, and managed to get across the pond once without falling again. The second time, it was easier. By the third time, he was moving smoothly and actually enjoying himself. He looked for Audrey but couldn't find her among the swiftly moving skaters. He turned in every direction, but she was still nowhere to be seen. A quick light jab in his ribs startled him and down he went again, sitting squarely on the ice with Audrey skating leisurely circles around him.

"I don't think I'll ever be in trouble at this rate," she teased, stopping to reach down with both hands and help him up.

"I don't think so, either. Let's go and get a—a hot *dog*?"

"It's not what you think. Come on."

The vendor threaded two red sausages on a long metal skewer and held them over the bonfire while he talked. "We're doin' a land-office business this year," he confided. "Never saw such a Christmas crowd. People're comin' from all over the ship for the holidays. Mustard and sauerkraut?"

Marik blinked. "Excuse me?"

"I say, do you want mustard and sauerkraut on your hot dog?" Marik looked at Audrey for help and she smiled.

"Either that, or it's chili and onions. Take your pick."

"I'll, er, take the sour Kraun and whatever . . ."

"And two hot ciders," Audrey assisted.

"Sauerkraut comin' up," the vendor caroled, tucking the money into his apron pocket. "And two hot ciders to go. You know," he continued, slathering mustard onto a bun, "when you think about it, we're lucky to have a bonfire at all, out here, way things are."

"Why is that?" Audrey wondered.

"Well—" He slapped the blistered sausages onto the embellished buns and stabbed each one with a pickle-flagged toothpick. "Here you go, sir! Ma'am! Well, we keep forgettin' we're way out in deep space. Now, that's worse than deep sea, when it comes to fire, see. Because if the fire should get out of hand, like a confla-gration or sumpin' like that, what would happen to the air? It would get all used up! And where would we be then? Not breathin', that's where! We'd all be dead as a doornail"—he snapped his fingers—"like that!"

"Only thing worse," interjected the stocky Security man, wrapping a bun around his blackened sausage and taking a substantial bite, "is explosive decompression. Blow the side of the ship right out, take all the air with it. Snuff a lot of good people."

"That would be a tragedy," Marik agreed. "Don't you have fail-safes, in case of accident?" The guard nodded, the wad of food making a knot in his thick cheek.

"Yep. The whole amphitheater, over there, is an escape pod. See, that big viewport is really a hatch. It looks pretty, overlooking space and all, but it just pops automatically when the internal pressure drops. Every level has one, and each race has its own seating area, because each seat is a little lifeboat, designed for that species. In case of decompression, a plastex canopy locks over it, and the internal air supply kicks in. They're rigged for re-entry and soft landing, with a Life-Glow and subspace beacon, and food and water and stuff inside. Supposed to work like a charm." He shoved the last bite into his mouth and started making himself another. "But I hope to God we never have to find out."

"Damn right," the vendor agreed cheerfully. "That's why we got these Security and Maintenance guys hangin' around my fire all the time, makin' sure it doesn't happen. That, and the fact that they like to mooch my hot dogs."

Marik and Audrey laughed and drifted back to their bench, munching hot dogs and drinking cider, their skates crunching solidly through the snow. The music was sprightly and loud, and the chatter and laughter of the other skaters made conversation difficult near the ice, but Marik was content merely to sit beside Audrey and watch the skaters fly past.

Someone out on the ice screamed shrilly, and Audrey covered her ear with one hand, wincing, even as they laughed at the energy of the young. The scream came again, followed by the screamer, who came racing across the ice from the opposite side of the pond, and not bothering even to remove her skates, ran past their bench and out of the park. Marik caught a glimpse of her face and her thoughts, and realized that this was no squeal of joy but a shriek of absolute terror. The child was afraid—of what? *The Mask!* he thought. *Great T'ath! He's here!* He was on his feet at once, speeding across the pond and into the snowy trees.

It was much darker among the frozen trunks and black branches, and the bright lights had dulled his night-sight, but he could see a contorted figure moving away clumsily between the trees.

"You! You, there! Stop!" he called, as it limped away. He followed as best he could, but lost it in the shadows. He searched for a few futile minutes, and was turning around to go back when the monstrous masked thing jumped him from behind with a hearts-stopping cry and, lifting a dagger that seemed part of its very hand, stabbed viciously again and again at Marik's chest. Its very weight bore him to the ground, and,

giving one last stab to make sure of its victim, the dreadful
assailant scuttled away, leaving Marik prone on the snowy
path.

Audrey skated to the far edge of the pond, peering into the
trees, but she could see nothing. "Dao?" she called. "Dao, are
you all right?" Her voice was lost in the jolly noise around her.
He probably can't hear me, she thought. *I'll go and see where
he is.* 'The Skater's Waltz' followed her into the trees as,
awkward in her skates, she hurried into the somber shadows.
Some distance away, she found Marik just getting unsteadily to
his feet. "Dao? Are you all right? What happened?"

"That little girl who was screaming—"

"The one whose parents took her home just now?"

Marik nodded, carefully holding his chest. "She saw the
Mask. I followed him and he jumped me. Tried to kill me, in
fact. He had a dagger—or a scalpel—something awfully
sharp." He tugged ruefully at his shredded tunic, under which
she could see the thick plastex conformer. "If I hadn't been
wearing this, he would have had me cold. I can't believe there
wasn't even a trace of mental scent. I had no idea he—or
she—was there."

"*She?*" Audrey repeated. "A *woman?*"

"Hasn't it occurred to you that the murderer might be female,
Owdri?" he asked softly. "Remember, the female of the species
is always deadlier than the male. Besides, I caught a trace of
scent—perfume, maybe—behind the mask. Probably enhanced
by the exertion. You never know," he finished, pulling his tunic
together as best he could and leading her back to the light and
laughter of the frozen pond.

"No," she agreed, looking at him with a strange expression
on her face. "You really never know, do you?"

"How do we know he didn't fake the attack?" Wimet asked.
"It would be a great way to divert attention from himself."

"Impossible," Lassiter argued. "The man's integrity is beyond question."

"No man's integrity is beyond question!" Wimet retorted.
"As an Interpol agent, you ought to know that. You learn it on

Day One!" He finished his cold coffee and grimaced. "Who else besides Marik saw the Mask?"

Lassiter shrugged. "Well, nobody, I guess. Just that little girl he told us about. But his tunic was all shredded—"

"He could have done that himself. And there's no proof that the child saw anything, just that she was screaming." He slitted his eyes wisely. "In fact, *was there really a child*? No parents called to report anything unusual. Think, man! Wouldn't her parents have complained?

"Hell, even if there was a child, kids scream all the time when they're playing. All we have is Marik's word."

"That's good enough for me, Mister Wimet," Lassiter said.

Alan Wimet smiled his acid smile and put down the cup. "Unfortunately, it's not good enough for me, Doctor. I'm going to put a tail on Marik. Make sure he doesn't do somebody else in."

Big Artie Michaels was a mystery-novel fan, and thought of himself as a pretty good amateur detective. He'd been following the Mask case closely, and when Marik checked the Jevic child in, with the unlikely claim that a barong had attacked her, everyone but Big Artie had laughed in his face. Artie, who had an active imagination, had taken him seriously. So had Mutt, with whom he was having a steak-and-fries dinner in the crowded cafeteria.

"Mutt, what if—" he began, pointing at her with a french fry, "just *what if* Marik was telling the truth today?"

"You mean, what if the barong really jumped them—and the Krail wouldn't help?" Mutt assisted, shrugging. "Big deal, Artie. Krail don't help anybody, unless they can get something out of it." She sipped her malted. "But barongs don't usually attack people."

"But that's just it! Think about it! What if somebody wanted to set Marik up—and, well, I don't know—drugged the barong or something, so Marik would look bad."

"Sounds pretty thin." She grimaced. "Have some more fries."

"Thanks. Maybe so, but it's all I have to go on, and Marik's kind of an interesting character. I need to know. You want to help me?"

She propped her chin on a fist. "You bet! What do we do first?"

The old zoo vet, Hafne Bor, looked at them as if they were mad. "Why would you want a sample of barong urine?" he asked, rubbing moisturizer into his scaly blue skin. "Even the Security people didn't ask for a urine specimen."

"Security?" Artie feigned ignorance. "Oh, you mean the Marik thing. Oh, that. Well, I'm doing a different study."

"He is," Mutt assured him.

"He's not." Bor slowly capped the bottle. "I only *look* stupid, children. But I guess it's all right, since you're a doctor and all. Can I see that ID once more, please?" Artie flashed his ticket and his grin, and Bor relaxed, pulled a ring of keys from a thigh pocket and unlocked the barong enclosure. *They were in!* Mutt slipped a hand into Artie's and he squeezed it hard.

The barong got up from its corner and ambled toward them waving its tails. Rubbed against Bor like an affectionate cat. It nosed Artie's hand and laughed open-mouthed at Mutt, who was impressed by the number and size of its teeth.

"Now, does this look like a vicious animal to you?" Bor asked. "Something that would attack a child, no less?"

"Nah," Artie agreed, handing him the sterile catheter setup. "He looks like a cream puff." Bor made short work of draining off half a liter of blue-green urine from the patient barong, and returned the filled apparatus to Artie.

"Here you are, Doctor. I hope you can exonerate old Shoni, here." He ruffled the multiple silky ears. "He's a close buddy of mine."

"Exoneration's what it's all about," Artie said.

Fifteen minutes later, they had slipped into one of the locked labs at the Med School, using Artie's ATM card to open the portal.

"We could get into a lot of trouble doing this," Mutt whispered, and Artie regarded her patiently over his glasses.

"We've got to analyze this urine," he whispered back, "and

Wimet sure isn't going to let us in on the main investigation. For all I know, *he* could be the killer! Or—or Dr. Lassiter! Or anybody!"

"Oh, right," she scoffed. "It's gotta be either the Security Chief or a guy who can't even walk or hardly use his hands. It's gotta be one of them, all right. Or maybe Mrs. Lassiter!"

"Well, it's somebody! Turn on that minilamp, will you?" He ran the specimen through a full two-hour analysis, while they sat in the darkness, watching it go through its paces. Mutt yawned frequently, and twice had to rouse Artie, whose eyes kept unfocusing into a blank stare.

It was during the last test, a neriosh chromatography, that Artie suddenly sat bolt upright, fully awake. "*We got it!*" he shouted. He grabbed her by the shoulders. "There it is, Mutt, right in front of our eyes! See that opaque band in the spectrum? Well, combined with—look here—with this one, and this! *Do you know what that is?*" His eyes were shining behind his glasses. She shook her head dumbly, adoring him, excited because he was excited. "That's the chemical compound that makes up Parnevon, one of the most potent mind-benders in the galaxy!

"Look! Listen to this! If someone who knew about drugs gave the barong a shot of Parnevon, it would have gone absolutely mad, just like Marik said it did. Not only that, but Parnevon is totally undetectable after the first twelve hours. We got in just under the wire! Here, wait—!" He recorded the findings in the Medicomp, and turned back to Mutt. "We've got it, Mutt! We've found it! Now we can contact Mister Wimet with some hard evidence, and bail Marik out!" He wrapped her in a tight hug.

"Wow!" she said softly, and he let her go, pushing his glasses up. They shared an embarrassed laugh, and he continued diffidently, "You know, everybody calls you Mutt, but you have a real name, haven't you? I mean, nobody would name a baby 'Mutt.' "

"Barbara," she told him. "Ensign Barbara Ann Mutowski, GFN."

"Well, Ensign Barbara Ann Mutowski," he said softly, pushing his glasses up once again, "you're a helluva kid."

"But I really didn't do anything," she protested. "I was just there."

"Right. You were there. What say we get this stuff to Wimet, and then go celebrate?"

Her grin threatened to split her face. "Oh, wow," she said.

The main procedure this morning was a combination limb reattachment and eye replacement. Marik was looking forward to it. He was beginning to enjoy the routine, the order, of *Hope*'s medical facilities, and Sharobi knew it, and was glad.

The patient was brought up, heavily sedated, into the surgery, and Marik, seeing his face, thought he seemed vaguely familiar. He turned to Jenner, Sharobi's indispensable and voluptuous red-haired assistant. "The patient's name?"

"Garrett," she read off the screen. "Sergeant Alfred Joseph, GFArmy. You know him?"

"Yes," Marik answered. "I know him."

Now he knew where he remembered Garrett from, he thought, slipping his hands into the manipulators. The last war. He had wakened from a dream of fire and death and destruction, only to find himself broken and bleeding under the wreckage of his hospital. The sun had been warm and fine, and memlikti trilled sweetly in the fern forest as he lay dying. It was Joe Garrett's squad who had found him, dug him out, sent him up to the hospital ship. But for Garrett, he mused, Dao Marik by now would be only a jumble of broken bones among the ruins of Sum ChiT'ath, deep in the fern forest of Eisernon.

He looked up to see Sharobi's dark gaze fixed on him, and knew that he had caught his thoughts.

"This the one?" Sharobi asked aloud, just to be sure. *Yes,* Marik replied mentally. Sharobi glanced around at his team.

"This patient gets the VIP treatment, gentlemen," he ordered. "Let's get at it."

Jenner smiled at Marik and confided in her throaty whisper, "I just *love* it when he calls me a gentleman."

• • •

Marik was cleaning up afterward in the scrub room, deep in thought, when someone spoke just behind him.

"Ppriamm Mmarikk," whispered PprumBurr's wings, and Marik turned in surprised to see the Droso physician there.

"Dr. PprumBurr. Nice to see you."

"You, ttoo. You rr bettrr?" Its manipulators were working furiously around its mouth, a sure sign among the Droso of extreme agitation.

"Thank you. Yes, I am." He frowned and stepped closer, lowering his voice. "Is something wrong, Doctor?"

The manipulators froze for an instant and the wings made an abortive blur of sound that cut off abruptly. It bobbed its head this way and that, then regarded him solemnly with its faceted red eyes. "I—*we* Drrozzo would like tto nnvite you tto conzzert ttnnite. You mmuzzt come. *Mmozzt mmprrtnntt. Mmuzzt!*" PprumBurr's legs bent with the effort of trying to communicate just how vital was Marik's presence there. "*Mmuzzt!*" it repeated, in a louder whirr. "*Pleez!*"

"A Droso concert. That's the one that's been advertised all week, isn't it? Part of the big USO show?"

"Yezz. Come! *Mmuzzt!*"

Marik laid a friendly hand on its hairy skull, between the big compound eyes that kept flicking one facet, then another, at him.

"I had planned to go, as a matter of fact. But tell me something: why is it so important that *I* go? I'm just one—"

"*Nno! Onnly Domm* will nnderzztannd! Onnly!" It was wringing its manipulators desperately again. "Watch *careffly! Careffly!*"

Marik frowned again. Only a *Dom* will understand? This was no joke, no whim, nothing to be taken lightly. The Droso physician was nervous and insistent, and Marik couldn't think why. There was only one way to find out. He smiled. "I'll be there, Doctor. You have my word. And I'll watch as carefully as I know how."

One slender manipulator reached up and thumped him

between the eyes—the Droso equivalent of a pat on the back—and it made its polite little *demi-plié* with all six legs.

"Thnnkzz," it replied, managing to convey heartfelt relief in one long flutter of silver wings. Then it straightened itself up, drew its manipulators quickly through its mouth, and folded its wings tidily. "Well, back tto workk! When the *tuv'z* away, th *pprog's* will pplay! Zzee you ttnnite!" And without a backward glance, Dr. PprumBurr launched himself at the overhead and fluttered away down the corridor, leaving Marik puzzled and amused behind him.

Joe Garrett opened his eyes and focused on the overhead. It was painted an incredibly beautiful shade of green. He turned his head on the pillow and saw a magazine lying on the table beside the bed, its colors astoundingly vivid and deep. He started to sit up and found himself pushing himself up with both arms. *Both arms!*

He jerked his right hand up in front of his face. It was there! It was back! He made a fist with it. Extended his fingers excitedly and wiggled them. Beat a tattoo with both hands on the sheet. He had his hand! It was really there! He hugged it to his chest.

My hand, he thought numbly, *I have my arm and hand back! And ohmigod, my eyes!* he exulted belatedly, finally realizing the double miracle. *They did it! It worked! Oh, Lord, You listened to me just like you listened to blind Bartimeus. And why not? We made the same prayer: Lord, that I may see.*

And now he could see. Oh boy, could he see!

He punched the buzzer and a male nurse charged in happily. "Well, awake, I see, *Hom* Garrett! And how do you like your new hand and eyes?"

Garrett grinned, pointing at him. "Wtorkow! You're Wtorkow!" He laughed aloud. "I recognize your voice! And the smell of your after-shave! It's great! Just great!"

"Notice anything different about colors?" Wtorkow inquired, and Garrett, still examining his arm and hand, looked up.

"Yeah, I do. They're different, real bright and deep! I never saw anything like it before. Is this SOP with new eyes?"

"Well, not exactly," Wtorkow explained. "The Senn brought in a shipment of eyes, all right, but unfortunately, they didn't have any blue ones; just ten thousand pairs of brown, in all sizes and shades from hazel to black. So Sharobi gave you a pair of temporaries in hazel. That's light yellow-brown to you. and, you know, brown eyes see color differently than blue ones. If you don't request a change in two weeks, by the way, these become permanent."

"*Brown?*" Garrett frowned. "But I always had *blue* eyes." He looked around the room, drinking in everything there was to see, and reveling in the colors that had become so vivid. It was as if the world, which had been pastel all his life, and then dark, had blossomed. What the hell, he thought. It was enough simply to have regained his sight, never mind eye color. He had his eyes back, his heart exulted, and he had his hand. And he was still in the good old GFArmy. "I'll just keep these," he decided. "They're great."

"Well, you have two weeks to sign the final forms, if you should change your mind," Wtorkow said. "Now—it's been five hours since you came out of surgery, and since you're nice and stable, how about a ride down to the lounge in a hoverchair?"

It was late afternoon when Alan Wimet leaned back in his chair and put his booted feet on the top of the desk, regarding Dao Marik through slitted eyes.

"Now, tell me something, Mister Marik," he began mildly. "Why would a patient in this hospital—never mind the fact that you really are who you say you are, and have Priyam Sharobi's backing on it!—why would an ordinary patient on USS *Hope*—*who is not an actor*—be in possession of a blond theatrical wig?" Marik's gray cat eyes never left his face. He made no answer.

Wimet tossed the wig onto the desk. Marik recognized it at once. "We found this in your effects. Hidden way back in your sea chest. Why would you do that?"

"In my sea chest?" Marik sat forward, astounded. "Why—that's impossible! It was right there on my bunk!"

Wimet stretched to full torsion, like a man who has just won a grueling athletic contest, clasped his hands behind his head, and slitted his eyes wisely, smiling his Cheshire cat smile. "Shall we talk?" he inquired in a silky tone.

So—for over an hour—they talked.

Audrey appeared in the doorway of the morgue lab, surprising her husband. He had seldom seen her so animated. Her face was glowing and her eyes shone.

"Here you are, Charles! I've been looking everywhere for you!"

"Where else would I be, Audrey?" he asked with a trace of asperity. "I'm always either here or in my hospital room. Where did you think I'd be, visiting some woman?"

"No. No, of course not." She snapped her little jeweled evening bag open and shut nervously a few times. "Have you forgotten we're supposed to go to the USO show with Priyam Sharobi tonight? In just over an hour?" *Snap, snap*, went the bag, stopping abruptly when he scowled in that general direction. She caught her lower lip in the edge of even white teeth.

"Out of the question," he said, looking her over appreciatively. "You look real pretty, Miss Audrey, but I'm still not going. You go ahead."

She laid a hand on his shoulder, cajoling. "Please let's, Charles. We haven't been anywhere together for the longest while, and you're doing so much better lately."

"Which is why I can't walk," he answered shortly, shaking her off and turning away. "Which is why my hands barely function! Yes, ma'am, I'm doing just *fine!*"

Audrey plunged on to cover her embarrassment. "Barbara says they put on a wonderful show. You still have time to dress. I even laid your things out for you. I really think you'd enjoy it."

"I'm going to be busy for a long time here, Miss Audrey," Charles said, settling himself more comfortably in his hover-chair. "And you know I don't go in for theatricals." He paused to make a careful adjustment of the microscope with the tips of two fingers, peering into it as he spoke. "Why don't you get Miss Barbara to go with you?"

"She's doing something with Dr. Michaels again."

"Well, then, how about Priyam Marik?"

"Oh, I don't think that's such a good idea," Audrey demurred.

Charles lifted his head and smiled at her through his thick, fair lashes. "It's a wonderful idea. You've been going everywhere together anyway for two, three weeks. Why don't you give him a call?"

"Because . . . because . . . oh, Charles, there've been all these killings, and . . . and then you found Einai blood and skin under the Senn's nails . . . and it's Dao's blood type! And no one saw the barong hurt Liat, we only have his word for it! And now they've found a blond wig in his quarters!" She lifted swimming eyes. "I can't imagine it could be Dao, but—I don't know what to think!"

"Why, honey, I wouldn't worry about Mister Marik, if I were you. You'll be as safe with him as you would with me, maybe safer. And Priyam Sharobi wants him kept up and about. Why don't you go on and ask him?" He studied her stubborn expression for a long moment, and then teased gently:

"Unless there's another reason why you don't want to be alone with the good-looking Einai gentleman. You're not getting a crush on him, Miss Audrey, now, are you?" Color burned suddenly in her cheeks and she lifted her chin.

"If that's your idea of a joke, Charles, it's in very poor taste." He was immediately contrite, and patted her arm possessively.

"I'm sorry, honey, I didn't go to upset you. I was just being silly. I thought you'd laugh. Imagine: my little Miss Audrey in love with a—well, actually, if you look at it, with a half-caste alien! Why, technically, that'd be miscegenation, wouldn't it?" She searched his face as if she had never seen him before.

"Why, Charles! I thought he was your friend," she whispered, and he smiled, his eyes pale in the light of the overhead fluorescent panels.

"Well, sure he is. Man saved my life, of course we're friends! You ask him, see what he says, next time you see him.

Which"—he consulted his ticket—"should be pretty soon, if
you two are going to get there on time." His raised hand
silenced her protest, and he commanded firmly, "Now, Audrey,
I don't want to hear any more about it. The matter's settled. Go
on and have a good time."

She made a last stab at it. "What about your dinner?"

"I'll grab something here, don't worry about me. You-all get
dinner out. Go on, now. Scoot!"

And, as she had always done, she obeyed her husband. Went
back to the apartment and reluctantly placed the call to Marik,
steeling her will to hope that he would not be in, or that he
would have good reason to refuse. Even said a little wordless
prayer that was destined not to be granted.

For Marik was there.

And he said yes.

Liat Jevic lay all too still in the muted light of her hospice
room, her eyes darkly circled in her pale face, her head and arm
thickly bandaged. The blanket scarcely moved with her breathing. Her parents, who had been spelling each other watching
over her, had been called away by a puzzling telecom message,
and the nurse who had volunteered to stay with her had stepped
into the ladies' room.

There was a skitter and scratch at the portal, and it hissed
open, admitting an intruder, whose shadow made a formless
dark blot on the polished floor. As quietly as possible, the
newcomer staggered slowly across the room toward the bed,
eyes fixed hypnotically on the dying child. Halfway there, the
intruder paused to listen for approaching footfalls. A voice. An
alarm.

But no one was there, neither in the room, nor outside in the
corridor. The intruder—and Liat—were alone. Satisfied, the
intruder crossed the last short distance to Liat's deathbed and
commenced the bloody work it had come for.

Later that evening, Waylan Stubbs leaned against the counter
in the men's dressing room, drinking a cold Ennel's. "What I'm
glad to see, is," he told Mancini the juggler, "I'm glad to see ol'

Sid, up and around. You're tougher than I thought, buddy!" He finished off the beer and picked up his guitar. Fingered a slow complicated series of chords, then hit a few really hot licks, showing off.

"Whoa," Mancini commented. Waylan waggled his brows.

"Yeah, I'm up and around, all right," Sid agreed over the music, "but I'm going to look like hell out there under the lights!" He dabbed stage makeup heavily on his face and neck. "Look at this! It'll take three kilos of Camo to cover these bruises!"

"Fifteen minutes, Sid," came the call through the portal.

"Yeah, thanks, kid," he yelled back, carefully blending the Camo under his jawline. "I was lucky, the other night."

Waylan, absently noodling through a few snatches of country tunes, lifted his head and gave his slow, fallen-angel smile. "Luckier than you know, m' friend," he drawled, "luckier than you know. And maybe luckier than you'll ever get again!" He continued to strum, gazing out the window that overlooked the park, when suddenly he flung down the guitar and grabbed his fringed-suede jacket, making for the door at a run.

"Where d'you think you're going, Waylan?" Sid demanded. "We go on in a couple minutes!"

"I just remembered somethin' I got to do," he called over his shoulder. "I'll be right back."

"*Waylan!*" Sid yelled, but Mancini shook his head.

"He's gone."

"What the hell's he doing? He's going to louse up the whole show!" He hit the wall com. "Get me George Mikhailaides, on the double! Damn Waylan's— Hello, George? Sid. We've got a problem. Stubbs just ran out of here like a bat out of hell, and I don't know when he'll be back! We've got to reschedule things! I want to put the kids on right after my intro, *then* Mancini, then move up the big production number, *then* Stubbs, and let the Droso come in for a big finish— I can't help the lighting plot, Ed's in charge of lighting, let him handle it!" He rang off, scowled at Mancini, and flopped into the nearest chair. "I'm getting too old for all this unrestrained holiday joy," he said.

"Whoa," Mancini answered somberly.

• • •

Ulrika Drac looked up in surprise when the chime rang. Except for the rare door-to-door solicitor for this charity or that, it almost never rang. She was not expecting anyone. She touched her braids self-consciously and glanced around the spare, immaculate room, then went to the portal and peeked into the spy-eye.

No one was there.

"Who is it there?" she called, but there was no answer. *Pranks*, she thought. *Some ill-bred adolescent playing games with my patience.* She started back into the room when the chime sounded again. Again, she peered through the spy-eye with the same result.

Nothing.

No one.

Annoyance crept up her chest and burned hotly on her thin cheeks. *If I get my both hands on this creature*, she told herself angrily, *I will teach him to ring chimes here! I will make ringing his foolish head!* She smoothed her braids and started once more for her bedroom when the chimes rang yet again, and she whirled, snatched open the door with a torrent of fury ready on her lips—and stifled a scream.

The grotesque, convoluted mask rode on a body misshapen and bulky, and huge gloves covered the ends of the arms, if arms they were. One hung so still it might have been empty, and the other was lifted up near the head, as if to strike.

In the first instant of shock, the intruder had shoved her inside, knocking her to the floor, and quickly shut the door behind them, even as running footsteps approached from the far end of the corridor, hesitated next door, and stopped. There was a discreet knocking. Murmured conversation.

"Who do you think you are, Mister Hallowed-Evening?" Ulrika demanded, scrambling to her feet in indignation. "Breaking into my home—dressed up like a witching person! What the nerves you have! Get out! Now!" The lifted hand swung with catlike speed, knocking her down again, and the mask turned full-face to her, glove at the lips.

"Shhh!" it said. Outside, the owner of the footsteps was now talking in a low voice to the people a few doors farther down. The Mask leaned close to the portal to listen, while Ulrika, blotting her bleeding lips, gained her feet in a frenzy of rage.

"Nobody strikes me!" she ground out, snatching up the heavy emergency bar of her window. "Nobody!"

She came at the intruder, the bar above her head, and her first swing barely missed the terrible mask, gouging a hole in the bulkhead. She didn't get a second chance. The intruder's left hand shot out and struck her throat with incredible force, breaking her trachea with one blow.

She began to strangle at once on her own blood, but her rage was so great that even in her death agony, she found strength to rip off the intruder's mask. Her eyes widened in horror as she slipped to the floor, hugging the mask to her flat chest. Her lips formed the word *You!*—and the intruder smiled.

"Peek-a-boo!" he said.

CHAPTER

XI

THE AMPHITHEATER, LOCATED on the far edge of the park, besides being a work of art by the eminent architect Harmon Ward III, was also a miracle of engineering. It was so designed that its seating was eminently comfortable, its acoustics impeccable, and its lighting superb.

Its backdrop was constructed of four thicknesses of clear polyplastex, a huge curved bulkhead that served as an integral part of the ship's hull. Besides serving as hull and sound shell, (and general escape hatch, in case of disaster), the backdrop gave the waiting audience a panoramic view of near space, with the luminous planets Jambi and Ildefor slowly revolving below. The steady, unwinking stars seemed near enough to touch.

Tonight, the amphitheater was crowded and festive, humming with conversations in many different languages, and rich with furs, jewels and expensive fabrics. Wisps of elegant fragrance trailed behind ladies of every species, and people jostled past each other pleasantly in the aisles, murmuring their apologies. If there seemed to be an excess of Security people scanning the crowds, no one seemed to notice. Warmlights mitigated the chill and harmlessly dissolved the occasional blown flurry.

"I can't believe Debi Swanson still looks so young!" Audrey commented to Marik, as she leafed through her program in the lee of Priyam Sharobi's broad-shouldered bulk. "Why, she was doing tri-D's when my mother was a girl, and just look at her! She hasn't aged a bit! Do you suppose these are old pictures?"

"No." Marik smiled. "From what I've read, Owdri, many actors volunteer for United Star Organization duty because it extends their careers. It has to do with the space/time factor. While planetside audiences are aging normally, the actors seem to stay young forever. The people back home age seven years, you see, while the onboard actors age only one month."

Audrey's face lit with understanding. "*That's* why, when people sign up for duty on *Hope*, their families come along as well. I wondered about that."

Oh, yes, Marik went on, enlarging upon the idea. It was no small compliment to be invited to join the staff of USS *Hope*, for it meant you were one of the galaxy's best; it also meant that—forsaking all planetside ties—your family would have to sign on with you, for the speed of the immense vessel played havoc with the passage of planetary time. A man could leave for a routine voyage and return to find in the place of his young family only a wizened grandmother, with her children grown and gone.

So the families of the entire crew, staff and support people of USS *Hope* came and stayed and worked in the hospital or on the farm or in the shops, and *Hope* became a little world unto herself.

"If a man wanted to, say . . . marry, for instance," he went on, coloring a bit, "well, then, he'd have to resign his commission and try to get posted to *Hope*, or some ship like her. That way, he could keep his family intact while getting on with his career."

She moistened her lips, and turned her eyes away. "Sounds like you've thought a good deal about it," she suggested lightly. "Who's the lucky girl?" Marik made no answer. When she turned to look at him again, he was watching with narrowed eyes the cold gleam of the twin planets, out beyond the sound shell, as they revolved against the merciless stars.

"I'm sorry," she whispered. "Oh, Dao, I'm truly sorry." He covered her hand with his own and pressed it gently.

Sharobi, sitting beside them in the twelfth row, center, grunted soundlessly to himself as he watched the two young people murmur together over their programs. What a mess it was, he mused. Here was the perfect couple: Audrey adorable in black velvet, turning shining eyes up to Marik, who, quite passably attractive in his winter dress blues, could see no one else. Marik had told Sharobi, in a rare confidential moment, that he and Audrey had decided to remain simply friends, forever. *Friends! Bosh and pift,* Sharobi thought sourly. *No real man—and Marik was nothing if not that—could be simply friends with a woman like Audrey Lassiter.* He rattled his program open with unnecessary force. *Pity she was already married,* he thought grumpily. And, then: *Too bad Lassiter hadn't zilched on ErthPast. Would have saved the lot of us worrying about it. But, no, there it was. Marik had to play hero again. Well—no help for it now.*

He scowled and riffled through his program, just as Audrey sat forward attentively, and he caught the barest scent of her perfume. For one moment, he shut his eyes and inhaled it, recalling another night, another lovely woman. Both gone, long ago. Then he shook his head and cleared his throat. *Acting like a regular jackass,* he thought, hoping no one had been watching him. *Must be getting old.* In the orchestra pit, the musicians were tuning up

On the opposite side of the lights, sound men manned their booths and gaffers rechecked switches and connections. The lighting crew had set their cues and were talking via headphones to the booth and backstage as well. Grips gave their sets a last once-over, and prop men 'set' their properties on the appropriate tables offstage. The stage crew retaped the crucial spikes for performers waiting in the Green Room below.

The cool air fairly trembled with excitement. Music swelled out of the pit, the heavy tasseled curtains closed with a massive whisper over the back of the stage, and the USO Holiday Show was on.

Bassett was sitting behind the desk at the nurses' station when Semmy came staggering up. It appeared very upset, making the Droso equivalent of moans and whimpers, and leaned against the desk.

"Why, Semmy, what's the matter, are you sick?" she asked, and it turned its faceted red eyes up at her soulfully.

"Nno. Badd," it whispered. "Awwful."

"What's awful? What's happened?" Bassett pursued, getting to her feet, and Semmy said, "Nno juuzz ffrr Zzemmi, evvrr 'ggainn. Aaii dzzobeid rruulzz—"

"What rules? What are you talking about, honey?" Bassett demanded, but just then Liat's parents re-entered her room. There was a instant's silence, then a piercing scream and the heavy, dull sound of Ferri Jevic's senseless body hitting the polished floor.

Sid Behrman, the M.C., was at his best tonight, giving it all he had, Sharobi thought. Even he'd had to smile at the few jokes he understood.

"Now, imagine we're on Grukkining," Sid told the expectant audience, "way out in the outback, right? and these three Gruks, they're friends, they're always making deals together. This time, Chon is selling this horse.

"So he says to his friend, Hal, 'Hey, *tchum*, I'll sell you this horse for twenty-five credits!' And Hal buys. So later that day, Hal goes by Rin's house, and Rin says, 'Hey, that's a good-looking horse, Hal. What d'you want for him?'

"So Hal says, 'I'll give him to you for fifty credits.'

"Rin says, 'I'll take it.' So he buys, now he's got the horse.

"Well, next morning, here comes Chon, sees the horse in Rin's stable, and offers him seventy-five credits for it, and Rin sells. So now Chon has the horse again.

"And it goes on like this for a few days, and the price keeps going up, until a Xhole from the city comes by. And he offers Rin four hundred credits flat for the horse, and he sells it. Whereupon the other two guys, Chon and Hal, jump all over him.

"'You damn fool!' they holler. 'What'd you go and do that for? *We was making lots of money on that horse!*'"

The audience responded with good-natured laughter and the obligatory applause, and after the noise settled down, Marik leaned over to Audrey with a puzzled frown and whispered, "What did he mean, *'making money on the horse'?*" which started Audrey giggling all over again. People nearby joined in her infectious laughter, and on stage, Sid beamed. *Damn, I'm good!* he thought, *they're* still *laughing,* and launched into his next story.

It was promising to be one of Sid's best, when Sharobi's com signaled. He spoke under his breath, listened, then leaned past Audrey to tell Marik urgently, "It's the Jevic child! Let's go!" The three left in the middle of Sid's performance, and Alan Wimet watched them from the Green Room audience monitor, wondering who had found what, and what ultimately would have to be done about it.

Peds was quiet and dark, as usual, except for Liat Jevic's room, where an emotional Ferri and Noln Jevic, along with Bassett, Semmy, and Ellie Giambone, the special, were crowding around Liat's bed. Both Mr. and Mrs. Jevic were in tears, and Audrey prepared herself for the worst, but as the group shifted, she found herself totally unprepared for what she saw.

For instead of a moribund child lying flat between the sheets, Liat was sitting up in her parents' close embrace, her cheeks showing a tinge of healthy green and her eyes bright.

"Hi, Owdri, hi, Pri—I mean, servant," she caroled. "Look at me, I'm better! Umma came in and saw me sitting up and she screamed real loud and fainted! She did! Really! Right there in the middle of the floor! You should have seen it!" Audrey caught her hands and kissed them, her eyes welling, as Sharobi whipped out his 'scope and quickly scanned the child. Scanned again. Turned slowly, putting it away, and smiled his infrequent smile.

"Well, Mr. and Mrs. Jevic, we'll want to do some more testing, of course, but according to my scanner, your daughter seems to be completely cured of her Ensi-vo."

"Oh, thank T'ath!" Ferri wept, holding Liat close. "Thank T'ath!"

"But—how?" Noln Jevic asked brokenly. "When we left here half an hour ago, she was all but dead! What happened?

What kind of miracle did you people do? Great Tadae, I owe you—"

"*Aii* ddid!" Semmy piped up proudly, its right foreleg snapping up to its face in excitement. "*Zzemuii* nnot bbad! Ddid gguud! Pplaii *ddokkttor!*"

"It's true," Liat assisted gaily, pointing to a small hematoma on her throat. "Semmy stuck me in the neck with his nose-needle, and I felt really cold and bad at first, and I kind of fainted, but he held my hand, and then after a minute I got warm again and now I feel real good! Can I get out of bed now? Just for a little while? Just to the playroom?" Every face in the room turned to Semmy, and Noln Jevic's was dark with anger.

"Do you mean to tell me," he began in a rage, pointing at the cringing Semmy, "that this—this *creature!*—this *insect!*—came near my baby?—after I made my wishes abundantly clear? Well, you've done it now, Sharobi!! I'm going to call my lawyer! You have violated not only *my* civil rights, but Liat's as well! I'll have your—"

As he began shouting, Sharobi sauntered up to him, with a wry smile, put an arm around his shoulder, and dusted imaginary lint off his lapels. "Let me explain something to you, Mr. Jevic," he said, scarcely above a whisper. "We had done all we could for your daughter, and it wasn't enough." *Brush, brush.* "She had about three hours to live, until this young Droso"—*brush, brush*—"who had more courage than the rest of us put together"—*brush, brush*—"took it upon himself to come in here, against your will"—*brush, brush*—"and administer the Droso Solution, so he could save his little friend's life." He straightened Noln's lapels meticulously, pulled him close, and talked directly into his face. "But don't worry, Jevic. Don't fret another minute. We can fix it for you. We'll make it right again." He spoke over his shoulder. "Bassett, get me a sample of NCVO-834. It's in the safe. Use my code."

She hesitated. "Priyam, are you . . . Are you sure you want *NCVO-834?*"

"Positive. And promptly." His sour smile reappeared as he turned to Noln. "We'll remedy the problem for you right away."

Bassett returned with the hypo and Sharobi placed it against Liat's thin arm, staring at Noln Jevic with eyes like granite shards. "Now, you have a choice to make, Jevic. You say you don't want interference from the Droso, fine. Well, Semmy, here, didn't know that. He just wanted Liat to live to see her grandchildren. So he cured her. And that seems to annoy you, sir. So I have a solution to your outrage.

"I have here in this hypo a specimen of concentrated Ensi-vo virus, guaranteed to kill Liat in less than twenty-four hours. Since you are unhappy that she is cured, we'll just put her back on her deathbed for you! All I have to do is push this stud, and she's good as gone! No problem. Just say the word. What'll it be?"

"No!" Jevic shouted, snatching Liat protectively into his arms again. "What's the matter with you, are you crazy? You think I'd let you kill my child? *She's well, for T'ath sake, why would I want her sick again?*" He blinked as his own words sank in; then he buried his face against Liat's hair, and holding her fiercely against him, broke into big, heaving sobs. Ferri encircled them tenderly with both arms.

"Congratulations," Sharobi murmured, and gave the hypo back to a relieved Bassett. "Put this thing away." He waved the rest of them out, leaving only Giambone to stay with the Jevics. As they gained the corridor, Marik commented that Sharobi's bluff had worked.

"But what would you have done if it hadn't?" he asked.

"Probably admitted Jevic himself for psychological evaluation," Sharobi mused. "But I'm glad it wasn't necessary."

"Mmee, ttoo," Semmy enthused, its wings an excited blur. "Lliatt well, nnow."

Audrey stroked Semmy's head. "Yes, she is, thanks to you. You really did save her life, Semmy. What a wonderful thing to do!"

"Yes, an adolescent practicing medicine—in my hospital!— and without a license, too," Sharobi agreed sourly. "That's wonderful, all right. You're lucky I don't call Security!"

"Nnott withoutt laizznzz," Semmy corrected smugly. "Will

havv, one ddayy. Aii mmeerlii ppremmatturr. Bai effew yeerzz."

"So will you become a physician, then, Semmy?" Marik wondered aloud, trying to keep a straight face, and the great red eyes fixed themselves on him.

"Yezz, Aii will," it answered, and made the buzzing equivalent of a delighted chuckle. "Hemattologizzt!"

Their laughter was interrupted by a beaming Giambone, who came hurrying past them down the corridor from Liat's room. "She's hungry," she announced.

"She's *well*," Audrey answered.

Sharobi consulted his ticket. "Did you tell me something about not wanting to miss the Droso concert?" he asked Marik, who quickly checked his own ticket.

"You're right. I've got to get back, I gave PprumBurr my word. Coming?"

"No, I'll stick around. Not often I witness resurrection at Christmas time."

"Dao—would you mind if I stayed, too? For a little while? I'd like to be with Liat."

"No, of course not, Owdri. Make yourself comfortable, I won't be long."

"Take your time."

Some vagrant thought, some ominous mental scent nagged at him, and he took her hands in his own, "Don't leave, Owdri. Promise me. No matter what."

"I'll be here," she promised. "No matter what."

The children were ecstatic. They had opened the show to riotous applause, done several Erthlik and Sauvagi show tunes and some Christmas carols in their appealing young voices, and finished with two choruses of The Bandy Gruk Shuffle, which included a clever choreography as well. They clattered down to the dressing rooms, babbling excitedly among themselves, and Angelo hugged each one individually, even Gino, who pretended disdain.

"Hey! Angelo! Take it easy on the suit, okay?" he protested, brushing his tunic sleeve fastidiously. "I'm not no kid!"

Angelo gave him an affectionate slap on the side of his head as he smiled beatifically at the others. "I was so proud," he said. "You sound like a buncha angels! You *look* like a buncha angels!"

"Pick up your feet, guys, it's gonna get deep in here." Gino advised the others in an undertone. "Me, I'm goin' out for a smoke."

Waylan Stubbs came running backstage, sweating and breathless, only four minutes before his cue, splashed his face with cold water, and straightened his clothing. "How's the house?" he asked Mancini, who pursed his lips.

"We got a live one tonight. Sid did his horse routine. Local kids sounded great. I'm always good. Where'd you go, man?" Stubbs ran his fingers through his fair hair and smiled his familiar fallen-angel smile.

"I saw a lady I knew, who needed taking care of." He picked up his guitar and sat against the edge of the dressing table.

"*Fifteen minutes before curtain time?* Whou. She must be something special!"

Waylan bent his head, fingering a few dissonant minor chords. "You know how there's some women, just don't know enough?" he asked after a minute, and Mancini lifted his brows.

"Oh, yeah! I married one, once."

Waylan Stubbs raised his head. "Well, Pete, my man, I'm afraid this one knew *too* much."

"Whoa," Mancini said.

The Jevics were still with Liat and Priyam Sharobi, and Audrey found herself wishing she had gone back to the show with Marik. She was silly, she thought, to have stayed. She was close to Liat, but she wasn't family, after all. She considered going back to the show alone, but she'd promised Dao she'd stay here. Finally, she sauntered aimlessly down to the lounge at the end of the corridor. It was abandoned and completely dark but for several unshuttered ports that admitted a faint wash of starlight. She stepped in and crossed to the viewport, entranced as always by the uncountable numbers and colors of stars. *What a wonderful painting this would make*, she mused. *I'll bet Gordon Garrison would be willing to show it at the gallery*. She was mentally composing a note to him when she was distracted by a faint sound around the near corner. She turned. "Who is it?" she asked. "Is someone there?" There was no answer, just the brush of an uneven footfall. She stepped closer. "Who's there?" she asked again.

All at once, seemingly from nowhere, the horrible mask filled her vision, and before she could cry out, a hand like iron cut off the sound. She tasted blood from a cut lip, her eyes wide, as her assailant slowly removed both the mask and his hand from her mouth.

"Charles!" she breathed. "You! Where is your hoverchair? Where did you get that—that terrible—*thing?*"

He tossed it into a corner. "It belongs to the killer. Now, pay attention, Audrey. I came to get you out of here. Your life is in danger."

She shook her head, soothing her lip with her fingertips. "But-but, *how?* From whom? And *why?*"

Charles leaned close. "You know how you were afraid Marik might be the killer?" he asked. She nodded. "Well, we got in some new evidence. You were right. He came along with you tonight for one purpose only: to do you in. So—I came to save you—again." He took her hand clumsily. "Let's go."

She shook her head unbelievingly. "But, Charles, it can't be! Not Dao!" she said numbly. "Besides, I have to stay here. I promised. He said not to leave, no matter what."

"Of course he'd say that, honey," Charles explained patiently. "It's easier to get at you when he knows where you are. Do you know where he went?"

"N-no, I—" she stammered, suddenly cautious about telling him. She couldn't think why. "I'm so confused, Charles, I— Look, he'll be coming back. He promised me."

"Then we'd better not be here when he does. Come on." And

Charles Lassiter led his reluctant wife away through the quiet
late-night corridors. No one saw them go.

Marik made it back to the theater just as the Droso came on.
The house lights dimmed, the spotlights came up, and there
was a benevolent hum as five Droso came onstage from either
side, flying high and very slowly. Their hairy thoraxes were
powdered with silver dust, and their wings were painted with
translucent colors that shimmered in the spotlights.

Five more Droso, one of whom was PprumBurr, slowly
descended from behind the proscenium arch. These five were
dusted with gold, their wings outlined with some clear,
sparkling substance. The audience burst into spontaneous
applause at the sight of them. Behind them, presumably
hanging from the catwalks above and trailing down to the stage
itself, were fifteen gossamer lengths of the same silk the Droso
used to spin their treetop homes. Ten of the panels were white,
four were gray. The remaining panel was black.

Each of the five golden Droso took an end of the colored silk
and, with their wings providing the music, they performed a
sprightly aerial dance to 'God Rest Ye Merry, Gentlemen,'
weaving in and out with their silks as they flew. Next, they
offered a slower, more sedate pavane, with more intricate
weaving, to 'What Child Is This?' The fabric lengths were
drawing up, forming complex hitches, half-hitches and larks,
starting to make a familiar pattern.

PprumBurr kept glancing Marik's way, almost desperately,
and he wondered why. What was the Droso trying to tell him,
and how, and why did he not simply speak up?

They danced through 'Ode to Joy.' The beautiful silk
weaving was almost complete now, and absently, Marik
thought that it reminded him of nothing so much as a—

A *bun* tapestry!

He sat bolt upright. A *bun* tapestry was an Einai creation,
made only for the Emperor, or *Domne*. Marik's tapestry, back
at the Summer Palace, depicted the *Lei alden Han*, the Lay of
the Han, which was the Emperor's theme. He quickly read the
weaving onstage and realized that this *bun* was not a musical

selection at all, but several crude Einai words, knotted into a message unrecognizable to anyone but himself.

PprumBurr was sending him a coded message!

He made out the words 'two' and 'production,' then tried again. The weaving of a *bun* was difficult, to say the least, even for Einai. T'ath only knew how long it had taken fifteen determined Droso to learn even the crude technique demonstrated here. He tried again and his hearts sank. 'Killer,' it said, and 'put' and 'level.' He made out the word 'hurry,' in black, which color gave it greater significance.

And there was the word 'bombs.'

Stay calm, Dao, he told himself, trying again. *Stay calm.* He started putting words together, his mind racing. Then it came together, all at once.

Killer. Put. Bombs. Production. Level. *Hurry.*

There was only one more word, and when he read it, Marik's blood ran cold. It was the name of the killer.

Waylan Stubbs slipped into Alan Wimet's office without a sound and thumbed the portal shut behind him.

"What've you got, cowboy?" Wimet said.

"It's serious, boss. Looks like our boy stole some stuff from the ammo dump. We got two explosive devices, complete with timers, missin' and unaccounted for."

Wimet swore. "We got any idea where he squirreled them away?"

"Nope."

Wimet swore again. "He's good, you've got to give it to him. He hasn't given us a shred of evidence to hang him on. Where's Mancini?"

"He was on Marik, at the USO show, last time I checked." He pulled a flat plastex case out of an inner pocket and consulted it. "Nope. Looks like right now, he's high-tailin' it for the lifts. Prob'ly still followin' Marik." His face, like his eyes, went blank and still. "Uh-oh! Know what I think?"

"Yeah! Marik's found out where the bombs are! Let's go!"

They left at a dead run.

• • •

Marik stepped out of the lift into another world. The Production level was in night mode, to coincide with Earthscape's twenty-four-hour day. The farm-year stood at late autumn, which, over the next two weeks, would melt into a warm, lush spring. The constant demand for fresh food on *Hope* allowed Production no time for the luxury of winter.

Unless I find the bombs, Marik told himself, *Hope will have no time for anything, ever again.*

A half-moon rode in a cloudy sky, silvering the barn roofs, and corn shocks stood black and silent as Senn *tipis.* Crisp oxygen-rich air smelled of wood smoke and apples, and owls swooped noiselessly over fields nubbly with pumpkins, hunting mice. Somewhere among this bucolic peace, a killer had planted a bomb, scattered terror, sown wholesale death. Where had he hidden it? In the barns? Among the corn shocks? Not likely. Under the pumpkins? Up the flue? It was a big level, Marik realized with a sinking feeling at the pit of his stomach. It would take time to find it, and time was what he had least of, just now. *Think!*

Warm light and busy metal noises leaked through the windows of the big machine sheds, where the night shift was tuning up and polishing to be ready for spring planting. Would he have set them there? *Think, Dao! Where would a bomb do the most damage? If I were mad,* he asked himself, *where would I set a bomb to go off?*

And then he knew. The place where a well-placed bomb could do most damage was in the Digester Building. With the giant methane storage tanks at the killer's disposal, the bomb would act as merely a percussion cap for a larger catastrophe. Exploding those tanks would blow the entire ship wide open. He began to run.

Even this far away, Marik, racing at breakneck speed down the frosty road, could hear the distant, ceaseless sound of the pumps sluicing the ship's wastes into the huge digesters.

The waste digesters were Part One of the most important complexes on the ship. Housed in their own self-contained building, which abutted the ship's hull, they recycled the waste products of all nine levels of the ship, with the exception of radioactive and hazardous medical waste. These were routinely stowed in shielded torps and boosted into the nearest sun.

All other waste had a much more interesting fate. Funneled into the digesters, it was composted anaerobically to extract methane, which was stored in two tanks for alternating use by Environmental Control, since gas was clean, easy to handle and easily renewable.

The remaining slurry, having been composted anaerobically as far as possible, was mixed with grass and shrub trimmings, dead leaves and wood chips, courtesy of the Parks Department, and was composted again in the presence of oxygen inside special bins made of metal water pipes. The heat thereby engendered was donated to Environmental Control as well, and the final, fully composted result, now a sterilized and superior grade of topsoil, was spread on the fields for use in growing next season's crops.

The problem tonight was the methane tanks.

Marik struggled with the heavy doors of the Digester Building, for his shoulder was still weak, and had barely shoved them open when he heard running footsteps on the tier above. He merged into the shadows, thinking the killer might have come back, and was relieved when Wimet called, "Marik! Marik, you there?"

"Down here," he shouted back. "By the storage tanks." He examined every inch of the tanks and found nothing; got down for a close look at the bottom and saw, almost obscured by the shadows, a small, familiar black box with a digital readout on the face of it. *We have it!* The time stood at four minutes, thirty-nine seconds, and counting. He reached for the bomb, even as Wimet clattered down the metal ladder, but it was set back a few crucial centimeters too far. The killer was taller than he, with longer arms. He tried to get beneath the tank, but it was too close to the deck for him to squeeze under. Too, the rigid conformer compressed his chest, cutting off his breath. Wimet stooped beside him, and behind Wimet—Marik glanced up, surprised—was Waylan Stubbs, smiling angelically.

"What've you got?" Wimet demanded, and Marik stretched a little farther, reaching for the bomb, with no result.

"It's a bomb," he gritted. "Set to go off in about four minutes."

Wimet whirled on Waylan. "Sound the alarm. Red alert, all decks." Waylan ran. Marik pulled back a scraped arm and changed his position. No go. In a last, desperate attempt, he tore off the conformer and, face contorted, teeth bared, strained every fiber toward the black box. He was almost there—his fingers touched it!—slipped away—regained it—and with a superhuman effort, tore it free! The alarm sounded its repetitious note, and, over and over, the computer's calm voice announced, *Red alert. Red alert. All personnel to the lifeboats. Personnel in the Malls report by species to the theater. Please make all possible speed. Red alert—*

"Three minutes, twenty-seven seconds," Marik panted, turning off the triggering device and tossing the harmless bomb to Wimet.

"Damn!" the Security Chief said. "That was close. What about the other one? Did you—"

"The *other* one?" Marik demanded, and then he remembered. PprumBurr had said *bombs*, plural, not *bomb*, singular. There was another bomb, ticking away, somewhere down here. "Oh, great T'ath!" he muttered, diving flat on the deck to peer under the tanks. He could see clearly the silhouettes of both, and while this one was clean and smooth and rounded, the other—

"There it is!" With Wimet and Waylan close behind, he scrambled around to the other tank, which stood directly against the hull, and flopped belly-down on the chill floor. The small, square package of death was snugged tightly against its ventral surface, well out of reach. Marik jammed his arm and shoulder as far under it as possible, pushing with knees and feet, skinning his shoulder blade and raising a green weal on his forehead. His fingers barely grazed it. He tried several times more, but it was no use. The bomb, inexorably counting off the seconds, was just too far back.

"Let me try!" Wimet took his place and stretched as far as he could for the bomb, but while he had a longer reach, he was not as lean as Marik, and couldn't get to it. "Waylan, give it a try."

The guitarist shook his head. "I'm shorter than both of y'all," he clipped. "We better face it, gentlemen, we're not gonna get *to* it. We better get the hell out of here while the gettin's good!"

Wimet met Marik's eyes and the alien nodded curtly. "He's right. She's going to blow, and there's no way we can stop it." He stared with narrowed eyes at the display that read, two minutes, ten seconds, thinking fast; and when he looked up, his eyes were a blaze of gray light. "Mister Wimet, I need a G-suit, rigged with manual thrusters, double time! Waylan, get out of here as fast as you can!"

Waylan made as if to argue, but Wimet gestured with an imperative thumb, and he ran. Wimet grabbed a suit and helmet from a nearby emergency locker and thrust them at Marik. "What the hell are you doing?"

"I'm going to blow a hole in the side of *Hope*," Marik said. "Now you get out of here, too! And seal every port between this tank and everything else!"

Wimet began backing off. "You're out of your mind, Marik!" he accused. "You're going to kill yourself, trying this!"

"*Run!*" Marik shouted, and reluctantly, Wimet ran.

Even as he programmed the first bomb to go off an instant before the second, Marik could hear one after another of the heavy hatches being sealed behind him. He hoped Wimet and Waylan Stubbs would get away safely. He hoped his plan would work. He hoped he would survive.

He attached the bomb firmly to the hull next to the second tank and took cover as best he could. If his plan worked, the first bomb would go off and open the Digester Building to space an instant before the methane tank blew. With any luck, the near-vacuum of the cosmos would literally suck the explosion outside the ship, where it could do no harm.

On the other hand, he told himself, as he watched the last few seconds squiggle down to null, if he were wrong he would soon be awfully dead. At least, he thought, and the thought was a tender comfort, at least Owdri is safe. At least that.

Then there was a tremendous double explosion that blew

flaming methane, concussion, enormous shards of shrapnel, and Dao Marik himself, out of the ship and into the cold, uncaring void beyond.

Audrey Lassiter felt far from safe. Edging along after Charles in the semi-darkness of the ship's red alert status, she realized that no one else was on the streets. She could see from the overpass, as they hurried toward Transport, that everyone in Earthscape was already at the theater, each belted into an escape seat with plastex canopies firmly secured. Their Life-Glows burned bright blue above their heads. Jambi and Ildefor rotated slowly beyond the plastex shield before them.

"Charles, the alert has sounded! Something's dreadfully wrong! Shouldn't we be seated with the others?"

"Be quiet, Audrey," he snapped, gripping her hand painfully tight. "We're getting off the ship *now!* I'm taking a lifeboat and getting out of here!"

She tugged him back, making him stumble. "Oh, but you can't! The Senn—"

Charles whirled and backhanded her with his splinted hand, and some objective part of his tortured mind saw what was happening, as if in slow motion. He saw his own hand swing and strike, her face lift and turn; he appreciated the way her hair fanned out and around like silk as she spun, and the gleam of half-light that ran down her bare arm. He heard the muffled thud as she fell, and the whisper of her dress, dropping in soft folds about her. She did not move. Leaning down, he started to pick her up, but someone in the darkness whispered hoarsely, "Lassiter."

He looked up and was chilled to see a shadowy figure standing a few yards off in the access corridor. It was wearing the Krafcik death mask.

One dungeon, Tom Paige thought, was much like another. He had once been a prisoner on Eisernon in a dungeon much like this one, except that on Eisernon, he'd had no company, human or otherwise. He kicked at his latest visitor, which squealed and viciously attacked his boot, and Kodi dispatched it with one well-placed stomp.

"Are they edible?" he asked wistfully, and Salman shook his head. "Not for hu— er, not for us," he corrected quickly. "The guards will bring bread and water again this evening."

"Sizzling pan-fried trout," Esme breathed, "with asparagus and raw tarangi."

"Lasagna," Theresa echoed wanly, "antipasto, and a bottle of Dago red. And cannoli for dessert."

"Are you sure you can't eat these things?" Kodi pursued, picking up the small rodent by the tail, and Salman advised against trying it.

"Great hospitality here on Ildefor, Your Highness," Paige commented, his chains rattling against the slimy stone wall, and Prince Salman sat straighter.

"I understand your discomfort, Doctor. But think of this," he encouraged. "It has only been one day of imprisonment. As soon as my father is well, your star people will set off the fireworks, Hamid Vizier will see them, and we will go free! What a wonderful thing! My father alive and well! And all of us free!"

"*If* Artie remembers the fireworks," Esme put in from where she sat.

"*If?*" Prince Salman's face went pale. "We cannot have *if*, Nurse Esme! We must have *when*! Doctor, did you not tell your friend that we will die if he does not remember?"

"Oh, yeah, sure!" Paige assured him, more cheerfully than he felt. "Good old Artie wouldn't let us down! As soon as your father is out of danger, he'll set off the best pyrotechnics we've got! Guaranteed!"

"Good!" The Prince sighed, settled himself as comfortably as possible, and closed his eyes. "Meanwhile, I shall take a nap."

While I, on the other hand, Paige told himself glumly, *shall worry.*

Then the contingent of guards appeared at the door, flanking a black-garbed man with a scimitar, and Paige realized that he had very good reason to worry.

● ● ●

Marik was tumbling wildly, trying to avoid the largest chunks of spinning shrapnel around him by using his belt thrusters. So far, by luck and the grace of T'ath, it had worked—as had his scheme to save *Hope*—but he found the big ship growing smaller by the second. That was the measure, he knew, of how fast he was plummeting away from her. Pretty soon, unless he could manage to reverse his course, he wouldn't be able to see her at all.

He applied a quick pressure on the thrusters as a sharp piece of external hull passed him so close it scraped his sleeve, and another as a loose bolt whirled past at eye level, barely avoiding its shattering his faceplate. *Keep your eyes open, Marik*, he told himself. It wouldn't do to let down his defenses now, and be done in by a mindless piece of metal.

He used his thrusters in constant avoidance maneuvers for what felt like an eternity, and felt them begin to weaken, even as the debris thinned to almost nothing. He tried them again, and they failed him. He found himself floating free, without power.

At least he was alive, he told himself. Where there's life—

He could see the ring of Senn scouts surrounding *Hope*, and wondered if they knew he was there. *I hope not*, he thought. *They've promised to blow out of the sky anyone who tried to leave Hope.* He wondered if his unorthodox mode of departure would mitigate their decision, and decided not. The Senn, once they made up their minds, were implacable. If they saw him, he didn't stand a chance.

On the other hand, if someone didn't see him, and soon, he was dead, anyway. Either way, his prospects were dim. Therefore he was inordinately grateful when he saw, at a great distance, a military skimmer detach itself from *Hope* and start toward him at top speed.

Gino was leaning against the bulkhead, enjoying the last few drags of his cigarette, when Crow Dog and Walking-About-Early saw him. He tossed away the butt and leaned back into the shadows, but not before Crow Dog shouted, "Hey! Rat! Stay right there! I want to talk to you!"

"Yeah," Walking-About-Early yelled. "What happened to our wallets?"

"In your ear, pussycat!" Gino retorted, taking off down the alleyway with both Senn in hot pursuit. He gained the overpass and made for Transport, but halfway there he stumbled over something soft and yielding, like a velvet pillow, lying in the middle of the dark corridor and sprawled full length. He felt around. It was the body of a woman. "Uh-oh!" he mumbled. "Now I got trouble!"

"Who are you?" Charles Lassiter, standing over his wife's inert body, there in the dark corridor, demanded of the masked thing.

"Your conscience, Lassiter," the Mask answered. "I've finally caught up with you. I didn't know where you'd gone, or even what you looked like, but I knew *she* was with you, so I followed her scent. Her fragrance. Get away from her."

Lassiter laughed. It came out as a wolf's snarl. "Another one, huh? Miss Audrey's been real busy, hasn't she? All right, you want her? By all means, take her. But understand, she's already been had! You're getting an alien's leavings!"

The Mask swore roundly and swung at him, and Lassiter attacked him with all the fury of a madman, punching and beating his opponent to the floor. He straddled his chest and tore off the mask. "Where did you get my mask, you imposter?" he demanded, throttling him, and Garrett panted, "In the lounge . . . someone left it there. I knew it had to be you . . . because it had her scent on it. . . ."

"I'm innocent," Gino told them from the main corridor, but they didn't hear him. "I didn't have nothin' to do wit' this lady here!" The Senn were getting closer, and he made a decision. Hide in the open. Get into a fight, they'll never see you.

"Too bad you figured that out, hero," Lassiter giggled down at Garrett. "Like they say down on the farm, it never pays to smell too good." He raised his splinted hand to deliver the death blow, when Gino dove at him from nowhere, pummeling him with all his might. Charles recovered and slammed him reflexively into the bulkhead, knocking him cold. He would have finished him off, but there were running footsteps approaching, and he hesitated.

Then from somewhere many levels below, there came the sound of a double explosion, and, forgetting Garrett, Audrey, and the boy entirely, Charles Lassiter leaped up and galloped crazily down the corridor to the hangar deck, laughing insanely to himself.

CHAPTER

XII

"YOU LIED TO us, infidel," Hamid Vizier said, as the five of them—Paige, Esme, Theresa, Kodi and Prince Salman—stood in the public square before the assembled troops. Common folk leaned out of windows and perched on nearby walls for a better view of the executions, and the square was jammed with people bearing torches and placards decrying alien assassinations of local Caliphs. The black-garbed man swung his scimitar in a flashy display of deadly dexterity, drawing a smattering of applause from the crowd.

"That man is dis*gus*ting," Esme said disapprovingly to the soldiers tying her hands behind her. "Showing off like that!"

"Shhh!" Kodi advised, wincing at the bite of the ropes. "Keep it down, huh, Esme? We've got enough trouble."

"Well, he could *hurt* somebody!" Kodi made no answer, but simply shut his eyes and groaned.

"Hamid Vizier, loyal soldiers, my people," Prince Salman said loudly, "my honored father is aboard the *Hope* ship and will be back among us shortly, completely cured—" A chorus of derision from the crowd drowned him out, and they waved the placards up and down menacingly. In back of the crowd, someone started a rhythmic chant, and people began to join in. It sounded like "Kill the aliens!"

Voldi, making his way unobtrusively to the front of the crowd with Sethi and Kedar close behind him, handed Kedar his placard, which read 'Death to Alien Satans!'

"I'm sure the lizard will make a speech before he beheads them," he muttered. "Remember the plan: I'll grab him and cause a riot, and you two release Esme and the others. The horses?"

"Saddled and ready, Voldi," Sethi reported, making sure his dagger slid easily from its sheath. "Just beyond the wall."

"You're throwing away your life, young master," Kedar gritted, "and ours into the bargain."

"What good is life without adventure?" Voldi whispered. "And what better adventure— Hsst!"

The Grand Vizier held up both hands and the clamor of the crowd died quickly to nothing.

"I, Hamid Vizier," he proclaimed, "do hereby declare that these aliens—with the complicity of His Royal Highness Prince Salman—have conspired to do away with our illustrious Caliph, Ishaq ibn Muhammad al-Ghazi, and take over our planet Ildefor!"

"That's a lie!" Paige shouted, and one of the guards hit him in the mouth. There was an angry roar from the people, and the soldiers brandished their swords, their horses dancing nervously. When the noise died down a bit, the Vizier continued:

"These alien Satans promised that our illustrious Caliph— may Allah grant him a thousand years reign!—would be cured on their accursed ship, and that they would send a sign in the sky when it was accomplished. But there has been no sign! They have killed him—or worse!" Another roar, another escalation in frenzy, Paige noted. The Vizier was working the crowd with the best of them.

"Look at the sky," he went on. "Do you see a sign?" *No!* shouted the people. "A mark?" *Nothing!* "Anything but the selfsame stars our forefathers steered by? They have lied!" *Ya Allah, they have killed the Caliph!* There was a wordless, sustained roar of fury, and Prince Salman turned to the others.

"I'm afraid all is lost," he said sadly. "I am very sorry."

A commotion began in front of them. A man in a sand-colored burnoose leaped up and tackled the Vizier, while two others shoved past the guards and started slashing the prisoners' bonds. But the soldiers had the sheer weight of numbers, and the bold coup was over before it had begun. It took three guards to wrest the Vizier from the determined grasp of—Esme gasped—Voldi, who was quickly wrestled to the ground, bound and roughly hustled off to the dungeon.

"Voldi! Darling!" she screamed. "Thank you for trying!" His white smile was the last she saw of him as they shoved him headlong down the stairs.

"The thing is, you see," Lassiter said to no one in particular as he wove the skimmercraft expertly through the cloud of debris, "a skimmer is real easy to pilot. Nothing to it. Why, I got my first license when I was only fourteen years old. Are you listening, Marik? Can you hear me out there?"

"Sir, we have a transmission from an unauthorized skimmer," *Hope*'s starboard watch reported, and First Officer Tong snapped, "Hostiles?"

"No, ma'am, but there's something awful funny about it. Sounds like somebody's been blown out of the ship, and somebody else went after 'em to finish 'em off. Request your monitor, ma'am."

"Affirmative, starboard watch. Stand by and copy any and all transmissions. Mister Coto, alert search-and-rescue—"

"Negative," Captain Kris cut in. "The Senn quarantine forbids vessels leaving this ship until Te-o-tun-hko's killer is found and punished."

"But Captain," Tong argued in her reasonable undertone, "there's a man lost out there! And someone's trying to kill him!"

"My responsibility is to the ship and its personnel, Miss Tong," Kris said. "Anyone outside her is there by his own choice, and I must respect that choice—and it's consequences. As you were."

There was an interlude of static, and Marik's voice came in, faint but clear. "Charles. Is that you?"

"It surely is." He giggled uncontrollably. "I've come to challenge you to a duel, Mister Marik. A matter of honor, sir. For sleeping with my wife, as a matter of fact. I'm sure you understand." He laughed again and then sobered. "Your choice of weapons, sir. Whatever you've got. I choose this skimmer."

"Charles, Owdri has always been faithful to you. For her sake, you should know that."

"I had to borrow a skimmer to get my first license, you know. We couldn't afford a skimmer of our own. My family were poor folk. Tenant farmers. Hat in hand, backdoor folk. Like that."

"She's been terribly brave and decent, Charles," Marik insisted. "Nothing ever happened between us. Nothing."

Charles made a slight adjustment on his panel and sat back. "Now, Mister Marik, let's don't tell lies right before we meet our Maker, shall we? I know my Audrey. You think I haven't seen how she looks at you? She never looked at me like that in my life." His voice dropped to a confidential whisper. "She doesn't know what we know, does she? She doesn't even *know*!"

Marik watched the boat come closer by the second, expecting at any moment to be vaporized by its guns. "What do we know, Charles? Say it aloud. What's our big secret here?"

"Why, that you're really not a man, after all! I know who you are! You're the spirit of evil, who kept me from my martyrdom! I had it made, and you took me down off the cross! You think I don't recognize you?" He banked the skimmer slightly, trying to get a clear shot. "You know," he added in a casual tone, "it's really hard to line up on you. I don't suppose you'd hold still for me."

"I'm afraid not," Marik demurred. A large piece of metal hull plate slowly toppled his way and he grabbed it and cartwheeled with it, the stars swinging dizzily around him. Anything to keep him out of the direct line of Charles's guns.

"I didn't think so. Her brothers, Oliver and Roland, they wouldn't stand still, either. Took me and four Krail ten minutes shooting to bring 'em down. They sure were feisty. 'Course, Miss Audrey was, too, till I broke her stubbornness. Whole family was." He giggled again. "Even her fiancé, that Steven fella."

Realization hit Marik at the pit of his stomach. "It was you?" he said. "You turned them in to the Krail?"

"Well, hell, Mister Marik," came the puzzled drawl. "I had

to! How else was I going to get Miss Audrey, fella like me? I always wanted her, from the first time I saw her, riding by so clean and fine and pretty on a shiny bay mare, and me standing there with manure on my boots. You know what hurt most? She smiled down at me. Real sweet and nice. It made me hate her, can you understand that? And want her real bad, too. I knew I had to have her. Control her. Be her master.

"But see, we didn't have any family, or money, or social position. Only way to get her was to eliminate the competition, doesn't that make sense? And the Krail even paid me to do it. So I said, hell, yes, I'll turn 'em in, long as I get the girl. And the money. And I did, too." He giggled again, insanely.

"I see," said Marik. And then, "Charles, you've got to get some help. You're very sick, my friend, let me—"

"*No!*" His voice was suddenly harsh and rasping, the soft reminiscent drawl gone. "No, I've had your help, Einai. And you're not my friend. You've taken away my wife, my salvation, and my reason for living. Now you're going to get what you deserve for what you've done to me!" He locked the automatic firing mechanism onto Marik's Life-Glow and started the countdown. "Better say your prayers, Einai, if you know any. 'Cause you're a dead man."

Kee-o-kuk, the Running Fox, came alert at his station. He had waited and fasted a long time for this eventuality, and the Great Spirit had granted his request at last.

After a massive explosion on one of *Hope*'s lower decks, a military skimmer had sneaked out of her port quarter and was making for an infinitesimal energy source some distance away among the debris. Kee-o-kuk wondered briefly what it was, but discarded the conjecture as immaterial. The important thing was, the skimmer pilot had broken the quarantine, and Kee-o-kuk had his son's death to avenge. Chanting his Battle Song, he armed his weapons, banked his scout ship and set off after Lassiter.

They were lined up like fowl at a turkey-shoot, Paige thought, ready to have their heads amputated by the crudest possible method. Himself first, then Kodi, the girls, and lastly,

Prince Salman. The executioner was showing off again, pleas-
ing the crowd, and then all at once the guards grabbed Paige
and shoved him roughly to his knees in front of the executioner.

This is my body, Marik said to Tadae, inside his hearts. *My
life, my accomplishments, whatever good I have done. I offer it
to You in these, my last moments. Do with it as You will.* He
watched with steady eyes Lassiter's skimmer approach. *Here,
too, is my blood*, he continued, *the failures, the pain, the loss,
the inadequacies and ineptitudes. The death I am about to
endure. I'm willing to drain the cup to the bitter dregs, if that
is Your will. Only have mercy on my soul, for I am only made
of sand.* And Dao Marik, suspended amid the thousand
thousand stars, calmly waited to die.

Kee-o-kuk watched his targeting display as it sensed Lassiter's skimmer, centered, and locked on. "Te-o-tun-hko!" he
shouted, hoping his son, the Runner, could see and hear him
from the Rainbow Bridge. He hit the weapons' stud and the
missile fired. As he watched it seek its target, Kee-o-kuk sang
The Song for Going Away, for he was a civilized man, who
prayed even for his enemy.

Lassiter's display, too, had locked on to Marik's Life-Glow,
and his thumb was beginning to press the firing stud when his
ship exploded in a burst of actinic light, and Charles Lassiter,
and his weapons, and his skimmer, provided a fantastic array of
fireworks that lit up half the night sky over Ildefor.

"The sign!" the people in the square roared. "The sign! The
Caliph lives and is well! We have the sign!"

A great cry of rejoicing rose up from the people, who swung
their torches wildly, and Hamad Vizier, infuriated, gestured
curtly at the executioner. The man in black slowly lowered his
scimitar and helped Paige to his feet. Brushed off his uniform.
Smiled sheepishly. Soldiers hurried to untie the prisoners, and
Prince Salman, once more in charge, ordered the immediate
arrest of Hamad Vizier and the release of Voldi and his friends.

Theresa Paladino ran up and kissed the Prince soundly, and

Salman paused, regarded her with new interest, removed her glasses and then his own, and returned her kiss with surprising enthusiasm. Voldi came bounding up the dungeon stairs, only slightly the worse for the wear, and swung Esme passionately into his arms, and Paige, delighted at the turn of events, clapped Kodi on the back.

The Senn showed all his teeth in a menacing grimace. "Don't even think about it, Doc," he advised.

It was late afternoon of the final day. Nalinle put Mikai down on the carpet of evergreen needles, here at the top of the world, and stared at the formidable river before him. This was no little River's-child, showing them the way, nor was it the placid River of the Village. This was a monster, a giant, a grandfather of waters. It was the river the runner had spoken of. At the end of this river was the Hopeship.

He explored the downstream banks on either side, but they were mostly sheer cliff walls, with no way to pass. He returned to Mikai and squatted down, considering this new dilemma.

"Fa' . . . ?" Mikai prompted. *What is it, Father? Can't we go on? What's wrong?*

"These are new rocks, Mikai," Nalinle mused aloud. "And a new kind of river. There is no way to walk beside it . . . but at the end of the river is the Hopeship." He drew a magic picture in the dirt with a broken twig, of himself and Mikai walking on the river, as if it were a road. "We must find a way to walk on water," he told his son.

He gazed out over the river, thinking about the problem, vaguely seeing the purl of green water over hidden rocks, the splashing foam, the log that bobbed and ducked only to emerge again, riding high. *How does a man walk on water? How can he use a river god for a road?* And even, *Can a god be a man's road, his way, to get where he is going?* The log was sailing along, floating above the problems of rocks and shallows. The log, thought Nalinle, trusted the river god, and was safe. *The log!* he realized, his jaw dropping as at last he consciously saw it, instinctively rising to his feet. *The log! The answer!*

He grabbed his son excitedly. "Mikai! I can take trees . . .

maybe two, or . . . or even three!" He squatted beside him,
drawing pictures in the air with his fingers. "A tree—will *float!*
It walks on the water! Two trees—or three!—will float
together . . . *better!*" Mikai beat at the air, laughing.

He chose three young trees nearby that seemed lucky to him,
told them what he wanted and apologized for having to dig
them up. Then he scoured the edge of the river and after a while
came back with a piece of deadwood shaped like a hand. He
was sure it was a good sign.

He began to scoop at the base of the first young tree, but the
work went more and more slowly as he got down to the roots.
They were tough and fibrous, and Nalinle was tired. The sun
sank low behind the taller peaks. Long blue shadows trailed
cool fingers over their skins, for the mountain air was thin and
sharp.

Use a big piece of wood to lift it with, Father, Mikai tried to
say, but he strangled on his own saliva and went into a fit of
coughing. Nalinle patted his back until it subsided, and then
started back. "Fa'," Mikai croaked. He deliberately flopped
over onto the dry pine needles and reached his bird's-wing
hand toward a long, heavy branch that had fallen. "Fa'!" he
insisted, trying to communicate with his eyes. *Use this, Father,
to shove under the roots. If you lean on it* here, *where else can
the power go but* there! *To pull up the tree! It's obvious!*

Nalinle sat him up again and took up the branch. "This is
what you want me to see, Mikai . . . ?" *Yes, Father!* Mikai
laughed, drooling. His legs churned excitedly.

"Something about the tree . . ." *Yes, yes! Use the branch!*
Again, he laughed. His eyes were shining.

Nalinle took the sturdy branch and hit the tree with it.

"N!" Mikai bellowed. "N!"

Nalinle stood it next to the tree, watching Mikai's reaction.
"N!" his son insisted. Not that. He wanted something else.
What else could he mean? What more could you do with a dead
branch, in relation to a tree? As a last resort, and more to please
the boy than anything else, he began half-heartedly to dig with
it. Mikai laughed aloud, and Nalinle smiled in surprise.

That was it. Mikai wanted him to dig with it. "The wooden

hand is better for digging," he told him, and Mikai seemed fretful. Nalinle felt fretful, too, for the branch had now caught fast on the roots and was stuck there.

He tried tugging on it, to no avail. Striking it with a rock. No. Even working it to and fro. Still nothing. At last he climbed up and, holding the tree, jumped on it, making Mikai so excited that he toppled over again. Nalinle felt something give under his feet, and abruptly, the branch hit the ground in one direction and the tree in the other. Nalinle goggled. It was out! Dug up! Free! He was amazed. That was what Mikai had been trying to tell him! He ran over and propped up his son against the rock yet again.

"It is a wonderful thing, your magic," he said in admiration. And then tenderly, "Mikai, my son, what would I do without you?"

He finished the raft quickly after that, lashing three young trees together with the bandits' salvaged rope, branches and roots standing up at bow and stern. He glanced at the sky. The sun had gone down, but the sky was light. There was still time. There had to be time.

He tied Mikai securely to the raft with the last few meters of the rope and, standing protectively across Mikai's body, he took the sturdy dead branch and pushed off from shore.

"According to his diary," Alan Wimet told the sober group assembled in Conference Room Eight, "and Charles Lassiter kept an inhumanly detailed diary, he deliberately killed Te-o-tun-hko—the Runner—only to set you up, Mister Marik. He needed Einai blood and tissue under a dead man's nails to throw suspicion onto you."

Marik winced. "But why? Other than saving him from a hideous death, what had I done to him? And had I, in my ignorance, not done it, would Runner still be alive?"

Joskwa Gallatin shook his head emphatically, making his eagle feathers spin and twirl. "Runner's death was Lassiter's choice. It had nothing to do with you."

Mykar Sharobi picked it up from there. "I've had my psych people working on this for several hours, Dao, while the Senn were pulling you in and bringing you back. Seems Charles resented you from the first time he saw you and Mrs. Lassiter together. According to records, and the diary, of course, he was insanely jealous of anyone who associated with her, no matter how casual the acquaintance. Something to do with his humble beginnings: his feelings of worthlessness, his need to dominate a woman of high social standing and good breeding, et cetera, et cetera . . . well, you understand. I doubt he ever had any actual *love* for Mrs. Lassiter; she was simply an object, a trophy, a whipping boy—"

Marik's head came up sharply and Sharobi nodded. "I'm afraid so. Full-body scan shows marks of continuing physical abuse, going back several years." The Einai said nothing, but there were knots of muscle at the angles of his jaw, and his pupils dilated until his eyes were a glittering black. It was fortunate for Lassiter, Sharobi decided, that he was already deceased. He cleared his throat and continued:

"When you took Lassiter down from the synagogue door, that clinched it. You see, he always knew he wasn't good enough for her, yet he couldn't let her go. He had this emotional need to own her. To prove himself. To be as good or better than the next man. According to what we've gleaned from this diary, it was eating him up alive.

"Then, when he was finally given an honorable way out of his dilemma, a chance for a hero's death, and an admirable end to what he regarded as a life of failure and inadequacy, you—of all people!—came along and snatched it away."

There was a long silence in the room.

Wimet slitted his eyes at Marik. "Under those circumstances, I'd probably try to kill you," he said. He and Waylan Stubbs laughed an inordinately long time over that.

Joskwa Gallatin spoke next. "There is still the matter of Te-o-tun-hko, the Runner. His father. Kee-o-kuk will speak."

Kee-o-kuk stood up, Signing as he spoke. "I am Kee-o-kuk, the Running Fox. I have lost a son, and I have avenged him. I killed his murderer and now he is free to cross the Rainbow Bridge. But I, Kee-o-kuk, am still without a son."

"I'm afraid we can't bring back the dead—" Sharobi began, but Gallatin waved him to silence.

"Let the man talk, Mike," he muttered. "He is speaking from the heart. Just listen."

"I demand restitution. I have chosen a new son, from among your people." He gestured. "Bring in my son."

There was a scuffle at the door and Crow Dog and Walking-About-Early strongly assisted the entry of Gino Cangelosi into the Conference Room. Seeing the assembled company, the boy broke free and approached the table, spreading his hands.

"Look, this is all a big mistake. Here—" He took Crow Dog's and Walking-About-Early's wallets from his thigh pocket and slapped them on the table. "It's all there, okay? The money's all there! It was just a joke! And I didn't have nothin' to do wit' that lady on the floor. I never laid a hand on her. I got witnesses. There was these two guys fightin' in the alley, and—"

"Shut up, *babbaluche*," his uncle Angelo said, "and listen a minute. This man is makin' you a offer you don't wanna refuse."

"What kind of offer?" Gino asked, and Kee-o-kuk told him. Gino laughed in astonishment. "You want *me* to train to be a Senn warrior? To take pussycat lessons? You gotta be crazy—!" Walking-About-Early lifted him by the scruff and leered into his face at close range.

"I told them you'd be too scared to try it, Rat," he gloated, "but they insisted on giving you a chance."

"Scared?" Gino demanded. "I'm not scared! No way am I scared! I just don't wanna show you guys up, is all! I can do this! With one hand tied behind me, I can do this pussycat stuff!"

"Talk is cheap," Crow Dog observed.

Sharobi made much of aligning his control board with the edge of the table. "So, is that a yes or a no, Gino? Are you willing to be adopted into the Senn and to acknowledge Kee-o-kuk as your new father?"

Gino jerked free of Walking-About-Early, rearranged his

collar and sauntered over to where Kee-o-kuk was standing.
Walked around him, eyeing him speculatively. "Not bad," he
decided. "The old man's not too bad." He squinted up at
Kee-o-kuk. "I don't know, though, Grampa," he challenged.
"Think you can handle a tough kid like me?" Kee-o-kuk's arm
whipped out like a striking snake and knocked him flat. Neither
of the Senn's impassive expression nor his tone of voice
changed one iota.

"Maybe," he said. And after a stunned moment, Gino got to
his feet.

"You remind me of my old man," he grinned. "Okay. Okay,
I'll do it. I'll go learn to be a pussyc—uh, a Senn. And five'll
get you ten, I'll be the best damn Senn you ever had."

"I'll see you and raise you ten, Rat," Crow Dog said,
reaching for his money. "Put up or shut up." The steward
quietly refilled everyone's coffee cups and as quietly disappeared.

"Priyam Sharobi," Marik pursued, "I've still got some
questions."

"Go."

"You say it was Charles who killed Ms. Drac—and tried to
kill Sid Behrman. But why?"

Wimet tasted his scalding coffee and grimaced. "Right, it
was Charles; but he wasn't after Sid. He was after Dr. Paige and
Ulrika Drac, because they were the only two people aboard
who knew about the psych flag. Sid was a mistake. Remember,
he was using Paige's room that night, because Waylan had
brought a girl home."

"Yeah," Waylan smiled ruefully. "I brought a girl home, all
right. My Interpol command upline. We spent the whole night
goin' over procedure. That was my big romantic evening!"

Sharobi slapped his hands on the table and rose, and the
others followed suit. "Well, gentlemen, are we all agreed that
this matter can finally be laid to rest?" There was a murmur of
assent, and the various contingents made their separate ways
home, leaving Marik and Sharobi alone.

"Does she know?" Marik asked, and Sharobi moved his
heavy head.

"She knows he was killed. I told her myself. Me and Father Santino."

"How did she take it?"

"Like a thoroughbred," the Sauvagi said. "How else would you expect her to take it?" He toyed with his empty coffee cup and said gruffly, "You're going to have to give her some time, Dao. She's too wounded, too—"

"Yes. I agree. Does she know about Charles's betrayal of her family?"

"No."

"Good. Don't tell her. Let her keep whatever illusions of Charles she can salvage. T'ath knows she's paid dearly enough for them. In the meantime, I'd appreciate your posting me to one of the medical stations planetside. I'm the last person she needs to deal with right now."

"Consider it done. Anything else?" Marik hesitated.

"Can I see her—just for a moment?"

"She's pretty heavily sedated," Sharobi pointed out. Marik stood there holding him with his eyes, and Sharobi gave in.

"Five minutes, Marik," he warned, "and then I throw you out myself."

Audrey Lassiter was lying on her side, facing away from the door, when Marik came quietly into her darkened hospital room. Her hair was a tumble of silk on the pillow, and Marik gently brushed a few vagrant strands off her face. Blue smudges under her closed eyes and the livid purple-red bruise on her cheekbone stood out starkly against her ivory skin. He brushed his fingertips over it with aching hearts, willing the pain away. Pulled up the blanket a bit. Tucked her in snugly.

"I never meant this to happen, Owdri," he whispered, stroking her hair. "Charles was my friend, and rather than make you unhappy even for a moment, I would have died happily in his stead."

Her breathing was slow and steady. They had sedated her, Sharobi had said. She would sleep for a long while, and wake up a widow because of him. Marik felt a keen pain in both his hearts, not only for Audrey and himself, but for the loss of a

Charles who had never existed. The Charles who had been his friend. "I know I've made a terrible mess of things," he finished, "but—oh, Owdri, my own dear love—I do love you so!" He leaned over and kissed her gently on the forehead; then he turned and left as silently as he had come.

He did not see the single tear that crept slowly down her cheek, to be followed by another, and another and yet another, all through the long and lonely night.

The current took the raft, swinging it out into the fast concourse at midstream. Nalinle was excited and frightened, poling along as best he could and peering between two sets of tree roots at the blunt cliff walls slipping past on either side. "I will never tell anyone of this," he breathed, "for who would believe me?"

There was a roaring in his ears, faint at first and then growing steadily louder, and he looked around quickly, worried, for its source. The shoreline began racing by faster and faster as the raft was caught up in the tortured waters, and he could barely keep his balance as the raft whirled and heaved its way into the thick of it.

Roots first, the raft nosed into the overspill, throwing Nalinle to his hands and knees. Miraculously, he kept hold of his steering pole, as cold water streamed over his hands and drenched the tense but delighted Mikai. This was more adventure than Mikai had ever known, and he was enjoying the raw thrill of it even though he was scared half out of his wits. The roaring of the rapids filled their world as the raft spun, ducked and bobbed its way along.

Nalinle got up as far as his knees and saw a narrow channel between the rocks up ahead, with a huge boulder jutting up through the foam, and the raft barreling right for it. Nalinle stood up, ready to pole the raft past the rocks. But as he pushed against the river-bottom rock, the raft's momentum shoved back, entangling the push-pole in the forward roots and whipping the whole raft around. The pole, firmly enmeshed in the tangled roots, slapped him smartly back of the head. Nalinle fell unconscious across the loudly protesting Mikai, and the raft slewed around dizzily of its own accord and went plummeting downriver as fast as it could go.

The outpost stood on the bank of a lake, which was fed by a broad brook whose watery music gave the Medical Team something pleasant to listen to while they waited for patients. For there had been no patients. Of all the runners they had sent out (and paid well for their trouble, too!) not one native had come to ask for help.

It was the last hour of the last day of four weeks' waiting.

"I just can't figure it out," Phonu Calleg said as the Team sat around the fire. "It doesn't make sense. After all, we're here to help them."

"Amen to that," one of the nurses said. "What a waste *this* has been!" The other nurse made a wordless sound of affirmation. Marik wrapped his hands around his coffee cup and gazed into it with narrowed eyes for a long while.

"Some people can't bear to accept help, Calleg-*na-shan*. They would rather die—or kill—than accept the help they need. It's sad, but it's so."

"It's stupid, if you ask me," McDermott put in from across the way. "If they need help, fine, let 'em come. Otherwise, I say let's get back to our ship. Our tour is up in fifteen minutes, and I got this really beautiful blonde mechanic, see—"

"She'll wait," said Paige, who had skimmed down with Marik for the ride.

"Give it another hour," Marik suggested quietly. Calleg snorted.

"Easy for you to talk. You've only been here a couple of hours. We've been down here thirty days, doing nothing. Playing chess. Collecting flora. *Bird*watching. My damn mind's getting moldy." He threw a twig into the stream and watched it dance merrily downstream. The land was bathed in twilight, and the sky was a pale blue with a star pinned against the east.

"Perhaps we can afford to watch one last bird," Marik replied, "before your mind molders away completely."

"Yeah, well, listen, Mister Bleeding Heart," McDermott

jibed, "I heard about what you did for that Lassiter guy, how you went out of your way and all, back in the Past, and what did it get you? A knife in the back, that's what. Not for me, thanks."

"You may be right," Marik said.

Paige added, "People who cling to their decency against all odds, Dr. McDermott, often pay a high price for the privilege."

Marik poked at the fire, sending up a shower of sparks, and raised that steady gray gaze to Calleg. "One more hour, as a favor to me."

Calleg heaved a deep breath and looked away. "All right, Marik. One more hour." There were groans of protest from the other team members, and he went on: "In the meantime, we can start packing our personal belongings and striking the tents. I don't suppose," he said to Marik, "that you two'd mind helping us pack?"

"We don't mind at all," Marik answered. He followed Paige inside and began collecting instruments, all the while listening, with his ears and skin and mind, for something he could not name, could not put a finger on. A call, a summons, a reaching out by—what? He did not know. *Someone is out there,* he thought, and the thought was a certainty, *and they are calling us.* Whoever it was, he only hoped they would reach the outpost in time.

The lake reflected the wide night sky, and the raft had leaped out of the river's turbulence and settled into calm waters just as Nalinle dragged himself to his knees. Mikai, who had enjoyed the whole adventure, crowed exuberantly, mouthing words faster than Nalinle could possibly understand.

"Shhh, Mikai," he mumbled. "Hush. I must see where we are." He was frankly worried. What if they had gone beyond the outpost? What if the Hopeship had left, and his journey had been for nothing? *What if,* he thought, remembering Auken's merciless eyes, *what if it was all some terrible, brutal joke?* He looked around desperately. *Where are they? Where?*

Trees loomed black against the sky. Stars in the water mirrored stars above, and there, across the lake, an orange campfire wetly twinned its reflection. *A campfire!* The outpost! They were not too late, after all—were they? Nalinle's heart leaped and, wrestling his pole from the stubborn roots, he began to push the raft as fast as he could across the width of the lake.

The skimmer was loaded and ready, and the Team climbed in and waited expectantly. Marik slapped a hand against the side. "We'll have a last look around," he said. "Make sure we haven't left anything."

"You people go on up," Paige added. "We're right behind you."

The skimmer revved its engines and the pitch dopplered up until it was a piercing whine that flung the craft smoothly skyward with its burden of mercy. In moments it was only a bright blue speck among the stars.

Nalinle, running at full tilt through the forest with Mikai in his arms, saw the white dart strike upward from the ground, its tubes glowing phosphorescent blue, and disappear into the night sky. He stumbled to a stop, shaking his head in disbelief and panting from exertion. *Not after all this way!* he thought. *They would not, could not, leave us now!*

"No . . ." he mumbled raggedly; then, louder, "No! . . . Wait!" he shouted vehemently. "Hopeship, wait!" He took off toward the fire again at a dead run, calling "Wait!" every few steps. But for the night-birds, calling along the lake, there was no answer.

Paige watched the skimmer go, and then turned to Marik. "Okay, let's have it. What are you really waiting here for?"

Marik met the straightforward brown stare evenly. "I don't know, Tom," he answered. "It's just a—a feeling I have. A mental scent. A sense that we need to be here."

"Okay with me. I've got all night." Paige sat down cross-legged next to the fire, and after a minute, Marik joined him. For a long while they watched the fire and listened to the loons calling down by the water. At last Paige said, without looking up, "It was all my fault, Dao. The killings, the explosions and everything. I red-coded Lassiter's psych flag that first day. I was trying to protect his career. If I hadn't done that—"

"And if Ms. Drac hadn't confided that she knew his secret. And if I had been more discreet about my feelings for Owd—for Mrs. Lassiter—and if and if and if." Marik's eyes gleamed like a cat's in the firelight. "It was Charles's fault, Tom. We have to face that. He made the choices, and ultimately, he paid the price for them. Unfortunately, others also had to—"

There was the faintest of cries, off somewhere, and Marik's head came up sharply. "Did you hear that?"

Paige shook his head. "Hear what?"

"I don't know, I— There it is again!" He got to his feet in that single balanced motion of his that always made Paige feel rather like a monkey. "Over there!" Paige, who could see nothing, started toward the source of the sound, but Marik caught his arm.

"Let them come to us," Marik said. "We don't want to scare them off."

"Right."

"Key your translator." Marik switched on his own, as the cry came again.

"Wait! . . ." came the voice, and Paige grabbed a hand torch and shone it toward the sound.

"Here!" Marik called. "Over here!" The underbrush rustled and parted and Nalinle, wet, bruised and exhausted, stumbled into the outpost clearing carrying Mikai against his chest. He paused, staring in wonder for a moment, taking it all in, and then dragged himself forward and extended Mikai toward Marik on both wavering arms.

"Hope . . . ?" he croaked, too exhausted to say anything more, and Marik stepped close and knelt down, so that his head was almost level with that of the small green man before him. Nalinle looked from Marik to Paige and back. *Am I here? Are these giants the gods who will make him well? Is this, after all, the Hopeship?*

"Hope?" he begged again, the tears running down his face. Marik took Mikai carefully in both his palms and studied him for a long moment; then he met Nalinle's eyes and smiled.

"Hope," he said.